Death in Candie
Gardens

Also by Eileen Dewhurst

Death Came Smiling
After the Ball
Curtain Fall
Drink This
Trio in Three Flats
Whoever I Am
The House that Jack Built
There Was a Little Girl
Playing Safe
A Private Prosecution
The Sleeper
A Nice Little Business
Dear Mr Right
The Innocence of Guilt

Death in Candie Gardens

Eileen Dewhurst

PIATKUS
CRIME

First published in Great Britain in 1992 by
Judy Piatkus (Publishers) Ltd of
5 Windmill Street, London W1P 1HF

The map of Guernsey was drawn
by the author

**The moral right of the author
has been asserted**

*A catalogue record for this book is available
from the British Library*

ISBN 0-7499-0138-1

Phototypeset in 11/12pt Linotron Times by
Computerset, Harmondsworth, Middlesex
Printed and bound in Great Britain by
Biddles Ltd, Guildford and King's Lynn

For Joan Bagley

This book was written out of my love for Guernsey, and I am deeply grateful to the Guernsey Police, the staff of the Greffe, the Ushers of the Royal Court and my friends on the island for all the help they have so willingly given me.

I hope that as a result my picture of Guernsey life is accurate, but the characters and events in *Death in Candie Gardens* are entirely imaginary, and bear no relation whatsoever to real people or true situations.

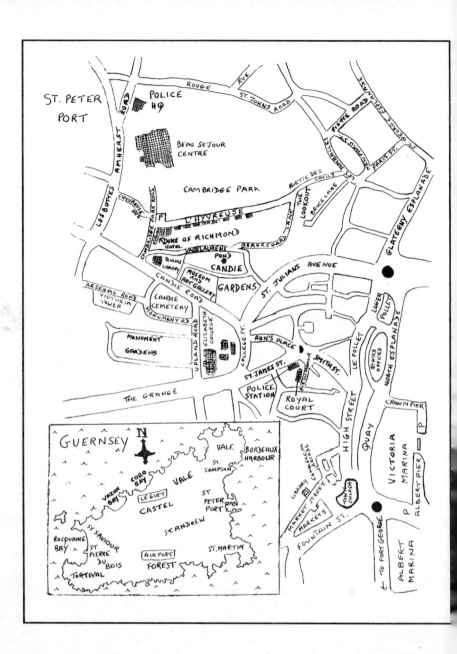

Chapter One

For a moment, when he saw the length of lead piping, he couldn't believe his luck.

He had been wandering about among the pines, scuffing his feet fruitlessly in the thick layer of needles as he searched for a fallen branch big enough to look threatening, then deciding to look more closely at the ruin of pinky-brown boulders built into the steep rise from the floor of the wood. (A wood called Le Guet, according to the board at the start of it. Was he in England or France, for God's sake?)

He had found the wood by chance earlier in the day, not thinking business. With other holiday-makers he had climbed to the lookout on top of the ruin and seen the great golden bites of the bays stretching up the west coast of the island, edged with the deep blue sea in which he had floundered, shivering, before his midday meal.

He had also seen a man on his own lose his footing over a tree root. He didn't want to spoil his holiday, the island seemed like a nice place, but he couldn't pass up these new opportunities . . .

So he had come back in the dusk. And been unable to find himself a weapon.

At last, reluctantly, he had called it a day and climbed back up the slope past the ruin. He had been put off investigating it on his first visit by the notice saying *Watchtower and Battery* and going into a whole lot of ancient monument sort of detail. But now it struck him that the Germans might have done something to it during the war like they had to most of the coastal forts and towers (the Occupation Museum had really excited him). So he walked round to the notice and read the last bit of it in the fading light. *In the Second World War the Germans added extensive new fortifications.*

This time he hared up the steps. But all the stuff on the top, including the barred shell of a prison that looked more like a cottage, seemed to consist of the same boring old boulders as the walls, with even the loose ones too big and heavy for him to lift. Laggingly he retraced his steps, and was going to start back to the hotel when something made him turn round for a last look down the slope.

To see the hard-edged concrete of the German bunker tucked in under a bulge of the old stone. With an oblong of black space for an entrance.

He half ran, half tumbled, his way down into it, cautious only as the blackness surrounded him. When he put out a hand it met sweating concrete wall, and his shoes splashed through stagnant water.

And kicked the lead piping.

He eased it out with his foot, then put his gloves on before bending down to pick it up.

Heavier than he had imagined, but not too heavy to lift above his head. And – the chief thing in its favour, putting it in a different class from any old tree branch – looking exactly what it was.

A lethal weapon.

Which he wouldn't use, of course. He never used the violence he threatened and he wasn't going to start now. Anyway, holiday makers would be more laid back than street-wise Londoners, far easier to relieve of their cash and bits of jewellery. And it was well known that people on holiday felt happier wearing their jewellery and carrying their money than leaving it in their rooms or even hotel safes. It would more than likely be Guernsey money, of course, but he was only three days into his two-week holiday and there would be plenty of time to change it. The waitress at his hotel had told him that banks always kept a stock of UK currency for people whose holidays were coming to an end . . .

As he tapped the length of piping against his left hand he reminded himself again that he mustn't spoil his holiday. That he had only brought his gear away with him because of the

London Bill starting to sniff around him and the lock on his door not being police-proof. That was why he had taken up the bargain offer in a travel agent's window in Tottenham Court Road. And he had got tired of working in the amusement arcade and felt he needed a break. If he hadn't seen that man lose his balance . . .

He was superstitious, and finding the piping told him he was doing the right thing, even though as it got darker it was more likely to be a couple than one man. He wasn't very tall but with his length of lead piping raised above his head he could terrorize a couple.

He went back inside to pull on the hood and black mackintosh track suit, but stayed close to the entrance because of not knowing the size of the darkness, or what it contained. Then, the old excitement pumping, he ran out among the trees.

It seemed light at first by contrast, but when he stopped and leaned against a trunk his eyes couldn't separate it from his dark body. That was good. A pity there weren't more trees. Another thing the waitress had told him was that Le Guet had suffered in the winter gales and half its trees had fallen.

He could hear faint laughter on the clear air. Hear it growing louder. Four people passed quite close to him, two men, two women, and a dog. Islanders – a pity there were four. The promotion for the cut-price holiday said Guernsey had come top of a poll to find the happiest population, so they'd be even more laid back than the holiday-makers.

But it was the holiday-makers who would be climbing to the lookout at night, as they had climbed during the day, to see how different the view was with a lightline instead of a coastline. If he could find a vantage point from where he could see a couple set off for the top of the ruin he could follow them, come up behind them while they were giving each other a geography lesson.

Darting about he found a tree close enough to the lookout. The trees gave off a good smell – stronger, somehow, now that he could hardly see them. He could wait quite comfortably, his weight against the trunk, his length of piping firm in his right hand. He'd give it till half eleven, he didn't want to be noticed getting back to the hotel too late, and if anyone was coming they would surely have arrived by then.

3

The night was mild, the light breeze only a whisper far above him. He had never been able to work out the moon, it didn't seem to follow a pattern like the sun, but it wasn't visible tonight. The darkness now was really thick, broken only by a faint glow from the direction of the lookout. Remains of the sunset? Reflection of the lights down below? Whatever it might be he needed it to tell him how many and what sort of people were climbing up to the view –

The rough bark of the tree hurt his back as he jerked against it. Two people had come silently across the pine needles. He heard their feet for the first time on the steps, still didn't hear their voices. He felt angry at them for giving him such a shock – they should have been laughing, talking, alerting him. Silhouetted against that faint light, they showed him they were male and female, hand in hand. Too in love for words, he thought bitterly. (He hadn't gone on the mugging game until after Jeannie had left him.)

The anger and the bitterness made it easy. They were talking when he came up behind them. 'Is that Cobo Bay?' the girl was asking.

Holiday-makers. And very young, he discovered when he told them to hand over their jewellery and their money and they turned their frightened faces up to the lead piping trembling above their heads.

'Feeling restless, darling?' Ballpoint poised, Olivia De Garde glanced up from the folder on her lap.

'Feeling hot. There doesn't seem to be any air.'

'It *is* hot. I don't mind it.' Because she conserved her energy, only moved when she absolutely had to. That was why her beauty was blurring at the edges. If Charles had ever indicated that she should do something about it she might have been able to. But he hadn't, and he never would. 'If you didn't pace about so much –'

'I'm sorry, darling.'

'Nothing wrong, is there?'

'Nothing wrong, no. It's just the heat.' He paused beside her chair, and lazily she raised her head to look at him and his unusually diffident smile. 'Although I did run across Joly Duguy at lunchtime and he did give me a pretty evil look.

Well, a look of utter hatred, if I'm precise. Without saying a word, even though I'd given him good morning before deciding I'd rather not say anything, either. D'you think implacably unforgiving people suck something out of the people they won't forgive? In two seconds flat I felt absolutely drained. And sort of – threatened. I hope he's not going to start haunting me again, hanging round the house and the office.'

'Joly Duguy . . . The police saw him off, he won't start that again, darling. And you know he's not entirely . . .' Olivia tailed off, yawning.

'I know. But I wish now I'd never published that wretched article.'

'You didn't name names, which you very well might have done. It isn't your fault that everyone in the island knew who and what you were writing about. Cecil Duguy during the Occupation is a horrible legend. And for goodness' sake, Charles, it's forty-five years since your father gave his evidence. Don't let Joly worry you, it's probably the moon. And do stop pacing the floor, I'm sure you're making yourself even hotter than you need be. If you go and stand in the front doorway you'll find there's a nice through draught.'

'I'm all right. When does this cousin of yours arrive?'

'Tomorrow lunchtime. I'm going to leave a note at the Duke asking her to dinner. She's a godsent partner for Tim.'

'I fancy Tim's too busy just now chasing this mugger to be interested in a partner.'

'What I really mean, darling, is that Anna will make us six rather than five, which is a better number.'

'Of course. I wonder what's she like?'

'If she's your type?'

'I wasn't meaning . . .'

'I know you weren't, Charles. Anna and I have only met once, at her mother's funeral, and then she was just a frightened little girl with long straight hair and skinny legs. She told me in her letter that her father married again eventually, and died a couple of years ago. She didn't mention her stepmother.'

'You didn't ask her to stay here?'

'Very languidly. And only after she'd told me she'd already booked at the Duke. She's giving herself a week's self-indulgence – I quote – before starting work with Bradshaw, Jones and Coquelin. Then she'll be moving to Brian Bradshaw's while she takes over for him. She had no idea the Duke was almost next door to her only surviving relative. I suppose it was rather nice of her to tell me she was coming at all.'

'Her only surviving relative? She was bound to, if only from curiosity.'

'Perhaps. I suspect she's rather independent.'

'So you might get on. Independent from her husband as well?'

'More than that, I think, so far as her husband is concerned.'

'Maybe something to do with the death of the child.' Ten years after the loss of their own child, Charles still sometimes tested the extent of his wife's recovery.

'Maybe,' Olivia repeated. Her eyes on his remained calm. 'I shan't ask her, of course.'

'So she'll probably tell you.' Charles kicked at the tufts edging a rug. 'Think I'll take a walk in Candie Gardens.'

'It's asking for trouble to keep going out at night on foot while this mugger's about. Walk in your own garden. Or take the car.' Olivia nestled more comfortably into her deep chair, pulling her bare feet up on to the cushion under the cream cheese-cloth flow of her loose dress. If she tried wearing dresses with waists again, or blouses and skirts, she might just shame herself into doing something about her weight.

'I want to stride out. No mugger's going to prevent me from leading a normal life.'

'You've been striding out so much lately you could just have used up your luck.'

'He hasn't discovered Candie Gardens. And he finishes by eleven-thirty. It's almost that now.'

'He could revise his time-table.'

'Obviously. But the parish will be bound to reverse their experimental round the clock opening of the Gardens and that will keep him out.'

'You've heard they're definitely going to?'

'No. But there's to be a meeting.'

'After the event, perhaps?'

6

'I hope not. But whatever they decide, it won't affect me.' Charles picked up a large handsome key from a side table and jiggled it about on his palm.

'You'll be glad to be able to use it again, won't you?' Olivia saw the flash of pride across his face, which always appeared when there was reference to his unique possession of a private key to Candie Gardens. His father had loved the Gardens too, and had done so much during the war to help maintain island morale that the key had been a parish gift following the Liberation. A hereditary gift, but the line had run out . . .

'What is it, Olivia?'

'Only a goose on my grave.' She hesitated. 'Would you prefer to be on your own tonight? Or shall I make an effort and come with you?'

'Couples don't deter him.'

Olivia roused herself slightly, letting some pages from the folder slide to the floor as she leaned forward. 'So you admit there's a risk?'

'That was a joke. Don't worry.'

'I shall, but never mind. Do I take it you prefer to be alone tonight?'

'Not necessarily, but you're comfortable where you are.'

'That's true, darling, and I have to get this printout read by the weekend. All right. Give me a kiss, then.'

Smiling, Olivia held up her heavy, handsome face. Always, even when Charles was in the midst of one of his insignificant affairs, they gave outward sign of their affectionate union in a myriad conventional small ways.

'I shan't be long tonight, darling. I just want to stretch my legs and try to find some fresh air.' He turned back in the doorway. 'If it makes you feel any better, Olivia, I've taken the family dagger each time I've gone out in the dark since the mugger first struck.'

'So you're not quite so contemptuous of him as you pretend to be. I think that's just plain commonsense.' Her smile dissolved his embarrassment. 'Thank you for telling me, darling.'

'Thank you for appreciating it. Don't wait up.'

'I won't.'

She followed his elegant back with her eyes as he went out. For more years now than she could remember, his pre-bedtime outings could have been romantic assignations and she wouldn't have minded. Although she still loved him, after the birth of their still-born son and the medical injunction to have no more children she had found the easiest and most congenial form of contraception was not to have him in her bed. So she had felt it was only fair to regard his short-lived *amours* as compensation for the loss of his conjugal rights. They were, too, her guarantee of his continuing indulgence of her sexual sloth, even of being able to invite him to her room from time to time for a cosy platonic statement of their mutual affection and be confident that their contact would go no further. The only forfeit she had extracted from him was occasionally to pity aloud his dependence on an activity she herself found both boring and unnecessary. But only on those rare occasions when to her shocked surprise a mild jealousy had overtaken her.

Tonight, though, it appeared that he really was going to Candie Gardens to walk alone. But Charles was a gambler, and he could have been gambling on her falling for his suggestion that she would be more comfortable staying put in her chair.

Smiling, Olivia leaned down to retrieve the scattered pages.

Dear Jane,
  You were right. I'm not used to travelling alone.
  But I think I could get to like it, with the prop of writing to you about it and knowing you're waiting to hear. Whatever the problems with Jimmy, he was always there, waiting to hear. One thing I've discovered this past couple of months is that after living for years with another person you get so that any interesting things you see and hear seem to need telling to someone in order for you to 'fix' them, be sure they've happened. An awful state of dependence, but could marriage be anything at all without it? I don't expect ·
you to try and answer that question, of course, because you haven't been without Clive and as long as you both shall live you never will be.
  Well, this is a nice, nice place. The plane comes in over blue and gold bays and small fields with high hedges and

enormous ginger cows, and even the airport fails to hassle – your suitcases roll towards you within minutes and there's an abundance of trolleys. And the chap who handed me my car keys suggested I drove the long way to the Duke of Richmond Hotel because it's prettier than the short way.

Before I set off he told me two things: that Guernsey has a thirty-five-mile an hour speed limit, and a mugger. The mugger is their first ever, which I can well believe, the island has such a good feeling. He apparently threatens his victims with a piece of lead piping, but doesn't actually use it. The car man offered me a sort of personal apology, which I found rather touching, and he was obviously praying it isn't a local.

Thirty five miles an hour feels like the clappers, even on the main roads. Most of the buildings are old enough to be attractive, and there's a lot of pink and white stucco with sash windows and curly gables. Going the long way you switchback downhill into St Peter Port and drive the picturesque length of it between the harbour and tall old buildings discreetly labelled Marks and Spencer, Midland Bank, etcetera, so it looks as if the developers are kept at bay.

The hotel is fine, high up above the north side of the town. My room is at the front, on the first floor, facing a friendly-looking green called Cambridge Park which is backed by trees and has the hotel car park discreetly blunting its nearest corner. When I first went to the window there were two women with five dogs between them on the sandy path that cuts the park in half. Nice. Surely I'll be putting fewer dogs to sleep in Guernsey than I did in London.

The green is just across a narrow road called L'Hyvreuse that leads to an enormous view of the port – after you've passed Olivia's house! Jane, she really does live almost next door to the hotel, it's right beside the end of her Georgian terrace. I saw 'Saxon Lodge' painted over the second front door when I set out for the lookout, and rather scuttled past so as to minimise the risk of a premature meeting – when I arrived I found a note from her inviting me to dinner tonight. I'm looking forward to it, but I'd have chosen another hotel if I'd known this one was so close – I want to

9

spend most of this week on my own, and I don't want her to feel she has to bother about me. Anyway, I'll be moving to the Bradshaws when I start work and I gather they live the other side of town.

There's a bronze direction dial set into the wall by the lookout – New York 3000 miles, London 180. More attractive houses go tumbling down the hill to the port and you can see most of the harbour, with a fortress called Castle Cornet strung out into the sea and island shapes on the horizon – Herm and Jethou straight ahead, Sark farther off to the right.

That was the moment I suddenly felt hungry. It's so long since my insides told me to look at my watch it seemed like a sign that I've done the right thing, coming here. It was a quarter past two, and when I got back to the hotel they'd finished with mid-day meals, but the girl in reception told me the nearest and nicest place for a snack would be Candie Gardens. So I went round the corner and through a green gate, and had a sandwich under a glassed-in Victorian bandstand, looking past a statue of Victor Hugo to the sea. I dithered afterwards in the doorway of the Guernsey Museum which is just behind the bandstand, but there'll surely be one day this week when the sun goes in. So I went back to the car, put my map on the passenger seat, and drove clockwise round the island as close to the edge as I could get.

To find the sea on the south coast you have to drop down steep narrow lanes. They tend not to have names, so twice I found myself embowered in greenery at the gate of a private house, and had to twist up the way I'd twisted down. But the other times I struck lucky and was able to stand on cliff edges and look down on perfect little coves.

On the west coast you're beside the sea and the bays are wide and there are a lot of people. I sat on sea walls and strode over clovery grass, and what I've done to Jimmy seemed less terrible than it seemed in London. Much less terrible than all those months of pretence.

The north of the island is at sea level and gives a great sense of space. So much contrast in such a small area is rather exhilarating. I found another marina and another town on my way down the east coast, but I was suddenly fearfully tired and I didn't stop to explore.

I'm sitting in my window now, and there are more dogs and owners on the green.

Jane, it obviously isn't going to be as easy as it feels just at this moment, but today I've at least started noticing things again. Mercilessly, so far as you are concerned! Sorry this is so long.

Jimmy's bound to ring to ask if you've heard from me. Say you have if you like, and that I'm all right.

Much love.

Anna.

Chapter Two

Charles De Garde went reluctantly up the short path, between the bright beds of marigolds and begonias. When he had first walked it the borders had held snowdrops and crocus, and he had found it a neat, sweet road to gratification. Not any more. He was here, now, only because the desperation in her notes and phone calls had reached a pitch to alarm him.

Distastefully he lifted the burnished brass knocker. The door opened as he let it go.

'So you've come.'

She stood aside. His reluctance now uncomfortably physical, Charles walked past her into her narrow hall, managing not to touch her, hating the sound of the front door closing behind him.

'Just to tell you again what I told you the last time. We're finished. No! Not that!' Her hands were above her head, pulling off her sweater. 'That's over, Linda.'

She flung the sweater to the floor, staring at him in anguished disbelief. He tried to keep his eyes from where her creased white shirt had escaped her jeans.

'Oh, God, Charles, I can't believe you. It was so wonderful! For you too, you told me. Well, I knew. Charles . . .'

'It *was* wonderful, Linda,' he responded wearily. Why for heaven's sake did he put himself in these pitiful situations? 'Nothing will ever alter that. But it's over. I told you when it began that it couldn't last. I told you exactly what I wanted.'

'And suddenly you don't.'

'Linda, you aren't married. My wife –'

12

'Your *wife*!' She kicked the sweater through the open sitting-room doorway. 'A fat lot you thought about your wife.'

'It may have seemed like that –'

'It did. Charles, *please . . .*'

'She's important to me, and sooner or later –'

'That's why you've taken up with that prissy piece who works in your office?'

'Oh, Linda.' He shouldn't have been surprised that she knew. In Guernsey, nothing remained a secret for long. 'Don't you see? It's because of my wife that I can't stay with any other woman.'

'Only ruin their lives.'

'My dear girl, I haven't ruined your life. You'd learned the score a long time before you met me.' As croupier at the Magali Club. As ex-girlfriend of its boss. 'And I never pretended it would be anything but an agreeable interlude for either of us. In a month or so's time the only thing you'll feel about this will be embarrassment.'

'Like you're feeling now.'

'Linda . . .' He couldn't deny it. Looking at her as poignantly as he could manage, he thought how attractive she was with her pointed, delicate face, pale and lightly freckled under the tumble of dark hair, and her marvellous lithe body. It was simply that he had reached the inevitable stage of being able to appreciate her only as a work of art. 'Any affair gets embarrassing when one of the people involved tries to stretch it out beyond its natural end. Ours is over. Let's keep the good memories.'

'OK.' He saw the effort it took her to make the two syllables sound light. She came towards him. 'After we've made one last memory . . .' Her hands were at the buttons of his shirt.

'No!' He wrenched away so violently she stumbled, enabling him to claim the door. 'I'm sorry, Linda, but that really is that. You're a sweet girl and I'm grateful, but please don't ring or write any more.' He put his hand on the catch.

'Simple, isn't it?'

She was breathing like an asthmatic and he didn't like the look in her eye. 'I'm afraid it is. It happens every day, to hundreds and thousands of people.'

13

'You're a bastard, Charles De Garde.'

'Hate me, then. Although wouldn't it be better just to enjoy our memories, as I shall?' His insincerity was making him feel sick. 'Goodbye, Linda.'

With a last lingering look into her angry eyes he put his hand on her shoulder, then opened the door and slid out. As he made himself walk slowly to the gate he felt an unfamiliar pang of self-disgust, thinking of her look of youth and vulnerability, needing to remind himself that it was deceptive.

And to reassert his normally strong sense of self-preservation. Thank God she wasn't opening the door again and shouting after him. He'd been fortunate that his professional reputation on the island had so far neutralized his reputation as a womaniser, but the Magali Club's boss had set Linda Parrish up in a fashionable part of town and allowed her to stay there. If his wretched private life ever spilled over into his public persona people might not be so generous . . .

Shuddering, Charles got into his car and drove rapidly away.

'Charles! Oh, darling!'

She had closed the thin curtains and was a shadow in the wide bed, turning towards him.

He slipped in beside her, taking her in his arms. 'I love you,' he said. It was so good to mean the words he felt tears behind his eyes.

'I know. I love you, too.'

'I know. I wish I hadn't been –'

'Hush. Don't let's talk. No need to talk.'

'No. Thank you, darling.'

They lay still, stirring themselves only to hug more tightly, while beyond the curtain the sun travelled slowly to the right.

As it disappeared and the room darkened, Charles turned on to his back, his arm still round her shoulders. 'I think I went to sleep.'

'I think I did too.'

'We'd better start moving. You'll want to be getting ready for the dinner party, and I haven't decided on the wine.'

'I'm organized. It won't take either of us long.' She laid her head on his chest.

'All right, then. Another few minutes.'

He didn't deserve her, but one could get more than one deserved in life as well as less. Sighing his gratitude, he took her back into his arms.

Dear Jane,

It's just as well I posted my first letter the moment I put my pen down, or you'd be getting a really unmanageable screed. I've just got back from the dinner-party next door but one, and there's so much to talk over and no one to talk it over with.

Don't misunderstand me. I'm glad Jimmy isn't here. I'm not missing him, but I'm missing communication – hence another letter so soon. At least you know that I'm a good listener, too! I miss that, as well.

I'm rather pleased with my only surviving relation. She's a large lady with clever, sleepy brown eyes in a beautiful face that's threatening to lose its contours but hasn't quite done so yet. Wavy gold-brown hair that the fashion magazines would say was too long for someone past forty but which is absolutely right for Olivia. Clearly very much in control, but not having to demonstrate it, if you see what I mean. There was a comfortable sort of woman hovering about during dinner, bringing things in and out and helping to serve, but Olivia had obviously done the cooking and very good it was too. Watercress soup, superb boeuf en croute, and a choice of light or heavy pudding – crème brulée or blackcurrant pie. I'm rather glad that I'm not going to be in the position of having to cook in return!

Olivia's husband Charles is an advocate, as they call both barristers and solicitors here, and kept us very well supplied with drink. He's tall, handsome, silver-templed, and impeccably dressed. Self-aware, but not objectionably so. I found myself thinking of the heroes of black and white thirties movies – he has that sort of debonair manner.

The other couple were a Douglas and Janet Chapman. Not Guernsey people; Douglas is on a five-year civil engineering contract. His firm in England found them a house in a place called Fort George the other side of St Peter Port, which Tim Le Page described to me in an aside as a rich man's fantasy. 'Tim Le Page!' you'll be saying, pricking up your ears. Yes, he's another good-looking chap but in the boyish mode – floppy hair and cheerful smile – until you're sitting next to him at dinner and can see the grey in the hair and the lines round his eyes and mouth. Even so, I should say that he's ten years or so younger than Charles. Unattached, too, and Charles's cousin, which makes it all beautifully symmetrical.

But you know that I'm not in the market for boyfriends just now, and that I'm joking. Actually, he seemed to be quite agreeable, if a bit shy. A bit distrait too, not surprisingly, as he's a detective inspector in the Guernsey police force – the detective inspector, in fact, isn't that marvellous? – and very concerned about catching the island's mugger. That's why he arrived late. He also left early, but for another reason that I'll tell you about in a minute.

Judging by what was said the Chapmans seem to be close friends of the De Gardes, but I thought I could sense something strained in the atmosphere between them. I kept catching myself listening to the conversation as if it was the ever-so-slightly stilted dialogue of a not very well rehearsed play. I suppose that sounds ridiculous, but I'm sure I wasn't imagining a sort of carefulness in the way they spoke and looked at one another – the two women and Charles, that is. Douglas Chapman didn't pay much attention to anything except his dinner and, for a moment, me: when Olivia announced over drinks in the garden that I was a vet he nearly fell off his wrought-iron garden chair, and during dinner I caught the odd look of amazed respect. I rather think the reflex public perception of a vet must be of a man with his arm up to the shoulder inside a pregnant cow. Given that, though, I still suspect Douglas Chapman of being a bit of a male chauvinist. I should say he's about Charles's age – forty-five? – but although he's tall he's totally unglamorous, and so far as I could see past a large moustache (a lot more luxuriant than the hair on his head) he has a permanently pursed-up mouth and the sort of pale suspicious eyes that seem to be constantly appraising the world and finding it wanting. Even when he asked for the

16

salt it was as if he suspected there was a conspiracy to keep it out of his reach.

Janet Chapman works as a PA for one of Charles's partners. She's small and slim and naturally blonde and one of those contained women you don't notice much at first and then when you do you realize they've got quite an intriguing look to them – perhaps because you can't tell whether they're interesting or not. One thing I could tell was that she was on edge. Perhaps that's how she always seems, but I got the distinct feeling it was something to do with the general sense of strain.

I haven't said anything about the house, have I? It's much bigger than it looks from the street because it's deep, and the sitting-room opens on to a wonderful walled garden the street doesn't give you a clue about. The decor is quiet and appropriate, all the furniture's old and good-looking, and I'd like to have a proper look sometime at the pictures.

Oh, Jane, I haven't thought about myself all evening. Or about Mickey, which I'm suddenly paying for. But not to think about myself has been wonderful.

I think Olivia and I are going to get on. I also think she's as independent as I am, and that she's aware I want to do my own thing until I start work. It's a bonus that she's fond of animals, and she asked me if I'd like to go to the Zoo and the GSPCA with her tomorrow. She asked in such a way that I could easily have said no, but of course I said yes. Whereupon she asked me if I'd mind driving. She has a splendid aura of relaxed lethargy, and didn't appear to be in the least put out by this indefinable atmosphere I keep mentioning – which I can't quite say of her husband, despite his ready quips. I don't think it had anything to do with Tim Le Page, by the way, although I noticed him look round the table now and then a bit unhappily.

Keep going! I've only got to tell you, now, why the detective inspector left early. We didn't finish dinner until well after ten, and we went back into the sitting-room for coffee. After a few minutes there was a muffled banging at the front window, which faces onto the street, and a man's voice shouting.

Charles said 'Oh, God, Joly,' and he and Tim jumped up and went outside.

Olivia said not to open the curtains, and went into the hall followed by the rest of us. The shouting was still going on and I could hear scuffling. Then I saw Charles and Tim through the open door, holding on to a scruffy-looking young man with a lot of curly black hair. The young man was shouting 'God damn you, you bastard, De Garde,' and things like that. Then the fire suddenly went out of him and they managed quite easily to bundle him into a car parked almost outside which I presumed was Tim's. He just sat there in the passenger seat, his head drooped on his chest, and Tim drove him away.

The rest of us went back into the sitting-room, and Charles and Olivia explained. The lad's father, Cecil Duguy (pronounced Doo-guee), was arch-collaborator with the Germans during the Occupation. Everyone knows this, but Charles has just published an article about collaboration and its aftermath in some island journal which has rather raked it all up again, even though he didn't name names. The father died years ago and the son is furiously loyal to his memory – criticism of his father is the main trigger for the lad's off times, of which tonight's episode was an example. Nothing schizoid, just 'a tendency to dramatic changes of mood', as Charles put it. Charles's father played a leading role in bringing the collaborators to book after the war, which of course started a Duguy-De Garde feud. Joly has done his feeble best to keep it going, which up to now has only meant hanging around and following Charles about. Obviously the article really got to him. As you can imagine, he's something of a local character and I think people here feel rather protective of him – he wasn't born until long after the war and he can't help his dad. I gather he's very skilled with marine timbers and has a little boatyard north of town. Olivia said Tim would probably just take him home.

That was the point at which the day suddenly caught up with me. Olivia noticed me trying not to yawn and told me to go home to bed. As all the above bears witness, I found I wasn't so tired after all, but I'm suddenly dead tired now. As are you, I've no doubt, if you've ploughed loyally through all this. I'm afraid there'll be more tomorrow – perhaps I should start keeping a dairy until I adjust to being on my

18

*own? I hope I never get like those sad people who tell
strangers their life histories on trains and buses. No, I don't
really think there's much danger. I'm talking to you now
because I was talking to you before I met Jimmy, before I
met anyone.*
Much love, as aye,
Anna.

Tim Le Page nosed into L'Hyvreuse and paused in front of
the Duke of Richmond Hotel to see if the light that had
attracted Joly was still on in the sitting-room at Saxon Lodge.
When he saw that it was, he parked and rang the bell.

Charles came to the door. He looked tired and harassed,
but even before Joly's arrival the evening had been a strain.

'I thought I'd let you know he's safely stowed at home. I
didn't have any trouble with him.'

'I didn't like to see you going off on your own, but my
presence could only have made things worse.'

'I'm afraid so. Anyway, I could have radioed for help, but
it wasn't necessary.'

'You didn't have a brandy, Tim. Perhaps you'll have one
now? Anna's gone and the other two are on their way, thank
God.'

'I could do with a brandy.' Tim followed his cousin into the
house.

'Tim!' Olivia didn't get out of her chair unless absolutely
necessary, but she leaned towards him, holding out her hand.
'I've been worried.'

He took the hand and squeezed it before sitting down.
Janet Chapman was watching her husband pace the room.
'He was all right. Poor Joly – he isn't as aggressive as he
sometimes likes to make out.'

'He's a nuisance, though. I hope he isn't going to start
haunting Charles again.'

'There was no point in trying to speak to him tonight, but
I'll have a try when he's more receptive.'

'Had he been drinking?'

'Only his usual few pints, I should say. But enough to take
the brakes off. I suppose Anna was tired.'

'Yes. Long day with lots of new impressions. We're going
to the GSPCA and the Zoo tomorrow.'

19

'We're going to dinner with the Brightwells.' Douglas Chapman paused by the window. 'Which means we won't be home till well after midnight. They get so upset if one suggests leaving at a reasonable hour.'

Janet Chapman looked at her watch. 'Such as half-past eleven.' She got to her feet. 'Thank you both for a lovely evening. Delicious dinner, Olivia, as usual.' She hesitated. 'I'll give you a ring and we'll fix a date for you to come to us.' To Tim she had always been a cipher, but he thought he could see new lines of strain round her eyes and beside her mouth.

'It's tomorrow you're going to the Brightwells?' Olivia asked as she dug herself slowly out of her chair.

'That's right.' Douglas pulled on his moustache. 'Well, thanks, Olivia – Charles.'

'I must go, too.' Tim drained his glass. 'I've taken to hanging around St James in the evenings instead of going to bed, so as to be on the spot if a call comes in about the mugger.'

'You're not getting anywhere?' Douglas Chapman suggested.

'We haven't caught him yet. But if he's not a local he won't get off the island.' Tim wished he felt as confident as he sounded. 'And if he is a local it's only a matter of time.'

'A matter of time before he turns really nasty?'

'That will do, Douglas.' Olivia put her hand on his arm. 'Thank you both for coming tonight. Have a good time tomorrow at the Brightwells.'

MUGGER STRIKES AGAIN! WHOLE POLICE FORCE ENGAGED. WILL TOURISM SUFFER?

The headlines kept repeating themselves in his head, but he still couldn't really believe it. That this odd little island he'd come to just to get away from London had turned him in ten days into a wealthy celebrity.

Wealthy wasn't an exaggeration, and he was probably the most famous person the island had ever known. He couldn't say his name was on everyone's lips, thank God, but his occupation was. MUGGER STRIKES AGAIN!

It made it all the harder, deciding that this had to be his last night. But with just four days left of his holiday he knew it was

20

time to wind things up. Four days with the mugger not operating, and the police would lay off the ships and airport, thinking he had slipped through their fingers or that he was a local. He was ready for a search of the hotel but he mustn't push his luck. And it wasn't as if he had nothing else to do, there was that girl on the beach . . .

Grasping the length of lead piping even tighter in his right hand, he flexed his legs, straining his ears past the small night sounds of breeze in the trees behind him, the rustles caused by birds and small animals.

He didn't have to wait long. It was a couple of women, this time. (He'd become a victim of his own success – women had stopped going round on their own after dark.) They were so terrified one of them crumpled to her knees even before he had the piping properly up. In his hoarse whisper he told them to hand over their jewellery and their cash. He was so confident, now, the inevitable wait while trembling hands did their best to carry out his instructions made him irritable rather than nervous. At one point the younger woman, the one on her feet, was fool enough to start arguing with him, but the piping tapping her shoulder soon shut her up. When he brandished it again and suggested there was more, the older one on the ground looked like she could peg out and he decided to call it a day. They'd probably handed the lot over, anyway. He told them to get moving and not to look back, and when they had stumbled out of sight he legged it into the cover of the trees, where he took off the black gear before going a roundabout way to his hiding place.

It was more of a challenge to get there on foot. He liked using his skills. Not that he felt he had any choice – he didn't dare risk a taxi again. The chap he'd hailed the night before had given him a few nasty moments, the way he'd looked at him and hesitated, then started mumbling into his telephone the moment they set off. All the way across the island the eyes in the mirror had seemed to be on him rather than the road, and it had been tricky to unwrap the lead piping and have it ready in case.

At bay, would he use it?

He didn't know because it had of course been all right, while he was easing the piping into his hand he had got the man talking about football, and when the taxi stopped they were buddies and the driver was telling him you couldn't be too careful . . .

Tonight he made it into the hotel with ten minutes to spare. Mrs O'Malley unfortunately was in the hall, glaring at him suspiciously. But when he made a jokey remark about being one for the girls she endorsed it with such vigorous disgust he realized on a high of triumph that in her narrow mind he was pigeon-holed as a womaniser.

He turned to the stairs with an apologetic smile, but the high he was feeling had made him decide to have one more go. Three blank nights would be enough to make the police slack off the ferries and the airport so he didn't have to be too careful.

One final stand, in a place he could get back from on foot but where he hadn't been before – it would fill the afternoon nicely, finding it – and he really would call it a day.

Chapter Three

'I could do without the vast H for Hire on my car,' Anna told Olivia as she turned the corner out of L'Hyvreuse. 'It feels like an L for Learner.'

'I know. I had to hire a car for a few days recently when mine was in dock, and I felt I was sporting an F for Fool. Mind you, some visitors do need to be treated warily on the roads, so it's probably a good thing.' Olivia yawned and spread her legs. 'We may find as many boarders as patients in the Animal Shelter. People here tend to be properly responsible for their animals.'

'I like the sound of that.'

Anna liked Olivia as a passenger, too, sprawling relaxed beside her but never failing to issue instructions well in advance of their arrival at a junction, interspersed with comments on their surroundings.

'We're over the border now into St Andrew,' she told Anna, after ten minutes or so of floral suburb. 'It's the only landlocked parish, so you can get to a different sort of seaside quite quickly in all directions. I always think of it as the animal parish, it's got the Zoo as well as the GSPCA.' Olivia broke off to laugh, a throaty chuckle. 'I'm sorry, Anna, I sound like a travelogue. But over the years I've written various articles about the island and it all tends to come out on a reflex.'

'That suits me. Do you write other things, too?'

'Not much. My job is to read. For MacEwens. Superior female fiction.'

'What a suitable job for an island. Do you get to London much?'

'Not often, I prefer it here. But I've a trip I can't avoid coming up in a couple of weeks. Here's the GSPCA now, on the left. Park anywhere you can find.'

A young man was by her door before Anna had switched off the engine, his enquiring face breaking into a smile as he recognized Olivia. Anna wound down her window.

The young man spoke across her. 'Good to see you, Mrs De Garde. I didn't recognize the car.'

'Meet Mrs Weston, Don. She doesn't like the H for Hire on her car as she isn't a tourist, she'll be standing in for Brian Bradshaw from next week while he's in the States.'

Although more agreeable, the young man's interested switch of attention reminded Anna of Douglas Chapman's reaction the night before.

'Take Mrs Weston round in an orderly manner,' Olivia suggested as Don helped her out of the car. 'While I meander.'

'Sure. Brian's practice serves the shelter,' he told Anna as he led the way indoors.

She liked his bright, dedicated face. 'I know. I hope I'll be allowed to visit you professionally. Small animals are my speciality.'

The two girl assistants, Becky and Amy, seemed as glad to learn about her as Don had been. 'You run things very well,' she said, when they had toured the wounded and the homeless and she had watched them change a couple of dressings.

'It's a great place to work,' Becky told her. 'Individual animals are important in Guernsey, like individual people. Locals like Don take it for granted, but I'm an incomer and it hits you.'

'I'm looking forward to it.' Looking forward, as well, to working again. The last half hour had shown Anna that she wouldn't lament the passing of her week's holiday.

Olivia strolled up as they were admiring the boarders. 'I'm going to London in a couple of weeks,' she told them, 'and when I come back I want a kitten. My cat died last month, Anna. He was seventeen.'

'That rare ginger mother has two kittens,' Becky said. 'The ginger's a boy and he's gorgeous.'

24

'I mustn't look at him. If I do I'll fall, and then you'll feel you have to say no to someone who can take him right away. I'll come in again as soon as I get back.'

'I hope I'll come in again soon, too,' Anna said.

'So do we.'

Amy appeared as well to wave them off.

'All right?' Olivia asked as they drove away.

'Oh, yes.'

'Barry Jones is going back to Wales at the end of the year. If they couldn't find a locum on the island they may not be able to find a permanent replacement. You'll have a chance to find out if you'd be interested.' Olivia's bulk shifted slightly. 'Forgive me, Anna. I don't know anything about your long term plans, but I thought I'd tell you so that you'll have some idea of how you want to react to the news when you hear it in the practice.'

'At the moment I don't know what I want long term, but thanks.'

'Are you all right?'

'I don't know. I haven't been. Mickey was keeping Jimmy and me together. After he was killed it went really wrong. It's almost a year now. He was knocked down by a lorry. At least he died instantly.'

'That's terrible. At least my son wasn't meant to live.'

Anna heard Olivia's shuddering sigh. 'But never to have known him . . .' She mustn't start crying again or she mightn't be able to stop. 'I left Jimmy a couple of months ago and moved into a flat. That didn't seem to be enough, so I answered Brian Bradshaw's ad, and when I got the job here I left the practice where I was working.'

'A burning of boats. Or is it?'

'I think so, although I'm trying to keep an open mind through these three months. Jimmy's so miserable, Olivia, he's always relied on me too much, and I'm so bloody sorry for him. But I know that's the last reason to stay with a man. Since Mickey died he's hardly let me breathe. It helped when I moved out, but not as much as this last twenty-four hours. That's ridiculous, isn't it?'

'It's the island.'

'It did it right away for you, as well? I'm sorry, I don't suppose you came here for assistance in living.'

25

'I came here for a holiday, and I met Charles. Who have you met from the practice?'

'John Coquelin. In London.'

'John's a nice man, you'll like working with him. Are you gong to see them before you start?'

'I've an invitation to call on the Bradshaws any time this week. They want to tell me what I need to know when I take over their house. D'you know it?'

'Charles and I have been a couple of times for dinner. It's rather large but don't worry, it'll come with a daily help and a gardener. Turn right here, then immediately left. We'll stop at Vauxbelets and have a look at the little chapel. Just ahead at the T junction. Good, there's a space . . .' Olivia had stirred herself slightly to assess parking possibilities, and got out of the car more quickly than Anna had begun to expect, in a swirl of generously cut yellow-gold skirt. 'I'm afraid the summer one-way system will be in operation,' she said as they started up the path to the tiny steepled building. 'But you have to see it. It's supposed to be the smallest church in the world. A French monk had three goes at building it over twenty-five years, then had to decamp to France in 1939 before his third and successful attempt was completed. The other monks here at Vauxbelets finished it for him.' Olivia paused at the door to recover her breath. 'The core is clinker from the furnaces used to heat Guernsey greenhouses, and you can see for yourself that every last surface is covered with shells and bits of glass and china. Inside as well as out. Mind your head.'

The faceted walls of the chapel winked in the dim interior light. There was a small altar, and with the six people already inside Olivia and Anna would have made up a maximum congregation.

'If you took the permanent job with Brian,' Olivia murmured as they waited their turn to descend the steps to the tiny shrines, 'you'd be able to come in the winter and have it to yourself.'

Perhaps Janet Chapman was less than stimulating company. Or perhaps Olivia, like Anna herself, found comfort in the novel thought of a relative close at hand who was looking more and more as if she could double as a friend.

'Your father and my mother,' Anna said as they walked back to the car, 'they were quite near in age, weren't they? Do you know if they got on?'

'Yes. He was devastated when she died. I remember you at the funeral, Anna.'

'I don't remember you. I only remember a lot of people standing too close to me who had suddenly become large and dark and solemn and wouldn't give me back my mother. No, I think I remember your father. I think he was the man who seemed less dark than the others, and took me on his knee.'

'He offered to adopt you but your father wouldn't let you go.'

Anna stood still. 'I didn't know.'

'I thought you might not. My mother was willing – we were both only children. So we might have been sisters instead of cousins. Actually I was rather relieved at the time; I didn't much like the idea of sharing. Anyway, Father died soon after and it dwindled to Christmas cards. I hope I haven't upset you, Anna.'

'No. I'm glad my father held on to me and I wasn't much of a sharer then, either, but I think I'd be glad now to have had a sister.'

'Yes. Well . . .' Olivia turned away to squeeze into the car. 'Now for the Zoo,' she announced when Anna was beside her. 'We're almost there. Then we'll go on to lunch at a pub I like in St Peter's, if that suits.'

'It does.'

Olivia called the young man behind the Zoo's ticket window Jeremy, and introduced him to Anna. 'Nothing bigger than a goat or fiercer than an eagle owl,' he told her. 'You could find yourself here professionally.'

'I hope so, although I've no experience of exotic creatures.'

'John Coquelin has, he'll bring you.' Olivia waved away the Guernsey note in Anna's hand. 'No, you're my guest today. It's a nice garden as well, as you can see.'

The garden was revealed as the path widened out – slight slopes luxuriantly set with shrubs and flowers around the small enclosures.

'All the animals were born in captivity,' Olivia said as they strolled forward. 'I'm sorry, I like this place so much I didn't ask if you object in principle to zoos.'

27

'Only to the practice of bad ones. This is fine.'

'You have to see the meercats.'

Most of the meercats were satisfactorily on their feet, performing their impersonation of small human beings anxiously surveying the horizon. There were also wallabies, small monkeys, otters, sloths, and tiny tamarins. Before they left, Jeremy allowed Anna to handle a monkey.

'Now for the real country,' Olivia said as they turned off the main road. 'St Peter's is only a mile from the airport but really it's light years away. I love the pattern of lanes and little fields. I think I've worked out a route that won't get us lost, although it doesn't matter if it does.'

'I like the thought of being lost here.' Between tangled hedges half hiding fields streaked red, yellow and blue, listening to a frantic thrush.

'So do I, and it still happens, and then suddenly there's the English Channel into infinity. Yet people ask if the island gives me claustrophobia.'

Anna negotiated another narrow high-hedged bend. 'You love the island, don't you, Olivia?'

'Like so many latecomers to places and creeds – no one more passionate than a convert. For me it's the ideal place to live. I love its smallness, it makes me feel secure, and it has every sort of life style – town, village, country, seaside – in microcosm. It's out of the rat race, and the individual is still important.'

'I can feel that already.'

They ate outside an old inn in the shade of a beech tree. 'Perhaps you were aware of a sense of strain last night?' Olivia suggested, as the landlord turned away after setting their drinks and salads on the rough wooden table.

'Yes, I was.'

'Charles is having an affair with Janet. Janet handles it very well, don't you think? Though not as well as Charles, of course.'

'Olivia –' The immediate shock was the contrast between Olivia's lazy half-smile and what she was saying.

'Charles and I have a good marriage,' Olivia went on calmly. 'But after the death of our son we ceased to have sex. I didn't want it any more, Charles still did. In the same way that

28

he needs whisky to relax. When he has a whisky, Anna, it doesn't affect him and me. His brief affairs don't, either.'

'But – Janet –'

'Yes. It's the first time I've known the woman. I'd rather not. Poor Janet, I suspect she's making too much of it.'

'You're sorry for her?'

'No. But I know how charming Charles can be.'

'How are you able to carry on as friends?'

'Because that's what we are. Have been ever since Janet and Douglas came to the island three or four years ago.'

'Charles told you?'

'I saw it in his face one night the four of us were out together. I'd seen it before, a sort of – sudden absorption. His face never looks like that at any other time.'

It hadn't looked like that at last night's dinner table. Perhaps it was a sign that Janet Chapman was on the way out? 'I'm sorry, Olivia.'

Olivia's heavy shoulders rose and fell. 'It will come to an end, just like a bottle of whisky. Janet knows the score.'

'And she knows that you –'

'Oh, yes. It's all right, Anna.'

'Douglas knows, too, doesn't he?'

'I don't think so. He's just always on the defensive. But as everyone else in Guernsey seems to, I suppose it's only a matter of time.'

'Only a matter of time before the affair's over, you told me. So that could come first.'

Olivia laughed. 'Thank you, Anna. I don't envy Janet if Douglas finds out – he has an outsize *amour propre*. I suppose I am a bit sorry for her.'

'To the extent of not blaming her?'

'I wouldn't go quite as far as that.' Olivia yawned and stretched. 'It isn't important, Anna, but I thought it was sensible to tell you why there can be an atmosphere when the Chapmans are around. Save your imagination working overtime.'

'Thank you. It upsets Tim, doesn't it?'

'You noticed that? Tim's my good friend, and he's very straightforward. Now, I suspect I have a migraine coming on, so I think we should make for home.'

29

'I'm sorry.'

'They aren't usually very bad. I wasn't going to ask you to dinner anyway tonight, you're only at the Duke for a few days and the food is wonderful. I expect you've paid for the dinners, too.'

'Yes.'

'I'm paying for lunch. But if you'd just go inside and do it for me . . .'

Olivia was silent on the way home, except for her impeccable directions. Standing with her at her front door, Anna thought she saw pallor under the suntan, and there was a tic at work in her cheek.

'Thank you so much, Olivia. I enjoyed that enormously.'

'So did I.'

'You're sure you're all right?'

'Yes. I just need to lie down. If you want to go into town, by the way, it's easiest to walk. Go down through Candie Gardens and out of the main gate at the bottom. You'll find yourself at traffic lights on St Julian's Avenue. Cross it into Ann's Place, carry on downhill along Smith Street, and you're there. It's a ten-minute walk. I'll be in touch.' Olivia hesitated. 'Not because of thinking it's kind, or polite. I'm glad you're here, Anna.'

'So am I.'

Surprised by her continuing sense of relish, Anna parked in the Duke of Richmond's car park and set off immediately on foot along the side of the hotel.

Janet Chapman moved slowly about her large kitchen, automatically preparing dinner while she thought about Charles De Garde and what had happened between them.

Sometimes thoughts of Douglas and Olivia obtruded, but with less shock and shame than at first.

She also thought about her past life, because its dreariness was so brightly illuminated by the light her extraordinary experience was casting in every direction. How had she ever married Douglas, then lived thirteen loyal years with his dullness?

Because she had been dull herself, that was why. Average at school, competent at secretarial college, reliable in an

30

office. Boyfriends boring worthies or repulsive fumblers, nothing important or exciting enough to help her gauge the inadequacy of Douglas's comparative wealth and sophistication or diffuse the dazzle of being invited out by her boss. After dinner in a good Soho restaurant – she hadn't known, of course, that it wasn't really Douglas country – he had brought her home, and her mother, waiting as Janet had feared in the hall, had opened the door and secured herself an introduction. When Douglas had driven away in his Mercedes and her mother said 'Out of your class, darling,' Janet knew she would follow wherever Douglas led. Her life had to change – as it had to change now – and the only alternative to Douglas was a place of her own. For a less dull young woman this would perhaps have been more interesting than Douglas's house in Weybridge, but the Sunday before the dinner date she had driven quickly past it and seen enough to be more confident of its promises of comfort and status than of her own ability to galvanize her single life. They had become engaged within a fortnight, married within a couple of months.

It hadn't taken long for Douglas to relapse back into his pernickety, self-absorbed ways. And there wasn't enough difference in their ages – only eleven years – for there to be a fatherly element in his feelings for her which might have retained some sense of affection.

It hadn't seemed a bad bargain, even so. She was free from her mother and her office, and so long as she saw to Douglas's every small need – there were no large ones – he was pleased to be able to turn all his attention to his work and let her manage his handsome house and garden. She had quickly discovered a talent and a liking for interior decoration and a passionate love of gardening. She had awaited with mild curiosity the sensations and emotions of child-bearing, but no child had come. Douglas had refused to consider her tentative suggestion that they submit themselves to medical examination, but her instinct had told her that the fault was his.

No need to think any more about that. It was the past, another country to which she could never now return.

Her interests in her home and garden and various good works had been enough for her in England, but when they

31

came to Fort George with its ready-decorated house and professionally maintained designer garden she had been so bored she had started looking for a job. They had met Charles and Olivia soon after their arrival in the island, and when one of his partners lost his PA to pregnancy Charles had recommended Janet. For years it had been no more than a good post obtained through the kind act of a friend, but now it was her daily gateway to a sense of being alive she had never before dreamed of.

Janet was so absorbed in her thoughts that she failed to register the sound of Douglas's key in the lock of the front door. When he came into the kitchen she turned round with a start and he caught the tail-end of her reminiscent smile. A smile she had never bestowed on *him*, not even in the far-off days of their courtship. It killed the last shred of doubt he had clung to since Paul's lunchtime revelation.

'Douglas! You're early.' Her smile now was its usual self, determined and unintimate. 'I didn't expect you quite so soon.'

'That was obvious.' Seeing her standing looking at him in her usual way, so calm and modest, so much the same as always, he wondered if he could be dreaming. 'Paul Tostevin told me something at lunch today. About you and Charles. Is it true?'

'Yes.' No point in asking him what he meant. And she had been braced for it.

He seized her by the shoulders, pleased to feel them trying to shrink between his hands, and shook her so fiercely her head lolled and she cried out. 'Whore!' he shouted. 'Jezebel!' He had to push her into a chair to prevent himself really hurting her. 'You're disgusting. You disgust me!'

'I'm sorry, Douglas.'

'You're sorry! Good God, Janet, Charles De Garde! A by-word for adultery! Your friend's husband! How could you? And why? Why? Janet, for God's sake . . .'

'I wasn't looking for it, Douglas, it happened – before I knew. I've never been unfaithful to you before.' She was shocked that the man raging close enough for her to feel his spittle on her cheek could seem so far away, so unimportant. She had to make an effort to think of him as a real person, suffering the real torments of a wounded self-esteem. Not wounded love, she couldn't imagine that, and there was anger rather than pain in his eyes.

'You've lived a lie so cleverly, I'm beginning to wonder!'

'I promise you, Douglas, this is the one and only time. Perhaps if you and I hadn't been going through a bit of a sticky patch . . .' It was the only self-justification she would offer.

'So that's your excuse, is it?' His anger had made him even paler than usual, but now a pink flush suffused his face. She found it absurd that a man who had been married for fifteen years should be embarrassed to discuss sex, however obliquely, with his wife.

'I have no excuse, Douglas, and I'm not trying to make one. Perhaps I should have told you.'

Her body was trembling but her face was still calm. He hadn't shaken her spirit. And she hadn't even attempted to deny it. 'Perhaps you should. I mightn't now be looking quite so much of a fool.'

'I haven't told anyone else.'

'But everyone knows. Except, until today, your husband.'

'No. Olivia knows because she noticed, and then Charles told her. And I suppose in the office . . . Paul Tostevin breathes other people's business, you know that. He's a friend of my boss –'

'And so it goes on.'

'Douglas, I hoped . . .'

'That you might get away with it? Well, I suppose it was on the cards, Charles gets tired of his women pretty quickly.' At least he had made her wince.

'I'm sorry.'

'You're not! You're not!' He was shouting again. 'You're revelling in it, you're loving it. Oh, the delight of making a fool of your husband –'

'Douglas! Do you really think that's why –'

She was looking at him with pity. On top of everything else she had the impertinence to be sorry for him.

His fury welled up again so violently he had to move away from her, and went over to the window, trying to remind himself as he stared unseeingly out that it could only be a matter of time before she reverted to the old predictable

Janet, crushed to an even more amenable state of wifely behaviour.

But until that inevitable day, and probably for ever after, Janet's face as well as Paul's had told him that he would be an object of pity. Because his wife had had an affair with Charles De Garde. His wife. Janet! Who up to a few hours ago hadn't given him a moment's anxiety in the whole of their married life. Not, he had to admit, that he had been all that aware of her thoughts and feelings. But he had lifted her out of the ruck and she had been happy enough about that at the time. And contented ever since, until . . .

Charles De Garde. Joly Duguy had called him a bastard, and he had been right. A destructive bastard, causing havoc wherever he went and yet blessed with a wife like Olivia, accepting his infidelities and keeping both his love and her dignity. Dignity! A man whom people pitied had no dignity. By losing her own, his wife had robbed him of his. Charles De Garde had robbed him.

It was so unbelievable it kept hitting him as if he was learning it for the first time. Reluctantly he turned to look at her, trying to disguise the fact that a wave of physical nausea was making him lean against the sink. She was still on the chair where he had thrown her, looking back at him with her usual lack of expression, no sign of the shame that ought never to leave her face.

'How long will this go on?' he demanded.

'Not long, Douglas, I promise you.'

'He's getting tired of you?'

'You can't expect me to answer that.'

He had still not made her falter. 'I need a housekeeper.' He was raging so hotly inside, it pleased him to hear himself cold. 'You can remain here in that capacity.' He didn't want her near him, but neither did he want her to move out and destroy all possibility of the scandal blowing over.

'Thank you, Douglas.' She had been no more than housekeeper since before their arrival at Fort George, but she wouldn't ask for more trouble by reminding him. And for the time being it suited her. 'I'm sorry,' she repeated.

'Don't keep saying that, you don't meant it.'

'I do. I don't want to hurt you.'

34

'Olivia?'

'Or Olivia.' At least the thought of Olivia had made her shudder.

'What's all this food for?' The shudder made it possible for him to take a few steps towards the centre table. 'We're supposed to be going to the Brightwells. Not that I've any intention of going anywhere with you again.'

'Jenny rang this afternoon to cancel. Richard has flu, he's come home from the office and gone to bed. She'll be in touch when he's better.'

'I see.' *Jenny rang this afternoon.* Which meant to the office. Charles De Garde's office. So easy to tell Charles that the dinner party was off. And take the lift to the top floor and the executive suite . . . If he stayed in all evening she wouldn't be able to get out. Even this unbelievable new Janet wasn't shameless enough to leave the house for an assignation while her husband was at home.

But what did it matter? One evening of enforced wifely presence wouldn't alter things. And if he went to the Club she might go out as well, and he could perhaps catch up with them . . .

The Club . . . 'You've taken the Club from me, too,' he shouted in dismay.

'Of course I haven't. No one at your Club will know, or be in the least interested. Charles isn't a member.'

'But I am,' he yelled. 'I am!'

'So go! What I've done doesn't have to affect your member-ship of the Club. Really, Douglas.' His eyes were frantic and she was doing her poor best to empathise with the disturbing new sense of social insecurity she suspected was the worst think she had brought him. But it was hard to be sorry for someone who was so sorry for himself.

'You'd like to think that, wouldn't you, make yourself feel a bit more comfortable?'

'I know how much you enjoy going to the Club, and I don't want you to be afraid of it, there's no need.'

'Oh, I'll go. Don't worry. I'll go now.'

'Have dinner first please, Douglas, it's well under way.'

'I don't want any dinner. I'll go to the Club when I'm ready.'

35

He went through into the sitting-room to pour himself a large whisky – the only thing he could think of that might make his sense of outrage a bit easier to endure.

She was lying on her side in the wide bed, facing the door. The curtains were closed. When he was halfway across the room she spoke.

'I'm afraid I've got a migraine, darling.'

He stopped. 'I'm sorry, Olivia. Is it very bad?'

'No. But I think I'll stay here till the morning. The casserole only needs heating through, it's got everything in it.'

'I'm sure it has.' Charles completed his journey to the bed and put his hand on her forehead. 'Has it spoiled your day, darling?'

'Only the last bit. Anna and I enjoyed ourselves.'

'I'm glad she's here. I feel you could be friends as well as cousins.'

'It's possible.'

He bent to kiss her cheek. 'Is there anything you want?'

'Not at the moment. Perhaps you'll come up again later. It's still very hot, isn't it?'

'Yes. I'll probably go for a walk when it's cooler.'

'I'm sorry to desert you, Charles. I'll be all right tomorrow.'

'Of course you will, darling.'

He went up to her again at nine, and she asked for toast and honey. When he went to collect the tray she had eaten all the toast and told him she was feeling better. 'But I think I'll close my eyes again. Let me know when you're going out, won't you, Charles? I should hate to call you and not get an answer.'

'Of course I'll let you know.'

When he went up at half past eleven she was reading.

'I couldn't sleep,' she said, smiling at him as she put the book on the table beside the bed. 'I'll take a tablet now and try to settle down. You're going out?'

'Just for a walk in Candie Gardens. It's a glorious evening.'

'I'll say goodnight, then, Charles. Take care.'

'I'll take the dagger. Goodnight, darling.' He bent to kiss her.

'Goodnight, darling, ' she murmured, yawning.

'Have you stayed at the Duke before?'

'No.'

'This is my third visit.'

'Really?'

'Yes. It's a good hotel. Don't you think so?'

'Yes. Oh, yes.'

'So do I.'

Anna liked dancing, as opposed to discos, and at least her partner danced well, even though she had to be careful not to rest her chin on his ear – there were certain situations in which being five feet nine was a disadvantage. Not that he seemed to mind. He was the only man at the generously sized and spaced tables for one grouped together in the Duke of Richmond's dining-room, and he had homed in on her the moment she had finished her dinner and strolled through into the ballroom.

'My name's Harry Price,' he said as the music stopped.

'Anna Weston,' she replied reluctantly.

'Let's have a drink, shall we, Anna?'

There was admiration in the sharp-eyed, self-confident face, and a middle-aged married couple she had talked to in the bar before dinner were smiling at them fondly through the gloom. The situation was reminding her of what it had been like in her teens to feel trapped, awakening a flicker of regret for the protection she had walked away from. But a woman of thirty-four wasn't worth her salt if she couldn't spring a social trap, however unaccustomed.

'Thank you.'

She led the way to the table where the middle-aged couple were sitting, ignoring the murmur of dissent behind her. Her three companions were so fluent about themselves and their reactions to Guernsey that by the end of a half pint of lager Anna had still not been asked any questions.

When she glanced discreetly at her watch it was half past eleven and she got to her feet. 'If you'll excuse me now, I need to write some letters. Thank you for the drink, Harry. Goodnight.'

It was a relief to close her door behind her and feel happier alone, looking forward to the simple prospect of reading in bed.

But first she switched off the lights, opened the curtains and the window, and stood looking out. The feathered edges of

37

the trees beyond Cambridge Park were motionless silhouettes, the sky was high and starry and the air was sweet. On a flash of pleasure that was gloriously unfamiliar she thought of walking along to the lookout, then remembered Tim Le Page's dinner-table lecture about the danger from the mugger in dark and lonely places. Cambridge Park tonight was a dark and lonely place.

The silence was so total it revealed a myriad small sounds. The low call of an owl, the shriek of a small rodent, the sleepy murmur of a bird, the soft closing of a door – and the shattering rhythm of confident male feet passing from right to left under her window.

When the silence was restored Anna took a last long breath of the perfect summer night, closed the curtains, and groped her way to a light.

Chapter Four

Anna had asked for an alarm call at eight, but woke as usual at seven.

Over the past months the instinctive pleasure of returning consciousness had given way within seconds to depression and self-doubt, but this morning in her Guernsey hotel room the sense of zest with which she had gone to sleep seemed to have survived the night. So did her regained energy, and she leaped out of bed and across to the window.

All that remained of the night view was the stillness of the trees. The green was already bright with sunshine and the sky was all-over blue. Today would be as fine as yesterday and the day before. Anna washed and dressed without any of her accustomed pauses to stare into space, then ran downstairs.

A girl she hadn't yet seen was hovering in Reception.

'Mrs Weston – Room 112. I shan't need my call and I'll be back for breakfast.'

'Yeah. Fine.' The girl offered a sleepy smile as Anna hurried out.

She retraced her steps of the day before up the side of the hotel and down the hill to the green gates. She was prepared for the disappointment of finding them closed, but one was ajar.

This time she went straight ahead instead of cutting through to the café, learning as she walked that the gardens were set on a shallow slope. On her left a high boundary wall of variously shaped and coloured stones had plants and seats at its foot, to her right bright circles of begonias on sloping lawns shone among the shadows of trees and bushes, many of them unfamiliar. Anna left the path to descend a flight of stone steps flanked by pipe-playing stone satyrs, walking on tiptoe through the enchanted morning to protect her illusion that it was the morning of the world in the Garden of Eden – an illusion unshattered by the chimney-eared tops of the more splendid houses of L'Hyvreuse rising above the wall. They merely told her that paradise was nearer home than she had imagined.

Ahead was a tree-traced view of the harbour and the sea, and when she thought she must be parallel with the lookout Anna came upon a pond inside old-fashioned iron railings.

And upon the the body of a man, slumped across them.

She knew at once that it was a body. Not just because it failed to respond to the sharp sound of her shock against the bird song. Only a dead weight could have pushed the iron railing so severely out of line, only a corpse have lain so sharply jack-knifed across it, feet just off the ground, dangling hands just clearing the grassy rim of the pond.

And the head. She could see only the back of it, but it was enough to show her why the man had died. The silver-grey hair, immaculate at the sides, had disappeared in the centre into a red-brown crater.

'*Specializes in a piece of lead piping.*'

Anna turned away to be sick into the grass. Painfully, not having eaten. And with a sense of shamed surprise. Over her years of encountering dead animals she had thought she would be inured to an encounter with a dead human being. She had been wrong.

On an absurd hope that she might have been wrong, too, in her first diagnosis of a human death, that a living body would after all be able to balance itself as this body was balanced, Anna turned back to it.

But nothing of course had changed. The serpent really had entered the garden.

In the shape of a mugger?

'*Specializes in a piece of lead piping, but doesn't use it.*'

Well, there was always a first time.

The museum wouldn't be open, but there was a house just inside the green gates that could belong to the head gardener. If no one came to the door she would be at the Duke within minutes.

40

Anna set off up the slope of the gardens at a run, her ears filled with the sound of her own feet and breath, so that she almost collided with the other runner before she was aware of him. A tall young man with untidy hair wearing yellow shorts and sleeveless shirt, a dog at his side.

'Hey! Steady on!'

She was running to the police, but the police had run to her.

'Tim Le Page! Oh, I'm glad to see you!'

'Well, thank you. But forgive me . . .' The woman panting in front of him was no more than the series of points he had trained himself to notice about a member of the public behaving suspiciously: tall, thin but nourished, youngish, short smooth dark hair, breathless and with anguished eyes and mouth. Knowing his name. Putting her hand on his arm.

'I'm afraid I don't –'

'Tim Le Page,' she repeated. 'I'm Anna Weston, Olivia De Garde's cousin. I've just found a dead body.'

'Anna! I'm sorry!' Abruptly she was a person. Not much like the cool, sophisticated woman he had sat next to at Olivia's dinner table, but recognizable. 'What did you say?'

'There's a body slumped over the railings by the pond down there. The head's caved in, there's no doubt the man's dead. I was running for the police and – and I found them!'

Her laugh held a note of hysteria, but it made her look a bit more like the woman he remembered. A woman who would know a dead body when she saw one.

'I'm sorry, I'll have to ask you to come back with me.'

'Yes, of course.' It was the first time she had heard the policeman in Tim Le Page.

They ran side by side, the dog keeping pace. 'This is Duffy,' Tim explained. 'I come out as much for him as for me.'

'I like the look of him.'

'He's a fine Heinz Variety.' The dog, neither large nor small, had a shaggy ginger coat, gleaming brown eyes and nose, and pricked, expressive ears. 'Down and outs do tend to come into the gardens at night, I always thought it was a mistake to keep them open. *Cordammy!*'

Her Guernsey-born waiter had said that yesterday at breakfast, when he had spilt the milk. 'Not a down and out.' Tim halted on the grass the far side of the path from the railings. 'The clothes are expensive.'

41

The hard dry surface of the path was unlikely to yield footprints, and after ordering his dog to sit down beside Anna Tim gingerly crossed it. The dog obeyed him, but immediately raised its nose to the sky and began an excruciating lament, which it took Anna's reassuring practised hand a few moments to subdue to a whimper.

'Thanks.'

'Could the wound have been made with a piece of lead piping?'

'I should say so.' He was trying to lean over the railings without touching them, to look into the face. 'Some of my colleagues have been waiting for the mugger to turn violent, it's a classic –. Oh, God. Oh, my dear God.'

Tim had taken the body in his stride, as a piece of business, but now he was backing away from it and staring in horror at the maroon and silver head.

'What is it?'

His stare turned on Anna, but she didn't think he saw her. 'It's Charles. Charles De Garde. I can't see his face but I recognize the watch. I gave it him for Christmas.' Why hadn't the mugger taken it? 'That's why Duffy –'

'Oh, no. Oh, please no.' His cousin, the husband of hers. *'Charles and I have a good marriage.'*

They said the word 'Olivia' in shocked unison, but for the moment it was all the policeman could spare her. Taking Anna's hand and calling the dog, he started running back up the garden.

'Priority is to get the team here and the gates closed. If the murderer's still this side of them, all the better. It's unlikely, of course, but you'd better stick close to me even though in this gear I feel as helpless as a baby. We'll try the head gardener's house first.'

The door was opened by the head gardener's wife, sleepy-eyed in a dressing-gown.

'Detective Inspector Le Page! Ted's lying in, he's off duty this morning.'

'That's all right, Mrs Dunning. If I could just use your telephone.'

When Tim had made his report and requests he went into the kitchen and found Anna drinking a mug of tea. He refused one. 'I must get back to – the body.' The pause was for his own flesh and blood. 'The team will be here within minutes. Someone will come to see your husband.'

Outside, poised to run, he told Anna she would have to make a statement.

'I realize that.' She had to ask him. 'Would you like me to tell Olivia?'

He shook his head, smiling but sure. 'Thank you, but it must be me.'

'Yes.' She hesitated a second time, but they had met socially first and could just be called relations by marriage. 'Would it be helpful to suggest going for my car and waiting to chauffeur you to a change of clothes?'

'It would. I live quite close to the Duke, and it won't do Olivia any more wrong to get out of this gear and collect my radio before going to see her. If you drive past the lane where you came in and take the next left turn into Candie Road you come to the main gates where there's a layby. I'll see you there as soon as I can.'

Tim wished he could have got dressed before receiving the team, but that was the least of things. Waiting beside his cousin's body, he tried not to review what he reluctantly knew of his private life. He had been fond of Charles, and the mugger struck indiscriminately.

The Scenes-of-Crime officer arrived when his vigil was only five minutes old. Then a couple of uniformed men, one of whom went down with him to the main gates and locked them behind him. Anna Weston was parked where he had suggested. As she saw him she pushed the passenger seat forward for Duffy to leap into the back.

'Thanks.' Tim replaced the seat and got in beside her. 'You can't go up the way you came down. Carry on to the lights and turn right. I told them about you when I rang in, that you were first on the scene.' On a fleeting reflex he wondered if she could have known Charles in London. 'I also said I thought you'd prefer to go to the station to make your statement than have someone come to the hotel. That's St James, you go –'

'I noticed it yesterday when I walked down to town. The long low building behind the sunken gardens. Yes, I'd rather go there. Shall I go straight away when I've dropped you?'

43

'After you've had breakfast, if you want any. Left here, then right.' Skirting the old Candie Cemetery, where Charles was about to join his fathers.

'When I've finished . . . Should I go to her?' She and Olivia had had a good day yesterday – remembering it was like peering a long way into the past – but it was the only one they had ever spent together.

'Turn right here. I should think she'd want to see you, but obviously we don't know how she's going to react. I'll leave a message for you at the Duke.'

'Thanks.'

'Right again here, then stop halfway down by the red car.'

It was a steep hill lined with stout stuccoed villas, the port and the sea at its foot.

'Thanks,' he returned.

'I'm glad I could help. God, it's awful.'

'Yes. She loved him. Come on, dog.'

Olivia's front door opened as Tim reached it. It was the first time in their long friendship that he had seen her face disordered.

'Oh, Tim . . . I rang you at home and you weren't there and then when I rang St James they told me you were on your way to see me. Charles went to Candie Gardens last night. I took a sleeping pill and I didn't wake till after eight. He hadn't come back . . . Tim, why are you here?'

'Come into the sitting-room.' He led her to her chair and pushed her gently down.

'Tim. Please.'

'Olivia . . .' He crouched beside her, putting his hand on her firm brown arm. 'Charles is dead. I went into Candie Gardens for a run and I met Anna going for the police. She'd found Charles's body by the first pond.'

'His heart.' She had turned her face away from him on the word 'dead' and was staring blankly ahead. 'We both knew there was a chance of it.'

'No. Someone . . . The mugger . . .'

'No!' He felt the brief agitation of her body vibrating through the chair. Then she was still again. An utter stillness that appalled him. 'Not that, Tim,' she said at last to the wall. 'A heart attack. A stroke. Not – that.'

44

He moved his grip down her arm, took her unresponsive hand. 'He was hit on the head. He would have died right away. I should say several hours ago, but we'll soon know. What time did he go out? Olivia?'

She still didn't turn to him, didn't move. Her hand in his could have been a piece of warm smooth wood. 'I suppose about half-past eleven. I told him not to, I said it was asking for trouble. He said the mugger hadn't discovered Candie Gardens. Tim . . .' The hand came to life, convulsing in his as shockingly as if Charles's fingers had prodded the grass they were dangling over. Belatedly he felt his gorge rising.

'Hang on, dear.' He subdued the nausea, and her twisting fingers. 'He wouldn't have known. Health to heaven . . .' He wasn't sure he believed that, but for the moment comfort was all.

'Thank you for being the one to tell me, Tim.' She had turned back to him, had let him catch her staring eyes. 'You must have been tempted to let someone else –'

'Not for a moment. Olivia – he would have been alone?'

The fingers stiffened. 'Yes. I think that last night he would have been alone.'

'Thank you.' He held her head against him, murmuring and stroking her hair, until the expected sound of the front door. 'There's someone outside who'll make us tea.' Gently he drew away from her and got to his feet.

'Pour me a brandy, Tim. We'll have tea later.'

'All right. Just hang on a minute.'

He let the WPC into the house and led her to the kitchen. 'She's all right. Make tea, will you? Caddy on the shelf over the sink, milk in the fridge. Make it for us all and bring it in.'

Olivia hadn't moved and was studying the wall again. He went to the corner cupboard and poured two brandies.

'Here, drink this.'

He could feel the effort it took her to turn to him. 'Thanks, Tim.' Her mouth quavered. It was an attempt at a smile, but he would have preferred it to be the beginning of tears.

'WPC Gallienne's making tea as well. I know you don't need her but it's regulation.'

'Yes. Of course.'

He didn't think she had taken it in, but when the WPC arrived with a tray she showed no surprise. Which could be

45

shock, of course. They drank in silence, the WPC the most obviously upset. Olivia took a couple of sips then returned to her brandy, draining it.

'I'm all right, Tim,' she said as she set the glass down, but she missed the table and the glass fell on to the carpet. The WPC ran forward to pick it up, checking her speed halfway. 'I'm Jenny,' she said, kneeling where Tim had knelt. 'I'll make you a bit of lunch later on.'

'It's all right,' Olivia murmured. She turned past the WPC's anxious face towards the walled garden, slanted with sunshine which by lunchtime would have reached the french windows.

'Tonight,' Tim said, 'I can stay here. Or you can move into my spare room. Perhaps Anna –'

'It's all right,' Olivia said again, to the garden. 'I don't need anyone. Or to leave the house. Honestly, Tim. He – didn't die here.' Something at last flickered across her face. 'Die . . . You said his head . . .'

'Yes. The back of his head. One blow. It would have killed him then and there.'

'He wouldn't have suffered?'

'No.'

He saw her sigh, her heavy bosom rising and falling. 'Thank God at least for that. But, Tim – identification. I know someone has to, someone close. But I don't think I can.'

'You don't have to, I can. First cousin is close enough.'

'Dear Tim . . .' Her head fell back. The WPC's hand moved from waist to throat, feeling for something to loosen but finding nothing tight. 'I'm all right,' Olivia murmured again.

'Feeling able to give me a very simple statement?' Tim asked gently. 'Or would you rather wait a while?'

'No point in waiting, Tim.' Olivia's sigh rippled the length of her prone body.

'Thank you. WPC Gallienne will take it down. I only want to know what time Charles went out, if you actually saw the way he went, when you realized he hadn't come back. Take your time.'

'I didn't see the way he went.' Olivia remained slumped in her chair. 'I was in bed getting over a migraine and he came up

46

to tell me he was going to Candie Gardens. I looked at the clock by my bed and it was twenty-five to twelve. When he'd gone I realized I needed some fresh air and a break from bed before the night, and that I was well enough to go out. So I got up and walked along to the lookout.'

'You *what!*' He had to force himself not to shout at her. 'Olivia, you knew the risks! You have a garden!'

Her massive shrug. 'I know, Tim, I know. But I'm a fatalist. And the mugger hadn't been this side of town. I don't know how long I stood there, probably a quarter of an hour or so. It was so peaceful and beautiful. I – I thought about going on to Candie Gardens but I couldn't be *certain* Charles would be alone.' She stared at him, grave and unblinking. They had never put Charles's lifestyle into words between them, but Olivia was a realist and assumed that he and her friends were aware of it. 'There was just a chance he might come back via the lookout, as we sometimes did when we went together' – he heard her catch of breath – 'but I didn't really stay there long enough. When I got home I went back to bed and took a sleeping pill. I never try – tried – to stay awake when Charles was out. I woke at eight and went to his room. The bedspread was immaculate so . . .'

It was the only time she faltered.

'I have to go,' Tim said reluctantly when they had done. 'The Chief will be waiting.' An hour ago he had been in day-to-day charge of the CID, but a murder inquiry automatically brought the Chief Inspector of Crimes in over his head. It would take some getting used to – unless, as he hoped and suspected, his Chief's confidence in his detective inspector's abilities would leave him with most of his usual scope. 'Someone else may bring the statement for your signature, but I'll be back to see you the moment I can. WPC Gallienne will ask Dr Richardson to come and have a look at you.' He clasped her hand and held it for an instant. 'Would you like to see Anna, Olivia? And is there anyone you'd like me to ring in England?' The question was a formality. Anna Weston had been introduced to him as Olivia's only relation, and friends from England who stayed at Saxon Lodge had always seemed to belong to Charles. He didn't think there was anyone, apart from himself, for an occasion such as this. 'Janet?' he suggested, reluctant again.

47

'Janet?'

'After she's – been told.'

To his relief, Olivia raised her head and struggled slightly more upright in the deep chair, the WPC's hands fluttering ineffectually beside her. 'They'll tell her in the office, won't they? She can come if she wants to. I'd like to see Anna.'

'She'd like to see you. She's gone down to St James to give her statement. I'll leave a message for her at the Duke.'

Outside the Duke he met Janet. She was as neat and noncommittal as ever, but her thin sunburned face was white under the eyes, and somehow distorted.

'Tim Le Page. I'm glad you're here. On duty, though, I suppose.'

'On and off. They've told the office, then.'

'Yes. How is she?'

'Numb with shock. But prepared to see you.'

He hadn't taken very readily to either Janet or Douglas Chapman, but he knew he could be prejudiced by the fact that their temporary home was in the rich open-market enclave of Fort George – and, in the last months, by what had happened between Janet and Charles.

'Tim, can you tell me anything?' Her questioning eyes were unnervingly large and aware in her small, closed face. 'Anything to comfort her.' '*Anything to comfort me*', Tim amended savagely in his head. 'If there is anything. But I expect you've already said all anyone can say. Was it . . . Would it have been quick?'

'Oh, yes. Instantaneous. One blow to the back of the head.'

'Ah.' Shuddering, she leaned her weight against the wall behind her. 'So the mugger used his lead piping after all.' Her voice was so quiet he could only just hear it.

'Perhaps.' He didn't know why he said that. Already most of the island force were out looking for the mugger turned murderer, hoteliers and boarding house keepers being questioned again and more urgently about the habits of their current clients, the small core of indigenous potential trouble makers being summoned for their second interviews.

'The office has closed for the day.' She pushed her short fair hair back from her forehead, staring through him. She had had her hair cut and styled about the time rumour had begun to connect her with Charles – perhaps that was why he had noticed her. Tim could see that some men might find her attractive, but it strained his imagination to think of her as Charles's latest fling. Not surprising that he had taken so long to come round to it, rather than sweeping her off her feet the moment he set eyes on her according to his usual practice. Perhaps they had had a friendly drink together at the end of a long day, their hands had touched, and then, with the new hairstyle . . . He didn't want to think about it. He had never wanted to think about any of Charles's affairs, but this one was the most distasteful. Perhaps he was old-fashioned, but it shocked him that Janet Chapman and Olivia were still prepared to be friends.

'You'd better go in to her,' he suggested. 'But take it easy.'

He saw her wince. 'Of course. I'm sorry, Tim, you've lost someone close, too.'

Was she talking about herself as well as Olivia? If her affair with Charles hadn't run its course Janet Chapman would be suffering, but she must know as well as everyone else how fleeting Charles's feelings were for any woman other than his wife, and her suffering compared to Olivia's was the moon compared to the sun.

'Yes,' he said, forcing himself to pat her shoulder, 'I must go and see what I can do about it.'

When he went down to the beach he found the girl already settled at his favourite spot. As she had been the day before and the day before that.

'Morning, sleepyhead! Another couple of hours and I'd have to have said good afternoon. Slept off your night on the tiles, have you?'

The first time she had said that he had nearly passed out beside her before realizing she was only showing him her disappointment that he hadn't asked her out. He had recovered quickly enough to knock the ball back, tell her well, yes, but it wasn't all that much cop. He had said something like that the second and third times, too. Now he had finally decided not to work any more he could change the record.

'Nothing to sleep off. How about altering all that tonight by coming along with me?'

49

'I don't mind.'

It looked as if she was going to be easy, but he'd have been more pleased about it if he'd managed not to let his success go to his head and stopped work when his instincts had told him to, instead of waiting until he'd actually used the lead piping . . .

Shuddering, he pushed his thoughts away from last night. The last night for sure, this time. He didn't have to worry, he'd got away with it yet again, but he could have done without the extra aggro and he ought to know by now to trust his instinct, not let his vanity and sense of power overrule it.

The trouble was that he'd never had success like this before, and he'd come to relish the sense of power as much as the bracelets and rings and earrings he'd pack up on his last day and post off to Marilyn. If he hadn't been so full of himself he'd have had four days instead of three for the police to persuade themselves the goods had already left the island, and start slacking off.

But he was still confident of slipping unnoticed for the last and longest time into his hiding place and getting the stuff parcelled up. Luck had been so gloriously on his side all the way through this latest enterprise that it couldn't desert him now. Finding that deep high ledge in the bunker the Germans had built on to the fort at Grandes Rocques had been another piece of it, to match his finding of the piping. It had meant he would be able to show them a room like an open book – and look at him now, nothing on his body but swimming trunks, and his clothes lying there innocently in the sunshine.

'That's great, flower! Pick you up at six?'

Three days. Time enough, he was confident, to get as far with this second undertaking as he had got with the first.

Chapter Five

Reckoning on the obviousness of the cause of death getting Charles's body speedily removed from Candie Gardens, Tim went straight from Saxon Lodge to the mortuary. It was there, naked, labelled, and painfully recognizable, and he nodded instantly to the man who turned back the sheet. Charles's eyes stared at the fluorescent-tubed ceiling in shocked surprise out of a calm white face that looked uncharacteristically spiritual. Tim had always imagined that one day he would talk to Charles about the motivation behind his way of life, about what must have been the uneasy mixture of public service and private indulgence, but now it was too late.

'Would the killer have had blood on him?'

'Probably not if he was where you'd expect him to be, at arm's length directly behind his victim.'

Beside the neat pile of clothes was the familiar jewelled dagger from the glass-topped show table in the sitting-room at Saxon Lodge that had so intrigued Tim as a child – illustration of the fact that Charles tended to be more prudent than appeared on the surface. As well as his watch there were his wallet containing twenty-six pounds in Guernsey notes and four credit cards. It looked as though becoming a murderer had caused the mugger to panic.

At St James the Chief was awaiting him in the embryonic Incident Room, his anger at a killer being on the loose in Guernsey making his voice and gestures larger and more emphatic than their norm.

'How is Mrs De Garde?'

'All right. I wish she could cry.'

'Too close to home for you, Tim?'

'No, sir. Just the opposite.' In England he wouldn't have been given the choice, it would have been 'special interest' and he would automatically have been off the case. If special interest were to be declared in Guernsey it would be difficult to get anything done, with so many people related to one another, police included.

'Good. Everyone's here. I assume you'll be intensifying current strategy and I don't propose to get in the way of it so long as you keep me thoroughly up to date.'

'Of course, sir. I've just made formal identification. Nothing was taken from the body.'

'Hm. Panic?'

'It looks like it. Any sign yet of the weapon?'

'In the pond. The expected length of lead piping. Visible signs of blood and hair – I'm sorry, Tim. There's some more news that could tie in or conflict. DS Mahy will fill you in, I've an appointment to see the Bailiff.'

'Thank you, sir.' Tim crossed the room to the broad, ginger-headed detective sergeant, his usual anticipation of reliable back-up more welcome than it had ever been before.

'Sir!' Detective Sergeant Mahy got to his feet, his blunt-featured face a balancing act between commiseration and relief. 'I'm very sorry.'

'Thanks, Ted.'

'And glad to see you. The mugger was busy somewhere else last night as well. A chap out at Fort Hommet lost all he was carrying. He appears to have been knocked down and lost conciousness when he hit his head on stony ground. A warm-up act, would you say, Tim, for what came later?' He put the fax into Tim's outstretched hand.

'The Chief said "tie in or conflict".' His eyes skimmed the page. 'Eleven-fifteen, eleven-twenty . . . home at eleven-forty-five . . . Why the hell didn't he ring us then?'

'My guess is because he'd been drinking, and had used his car to get to Fort Hommet and walk it off. If the pain wasn't too bad he probably decided to wait until he could pass a breathalyser test. He rang us soon enough when he woke very early with a bad head caused by more than the alcohol still in his system – just before his wife took him to Princess Elizabeth casualty, where Sergeant Guilbert and your namesake Constable Bill caught up with him. No stitches needed, no fracture, but some pretty bad bruising.'

'I expect you're right, Sergeant. We'll get the door-to-doors organized for the area between L'Hyvreuse and Candie Gardens, then we'll go and see Mr. Terence Smith. Get them all gathered round, will you?'

The CID was officially based up on the Amherst Road, midway between Tim's house and the Duke of Richmond, but day to day police business centred on St James, where more often than not the detectives found themselves even when times were normal. This morning there was a noticeable presence of plain clothes among the uniforms that crowded around him.

'I'm afraid we're going to have to go back over all the ground we've already covered,' Tim told them. 'Murder concentrates the mind, and if anyone was deliberately withholding information it may make them think again. At least this time we can follow a pattern, radiating out from Candie Gardens. Priority of course is a house-to-house between the Gardens and L'Hyvreuse – every last property in it, both sides of Charles De Garde's house. De Garde always went into the Gardens via the green gate in Vauxlaurens, so that means covering the lane itself and Cambridge Park Road, plus the houses in Candie Road that face down towards Cambridge Park, and the Duke of Richmond Hotel and its staff. Most of the houses in Cambridge Park Road are staff quarters, and at eleven-forty-five last night there would still have been plenty of to-ing and fro-ing. There's a hell of a lot to do, so let's get down to deciding who's going to do it.'

It was mid-morning by the time Tim and his sergeant set off for the west coast. An indignant and immaculately presented wife let them into a large open-market house with a breathtaking view of Vazon Bay, which Tim guessed the national tabloids would price at about half a million.

'It's too bad, Inspector, really it is. We retire to Guernsey at enormous expense, and this is what happens!' She led the way into a sun room already uncomfortably hot from the first direct rays of the day. The victim of the Fort Hommet attack was huddled under the overhang of an elaborate basket chair, wearing a bandage and a look of suffering bravely borne. 'This is my husband. You'd better sit down.'

'We're sorry,' the DS said as he obeyed her, seeing the set of Tim's lips. 'This is the first mugger the island has ever suffered and you've been very unfortunate. He hit you with the piping, sir?'

'Well, no.' The man was having difficulty controlling his mouth movements, and could be in shock. 'He – he just tapped it against my head and I slipped as I tried to back away. I must have hit my head on a stone, the ground where he cornered me was covered with them. Big ones. Sharp. I knocked myself out and when I came to of course there was no sign of him. Nor of my watch and wallet, so I'm afraid I can't tell you what the time was. I suppose it took me about a quarter of an hour to drive slowly home' – Mr Smith's eyes slid away from Tim's – 'and it was a quarter to twelve when I got there. I'd looked at my watch just before it happened, and it was just after a quarter past eleven. So I must have been out for about ten minutes. I've said all this already in my statement.'

'I know, and thank you, sir.' This time Tim managed it himself.

'It was a very expensive watch,' Mrs Smith added accusingly. 'I hope it will be recovered.'

'I'm afraid we're having to give priority to a murder inquiry.' Tim hoped it was the one and only time he would find himself pleased to speak of his cousin's death. 'A man was killed with a piece of lead piping the other side of the island last night – in Candie Gardens, St Peter Port – half an hour or more after your husband's encounter. We can't make it any more precise than that until we get the forensic report. Do you remember seeing a vehicle nearby, sir? Or a cycle of some kind?' A motorcycle or a scooter might have made it in time. 'Or perhaps you heard the noise of an engine? We'll be grateful if you can think very carefully.'

But Mr Terence Smith was preoccupied with thinking of his lucky escape. It was several minutes before the policemen secured his unwelcome assurance that he had neither heard nor seen any sign of a wheeled vehicle.

'There's no doubt about the mugger being able to have managed both, is there, Tim?' Ted Mahy asked when they were back in the car.

'I shouldn't think so.' But Tim was aware of a sudden sense of unease that he tried to ignore. 'Whatever time the Path. lab comes up with for Charles's death, it couldn't have been before a quarter to twelve, because that was roughly when he went into Candie Gardens. If the lab does decide it was that early, I think mopeds and so on will have to be ruled out, but not a four-wheeled vehicle, although it could have been tight. Nothing on the Fort Hommet ground?'

'Nothing, except that the hospital's certain it did all the damage suffered by Mr Terence Smith. So no help there.'

'Wouldn't you know it?' He would have to fight, too, against the debilitating sense of frustration that had had so much to feed on since the mugger first struck. 'As soon as you hit the Incident Room, Ted, get Bill Torode to set up interviews with all taxi and car hire firms, find out who they drove last night at the crucial time. And then the folk they've driven since the mugger started work who just might have been him. Or her, we're not sexists. We'll also – God help us – have to contact hire car drivers and drivers of their own cars who've gone back to England or wherever but were here when the mugger began operating and could have given him a lift. That could take us from Land's End to John O'Groats. To say nothing of Europe and the USA. At least we can get Channel TV to appeal to motorists still here to let us know if they gave lifts between the relevant times last night. And ask anyone who happened to be at Fort Hommet round about eleven fifteen or in or near Candie Gardens at about eleven forty-five to get in touch. I'll set that one up myself. I want to see the local door-to-door people as soon as they report in, Ted.'

During their absence the Incident Room had reassuringly matured, but the door-to-door people had an identical and depressing message.

No one remembered seeing the tall and striking figure of Charles De Garde, known to have walked from his house in L'Hyvreuse to Candie Gardens at about eleven forty-five, nor his wife, who had walked the length of L'Hyvreuse and back a little later. Which meant that the negative responses on a possible pursuer of Charles De Garde were of no value at all.

55

'Olivia.'

'Hello, Janet. Good of you to come.'

'Of course I'd come.' Janet walked over to Olivia's chair and stood in an unprecedented pose with arms outstretched, while Olivia heaved herself up and the WPC turned her back in the sitting-room doorway.

When she had found her feet Olivia was just short of Janet's fingertips, so that Janet had to move forward in order to take Olivia's heavy upper arms into her hands.

'There's nothing I can say except that I'm sorry.' From the frozen wastes that she now inhabited, Janet noted that the comment was usefully ambiguous; she was apologizing as well as expressing her regret at the death of Olivia's husband, and Olivia could accept one or both interpretations as she chose.

'Thank you, Janet.' Olivia turned slowly towards the door, making the movement just large enough to free herself from Janet's grip. 'This is Mrs Chapman,' she said to the WPC's back. 'Janet, this is WPC Gallienne.' The girl swung round, smiling a little too determinedly. 'I think Mrs Chapman would like some coffee.'

'Of course.' The WPC hurried out of the room.

Olivia gazed gravely at Janet before turning again and with stately grace crossing to the french window. She pushed it open. 'Another hot day,' she murmured. 'But the sun's too high at this time of the year to get very far into the room.'

'Olivia . . . Can't you cry?'

'Not yet.'

'You should.'

'To order?'

'Of course not. But it's a release.'

'So they say.' Olivia was looking out at the garden. 'Perhaps I'll cry when I'm alone, Janet. I haven't been alone yet. How did you – find out?'

'The police rang the office. I saw Tim outside.'

'He came right away. You'll miss Charles, Janet. Friend and colleague.'

'Olivia. I –'

'Don't say anything. It doesn't matter. Forgive me, but it never did. Well, you've had a few years to get to know Charles.'

56

'Yes.' Janet made her first effort. 'You're right, Olivia, it didn't matter. But you're very generous.'

'I've no intention of spoiling a friendship for something that didn't count.' Olivia, turning to rest her benign brown eyes on Janet's bloodshot blue ones, registered no awareness that Janet had winced. 'Being fond of Charles did count. For you and for Douglas. I don't want you pretending to make light of that. Have you told Douglas?'

'No. I came straight here when I heard. The office has closed for the day.'

'A nice Guernsey gesture. You'd better sit down, Janet, you look whacked.'

'Shock.' Janet remained standing. 'You've reminded me I ought to ring Douglas.'

'Yes. You don't want him to hear from anyone else.' Olivia turned back to the garden. 'Go upstairs to my bedroom, you can talk there in privacy.' The privacy Janet perhaps needed. Olivia didn't know whether Douglas would be receiving the news of the death of his wife's lover as well as the death of a friend.

'Thank you, Olivia.'

'Your coffee will be waiting for you when you come down.'

Janet took the steep stair at a run, stumbling near the top and bruising her shin. At least for a moment the physical pain took from the mental. Charles's bedroom was nearest the stairhead. The only time she had been in it was with Olivia, to be shown Charles's extreme neatness and tidiness. Janet entered it again now, falling on her knees by the bed and burying her face in the smooth cover. Then rocking back on her heels as she imagined Olivia's heavy tread on the stairs. Foolish to risk making life more difficult than it already was. It took a few moments to restore the bed's pristine appearance.

Olivia's bedroom wore its usual luxuriously untidy look, generously cut clothes draped across the small period chairs, the teddy-bear on the bedspread lurched towards the window. The latest published volume from Olivia's employer sprawled open, spine strained, on her bedside table, beside a typescript and the notes she was making for her report on it. Squatting on the floor by the bed, Janet picked up the telephone and punched out Douglas's office number.

57

'Mr Chapman, please. It's his wife.'

He wasn't in his office and the wait seemed very long in a room so saturated with the presence of Charles's wife. Long enough, even, for Janet to be able to smell Olivia's perfume on her own sleeve.

'Janet?' Voice as cold as it had been at breakfast. 'What is it?'

At least he hadn't heard. 'Douglas – I have to tell you – Charles was walking in Candie Gardens last night and the mugger . . . used his piece of piping. Charles died.' There was no kind way to put it, for herself or for anyone else. 'I'm with Olivia now. The office is closed for the day and I came straight over. I should have rung you first but I just rushed out, I'm sorry.'

'Have you entirely lost your senses, Janet? Or are you trying to make a joke?'

While she was waiting she had imagined a myriad different responses. The reality hadn't been one of them. 'I can hardly ask Olivia to come to the telephone. You'll have to take my word for it. Charles had his head bashed in last night by a mugger.' She was suddenly choking, and finished the sentence on a whooping intake of breath. 'I'm not joking, Douglas.'

There was a short silence. Then, his voice without expression, Douglas said, 'It seems not. Olivia was glad to see you?'

She had to pause to think. It wasn't a question she had asked herself, although perhaps she should have done. 'Olivia isn't glad about anything at the moment. She hasn't thrown me out. I wasn't a threat, you see.' The effort again. 'She said our friendship was important.'

'Quite right. It is.' Douglas cleared his throat, so often a preliminary to something he found difficult to say. 'Janet . . . Are you alone?'

'I'm alone. Upstairs.'

'Right. You say Charles was walking in Candie Gardens. So far as you know he didn't have an – appointment – there?'

'Not so far as I know, Douglas.'

'Because if he did, the person he was meeting might have seen something, might be able to help the police.'

Her husband wasn't clever in the sense that Janet understood the word, but to cite public spirit as the motive for slaking jealousy showed some native cunning. 'Of course they might. But if he was meeting someone, Douglas, I don't know who it was.'

'You didn't go anywhere yourself while I was out last night, Janet?'

'No.' If Olivia had lifted the sitting-room receiver . . . Not with the WPC about, and anyway it wasn't Olivia's style. 'Did you go anywhere on your way home from the Club? You were very late back. If you were anywhere near Candie Gardens you could have seen –'

'I was nowhere near Candie Gardens. When I left the Club I drove straight home.'

'Where you arrived at half-past midnight. All right, Douglas. Perhaps you'll call in and see Olivia on your way home.'

'Of course. Good God, it's terrible!'

'Yes. Appalling.'

'If the mugger had only been caught –'

'Yes, Douglas.'

Alone in her sitting-room Olivia remained at the window, staring out. Dew still sparkled along the edges of the shadowed eastern border, but the sun had picked out the richness of the planting on the west side of the garden and some of the more precocious flowering shrubs were looking tired. The garden would miss Charles's loving attention; she would have to get Sammy to come more often. If she was living in England friends and acquaintances would urge her to find a smaller house with a smaller garden, but here she would be spared all the well-intentioned advice. Charles had put Saxon Lodge on the open market, making it impossible for her to buy modestly on the local. Not that she could imagine ever wanting to, even without him.

Without Charles. The only man she had ever loved.

Coming in with a tray of coffee, the WPC saw the motionless figure at the garden door suddenly start to tremble. Mrs De Garde's feet didn't move from the spot where they were planted apart, but her whole body was quivering and the WPC could hear moaning sounds. She put the tray down and sped across the room.

'There, there, dear, it's all right. It's all right. Come and sit down.'

59

The eyes were opening and closing and the face was pale under its tan, glistening with sweat that Jenny Gallienne wished was tears. It was a strenuous exercise helping Mrs De Garde over to her chair, and when she was lying back in it the WPC picked up the glass from the table beside her and went to the corner cupboard.

'I'm all right,' Olivia murmured to Jenny's relief, choking on the brandy. 'I just realized . . .'

'I know, I know,' crooned the WPC, chafing the now motionless hands. 'That's how it goes.' She felt good in the role of comforter, but it was a relief to hear Mrs De Garde's friend coming down the stairs.

Dear Jane,

I hadn't intended burdening you so soon with another letter, but now I do really have to talk to someone and there's no one here. You see, I went for an early walk this morning in Candie Gardens and found Charles De Garde jack-knifed across some railings. Dead. The mugger had finally used his lead piping.

I feel I must be mad or dreaming to have written that, but it's true. I didn't realize it was Charles – I just saw a well-dressed, well-groomed man with the back of his head caved in.

I started running back up the garden to where I'd noticed a house, and bumped into a jogger with a dog. Tim Le Page!

The moment I'd told him, he became a policeman; the transformation would have been interesting any other time. I took him to the body and the dog set up the most terrible howling, I suppose it recognized Charles before Tim did. Actually it was Charles's watch he recognized – he'd given it to him. Odd that the mugger hadn't taken it, but I suppose after turning killer he must have panicked. Then we ran to the house – it was the head gardener's – and when Tim had summoned his team I drove him home to put some clothes on before going to tell Olivia. I offered to go but I was relieved when he insisted on doing it himself. I think they really are good friends. So I went down to the police station to make a statement. Very easy, except for feeling I should

60

tell them I'd been sick into a patch of grass so that they didn't think it was a clue. The uniformed sergeant told me there was no need to include the admission in my statement, but that if other people followed my conscientious example his task would be a whole lot easier.

Jane, I don't feel anything like as flip as I sound. When I got back to the hotel there was a scribbled note in my pigeon-hole from Tim saying Olivia would like to see me. There was also a journalist plus press photographer awaiting me in the lobby. From the local paper, the Guernsey Evening Press, asking me to help them make the most of their advantage before the nationals moved in.

They'd been admirably quick off the mark and obviously I couldn't say no, although I think I managed to make my agreement conditional on their leaving Olivia alone for a while. The young management were super-sympathetic and put a room at our disposal, and I just gave them the facts and let them take my photograph. When we came out of the room a man and a woman and a camera from Channel TV were waiting, so I went back in again.

'It's the coincidence, you see,' the woman told me. She obviously wasn't a local. 'I mean, Charles De Garde's body being discovered by his wife's cousin the day after her arrival from England . . .'

I didn't think this sounded very good, especially when I thought how it might strike my employers. But that's how it is, and how it will come out with or without my co-operation. I wasn't surprised when the man went on to mention my encounter with my fellow-cousin 'near the body of the victim'. 'Makes a sort of symmetrical pattern,' he said. At least no one got on to the symmetrical pattern of Olivia and me having both lost our sons. I tried again to make my co-operation dependent on their laying off Olivia, and they undertook not actually to ring her doorbell.

So I suppose I could have been on TV at lunchtime. I didn't tell Olivia about my encounters with the media, and I suggested to the WPC and Mrs Moleson that it might be a good thing if they didn't, either – she'll see and hear enough in due course – so I didn't see the one o'clock news. The Channel TV people said that tomorrow, if not tonight, I'm

*likely to be on in England, too. I didn't think you'd be
seeing my holiday pictures so soon.*

*I've only spent one day with Olivia, but I knew she'd be
magnificent. Calm and controlled, able to think about
whether I'd had breakfast, about Janet Chapman looking ill.
There might just have been an edge to her concern about
Janet, of course, who was there when I arrived, another pair
of wide dry eyes staring through me – I was glad to discover
that she was about to leave, it couldn't have been good for
either of them. (So far as Janet's concerned, it must be pretty
awful not to have any right to suffer publicly, however much
you've brought the punishment on yourself.)*

*In normal times I shouldn't think Olivia and I would ever
have got around to touching one another intentionally, but
when I saw her trying to struggle out of her chair I found
myself on my knees putting my arms round her. For a
convulsive moment she responded, and after that there was
no embarrassment. 'You know how it feels, Anna.' Stressing
the pronoun, excluding Janet, whether intentionally or not I
couldn't tell. But I shouldn't even be wondering about that,
it isn't important now, and Olivia would have said the same
thing if Janet had already left. That was when she did go,
calm and quiet but looking as if she might collapse if she
didn't sit down again pretty quickly. I could imagine Tim Le
Page saying 'The wages of sin . . .' No I couldn't, of course,
but I suspect hm of having views on the matter.*

*There was a WPC there, a nice local girl called Jenny
Gallienne. Olivia asked me to stay for lunch and suggested
we could manage on our own, so after a lot of reassurance
WPC Gallienne left too. Olivia's Mrs Moleson was in the
kitchen and made us sandwiches which Olivia played with.
It worries me, Jane, that she hasn't wept. It was a day and a
night before I could weep for Mickey, and it helped when I
did.*

*I kept quiet and let Olivia talk or not as she felt. As soon
as Janet had gone she asked me to tell her exactly what I saw
in the Gardens, and she asked me several times afterwards if
I was sure he would have died without suffering – the way I
had to keep asking Jimmy about the expression on Mickey's
face. You know, but somehow you have to have it*

*confirmed. I suppose because of not having seen it yourself
and being afraid people are trying to spare you. Olivia sat
silent for moments on end, then suddenly started telling me
what good friends she and Charles were and how well they
understood one another. You know how that feels and it
must be devastating to be so suddenly bereft. But at least she
was talking about him.*

*I think she was glad to have me there, not just because I'm
her cousin but because I understand bereavement, so at least
I've been able to do something good with Mickey's death. As
for the cousin bit – the shock made me forget until a moment
ago that she's lost her child, too, so now I really am the only
family she has left. I'm not sure that she's properly taken in
what's happened, and the worst could still be to come. I
offered to move in with her but she didn't hesitate to tell me
she preferred to be on her own.*

*After lunch she asked me to walk down the garden, and
showed me an enclave where she works and relaxes when the
weather's good. 'I am by nature indolent, but fortunately I
can think quite clearly in the sun.' I can still hear her saying
that; she's unusually easy to quote. Her voice is naturally
deep, but was even more so today – the only outward sign of
her shock apart from the way she stares through one.*

*The garden is gorgeous, and completely walled in rosy
brick. The wall at the bottom is newer than the rest, and she
told me that Charles never got over his anger at his father for
having sold off the part beyond it. The garden once went all
the way down to Vauxlaurens, almost opposite the green
gate into Candie Gardens, but now there's a bungalow in the
way and no access. Olivia told me Charles used to be taken
into the gardens in his pram, and asked me if I thought the
future could have hovered over him there, if the baby could
have started crying without any reason. When I told her to
stop it she reproached me for not understanding, and of
course she was right. As I'm sure you remember, I had my
own dreadful fantasies.*

*When we got back to the house Olivia said she'd like to be
on her own for a while, and anyway she needed to rest. That
was the moment I really felt for her. Rest times are so
terrible, yet one has to try and have them just in order to*

63

keep going. I asked if I might go back later and she suggested after dinner – she still seemed concerned that I should get my money's worth at the Duke. Her Mrs M clearly adores her and was dug in for the afternoon, but I suspect we needn't worry about Olivia and food when Mrs M isn't there – she told me she finds the kitchen a solace and that in a day or two she'll probably be eating more rather than less.

It's half past two and I'm going to ring Bradshaw, Jones and Coquelin to suggest looking in on the practice as well as arranging a visit to the Bradshaw house. I've decided it would be preferable for me to meet them all before they see me on TV. (Let's hope everyone was too busy to switch on at lunchtime!) I'd rather give them a personal account of what happened than have them hear the public one and start wondering if at the very best they might be taking on someone who tended to be accident-prone.

Oh, Jane, what a mess. I hope Tim Le Page manages to make use of his anger.

Much love,
Anna.

Chapter Six

After his mid-day meal he took a bus out into the country, then went for a walk. Stupid to come all this way and not have a proper look around. He'd covered quite a bit of the island while working, of course – St Peter Port and the bays north and south of Cobo – but sight-seeing was something else.

The weather was still perfect and it was all very pretty. On a small scale, which might get you down after a time, but fine when you knew you were soon going home.

Home. He always looked on the bright side, and police interest in London would have to have died down by now. Anyway, he'd have posted the goods to Marilyn, and arranging their disposal would involve no more than an innocent visit to a girlfriend.

When he had first arrived he had thought the people were friendly, but that seemed to have changed. Because of him, the people at the top of the happiness poll had dropped to the bottom, started to look at every man jack as a possible mugger. Because of just one man! Well, history had proved that it only needed one man, the right man, to affect a whole nation. Napoleon. Hitler. He had always been interested in Hitler and now Hitler had given him a helping hand. He'd have another look tomorrow at the underground museum.

People were even more miserable-looking today than they had been yesterday. On the bus, in the café near the bus-stop where he had jam and cream and scones and a pot of tea, he didn't see anyone smile and little groups of people were talking anxiously together. He kept getting a crazy yen to shout out to them that it was all right, they needn't go in nightly fear any longer of their precious possessions, the master mugger was on his way.

He was the only one who was smiling. Trying to make the bus driver, the waitress, the people around him, look at him less suspiciously, but he was beginning to think his contentment could be making him stand out.

He even began to feel anxious about the girl, to wonder how she would be. It was a relief to see her standing at her hotel gate as she had promised. And even better to have her run up to him and hang on his arm.

'Hi, flower! Ready for anything?'

'Oh, Dave, I'm glad to see you! What about the news?'

'What news, flower?' He had meant to get a local paper, see what they were saying about him today, if that chap was all right, but the one newsagent he had come across had sold out.

'You mean you don't know?'

'Don't know what? Don't tell me the mugger had a night off last night?' Or that he'd really hurt the man . . . He knew he hadn't. 'Flower? Are you going to tell me or aren't you?' But he didn't care, it couldn't be anything to do with him. Probably one of the Royals was starting another baby. 'And where do you fancy going?'

'The mugger used his lead piping last night. Killed a man. Murdered him. One savage blow to the head. I just saw it on TV. I'm glad I've got you to protect me, I can tell you! Oh, let's go into town. Dave?'

It had never needed such will power to carry on at the same relaxed stroll as if he hadn't just walked into a nightmare, to try and hide his panic from the dangerous, prattling creature at his side. 'I'm just shocked. That's awful, flower.'

'You've gone quite pale, Dave. Not scared, are you?'

'Me? Of course not. Come on, there's the bus.'

He drank more than he was used to, but it didn't make him drunk. All it did was hold him mercifully outside what had happened while he couldn't give it his attention, help him go through the motions of ordinary life, even make it passably with the girl down on the beach after dark.

When he left her outside her hotel after the longest evening of his life he wanted to go on the beach again and run and shout, but instead he went back to his own place – he couldn't risk, now, being out late – and got into bed and lay there shivering all night in the heat, trying to work it out and seeing the hiding place of his booty and his weapon shining out along the coast like a bloody lighthouse.

The pain was suddenly physical and Janet had to sit down, leaning forward and cradling her body in her arms. She heard herself groaning as if the sound was coming from a long way off, and eventually she slid down on to the floor. When the groans became screams she knew she must get to the cloak-room.

She used the furniture to help herself up on to her knees, and hobbled on them the width of the hall. She was in the cloakroom a long time, and when she came out she was too weak to go upstairs to bed but just managed to crawl back to the sitting-room and on to the sofa, where she lay curled up, shivering and feeling more alone than she had ever felt before.

The pain had gone but a pain was still there, defining the boundaries of her lifeless body. After a time her exhaustion put her to sleep and her sense of loss became a succession of brief dreams. A house falling down, a dog at a closed door, a man with an axe to a tree. To save the tree she cried out, and woke to a weakness still so profound she slid off the sofa again and crawled across to the drinks cupboard to get herself a brandy and the chance of some energy to face Douglas's return.

Her heavy eyes took a few moments to focus the clock and tell her he must be on his way, that she hadn't much time left in which to prepare for her complex yet subordinate role in what was bound to be the drama of his outraged sympathy for the widow. It would be even more uncomfortable than the role she had already played of penitent comforter to Olivia, and her need to play that would at least be reduced by the presence of Olivia's cousin. But it would be months before either role could be abandoned. Months of pretending Charles had meant as little to her as she had meant to him. And months of life with Douglas in the unreality of Fort George until it was time to go back to years of life with him in England.

Douglas must not suspect the real extent of her loss. Forcing herself upright, Janet tottered to the patio door and gripped its cold handle, as supportive a prop as anything else in this icy world. How could she go on living in it, perhaps for decades into the future?

She hadn't the strength to push the handle, let in the heat of the day. Beyond the glass, the pink-and-white floored terrace with its patio suite in simulated cast-iron, the perfect green lawn, the symmetrical curves of the flowerbeds to each side of it, mocked her misery, confirmed her anguished knowledge that she had no real role in life. The silence was so terrible it was even a relief to hear the front door, followed in the usual way by the door of the cloakroom.

Letting the handle go, steadying herself unsupported, Janet ran her hands down her hair and under her eyes as she stumbled out to the hall just as Douglas appeared to the sound of a lavatory flush.

'Douglas.'

'Janet!' To her amazement, irritation was still the dominant emotion in his face. 'Forgive me for mentioning it, but the cleaning brush was in a prominent position in the middle of the toilet floor. It doesn't matter to me, of course, but you know I sometimes bring clients home for a drink.'

'I'm sorry, Douglas. It won't happen again.'

'I hope not.' He marched across the hall and into the sitting-room without his usual peck to her cheek. Following humbly in his wake she was able to lean undetected against a succession of supports. She found him plumping up the devastated sofa cushions, and collapsed back on to them as he went over to the window complaining about the lack of air.

'This is a bad business,' he announced, when he had pushed the patio doors wide. 'How is poor Olivia? I decided not to disturb her in her sorrow.'

'All right on the surface.' Janet was surprised by the normality of her voice. 'Which one would expect. I wish she could cry.'

'Yes.' Douglas had turned to look at her. Coldly. 'Like you.'

She gasped as the ice thawed to a jet of cold water. 'I had a pain. And Olivia and I are different people.'

68

'Yes. And with different parts to play. Don't forget, Janet, that Olivia is the heroine, and yours is a bit part.'

'I won't forget.' He had even used her own metaphor. Slumping back on the sofa, Janet tried to tell herself that he wasn't being cruel, that he was bitterly hurt and was merely giving her what she deserved. And coldness and hostility, anyway, were more congenial to her now than anything else.

'I don't intend to go on at you, Janet. And I hope soon to be able to act towards you, in public at least, as if none of this had occurred.' Douglas's awareness of his magnanimity shone warmly in his eyes. He was always at his happiest when right was patently on his side. How she despised him! She didn't hate him, or even dislike him, he wasn't important enough for that. Not important enough for her to go on subordinating her life to him. As she realized that she was ultimately going to free herself, a shaft of warmth briefly penetrated the surrounding cold. There was after all, dimly ahead, the prospect of something better than the bleakness of the moment.

'Thank you, Douglas.'

'What I can't understand,' he said on an irritable rush – exasperated, Janet suspected, as much by his inability to keep quiet as by what he was asking her – 'is how you could have known Charles all this time and then suddenly gone mad.'

'Because he went mad too, I suppose.'

'So it was all down to Charles?'

The question was so irrelevant she might as well answer it as soothingly as possible. 'I wasn't looking for trouble, Douglas, as I told you yesterday.' Light years ago. 'It just happened. And I knew I couldn't hurt Olivia.' The effort again.

'You hurt me, Janet, but I suppose that doesn't count.'

'Of course it counts. I'm truly sorry. I hope you really will feel able eventually to forget it.' He would think she was grovelling, he had never known when her tongue was in her cheek, but in this new icy world it didn't really matter what anyone thought if it suited them and left her to shiver in peace while she made her plans.

'I'm glad that is how you see it. I think I shall have a drink.' Each evening he made the same announcement, as if of a rare event. 'You'd better join me with a small brandy, you look terrible.'

'I'm sure I do. Thank you, Douglas, yes, I'll have a brandy. You needn't make it too small.'

She had earned herself a partial absolution. Even in extremis her instincts of self-preservation had come to her aid, and would help her to reach her only remaining goal: to be rid of her husband.

The commentary accompanying the pictures of Anna on Channel TV placed her so precisely in her temporary setting she decided to go straight into dinner without a repeat of her last night's visit to one of the Duke's attractive bars. Even so, of course, she was the cynosure of most residential eyes, one old lady even grabbing her arm in a pinching grasp as she went past, to hold her still for a moment while she expressed her concern. As she sat down Anna was aware of her dancing partner of the night before wrestling with the dilemma of whether or not to come over and speak to her, and decided the matter for him by opening the paperback novel she had brought down with her in order to save embarrassment all round. But all through her excellent dinner she was aware of his anticipatory eye on her, and even though her sense of annoyance was academic – her return to Olivia's that evening meant she would not have to endure his company – Tim Le Page on his way to her table was still a comfortable sight.

'Hello!' But why was he here? 'Olivia . . .'

'Olivia's all right. I've come to tell you that she's gone to bed and hopes you'll go and see her in the morning.'

'Of course.' He looked tired and drawn, less boyish. 'Do sit down, I'm conspicuous enough as it is. You'll have some coffee?'

'Please. I've just had some with Olivia but I've lived on it all day and I think I'm becoming addicted. I – Ah, thank you.'

Anna's waiter, unprompted, was already putting another coffee pot and more chocolate mints on the table, setting a cup and saucer in front of Tim before he was settled in the other chair.

'I see what you mean,' he murmured.

'It's awful, but I want to laugh.' At the increasingly elaborate pretence by her fellow diners of being deeply absorbed in their meals.

'It must be very frustrating for them. I haven't had a chance to see the news yet, but you've obviously appeared on Channel TV.'

'They were here when I got back after making my statement. A close second to the Guernsey Evening Press. Your appeal came over well. Have you had any responses?'

'A crop of them. People tend to take this sort of opportunity to settle old scores. Unfortunately they've all got to be looked into. But the people we want to hear from are getting in touch, too. Car owners. Taxi drivers. The only way our man could have managed both jobs was with wheels.' Again that shaft of unease. 'I'll apologize now for the possibility that my phone may ring.'

'Apology accepted. Have you had anything to eat?'

'I shoved a sandwich together when I went home to feed Duffy, then when I looked in on Olivia she wanted to make me something and I thought that if I let her she'd make something for herself. So we had omelettes and she ate a few mouthfuls. Then she suddenly flopped. The doctor came earlier and prescribed something so she should at least have a long sleep.'

'And then the waking up and remembering.'

'Yes, I suppose . . .' Even though he had been sitting opposite her for several moments she had been no more than the vaguely attractive fuzzy background to the clear picture of his investigation. Abruptly the focus changed. 'Yes, you know about that, don't you? Olivia told me before – before the dinner party. I'm so sorry.'

'Please don't be, I hate sympathy and it's all over now.' She hadn't been thinking about herself, she had only been anticipating Olivia's experience from her knowledge of her own. 'It's just that it's worse after a rest from it.' Her defiant eyes drove his down to his coffee. 'I tried to make my interview with Channel TV conditional on their leaving Olivia alone. D'you know if they did?'

'She didn't mention them, so let's hope so. A gesture like that ought to be respected.' He looked up at her with a smile. 'I'm impressed.'

She returned it. 'Thank you. I hope they stick to it.'

'I'm afraid the national press won't, but at least she's had today unhounded. Are you all right?' he asked belatedly,

71

realizing she still didn't look as she had looked at the dinner party.

'Yes. Are you?'

'Yes. I'm lucky to be so busy. When do you start work?'

'Wednesday next week and I'll be glad, although I won't be able to see so much of Olivia. I felt a bit concerned about my new employers seeing me on TV before seeing me in the flesh – apart from John Coquelin, I met him in London – so I called on them.'

'They look after Duffy. You'll be happy there. I don't suppose they were worried that your notoriety might affect your veterinary skills.'

'No, but I've felt better since I went. I also went to Brian Bradshaw's house, where I'll be living in style while I take his place. Have you found anyone who saw Charles last night?'

'Not a soul. Not even anyone living in L'Hyvreuse or Cambridge Park Road, which includes most of the junior members of the Duke of Richmond's staff. So I'm afraid the fact that nobody noticed anyone who could have been the mugger, either, doesn't have to mean he wasn't about. Olivia will have told you that she went out too after Charles had left. She felt better and walked to the lookout for some air.'

'She didn't listen to your lecture.'

'Oh, she would have done, but that's Olivia. No one noticed her, either, but of course she went the other way, where there's only one row of houses, so that's not so surprising. There *is* just the possibility that Charles went that way too, perhaps to look at the view en route. If you go the length of L'Hyvreuse and turn right past the lookout you come to the bottom of Vauxlaurens – well, it's called Beauregard Lane at that point – and you get to the side gate of Candie Gardens from below. But a pointer against Charles having gone that way, apart from its being quite a bit longer, is that if the mugger had spotted him he would have been pretty well bound to have accosted him somewhere between the lookout and Vauxlaurens. He couldn't have found a more suitably remote spot, and he couldn't know Charles was on his way to the Gardens. On the other hand it could just explain why no one seems to have seen Charles, if like Olivia he turned right out of his front door instead of going round the corner where the young hoteliers were coming and going.'

'Turned right . . . Tim!'

'What is it?'

The band was tuning up invitingly beyond the curtain, but the surrounding diners continued to be more interested in their coffee. 'I might have something useful to tell you, but I feel as if we're rather in the spotlight here.'

'So do I. I'll have to go soon but there's time for a drink. A corner of the ballroom near the bar should be noisy and dark enough to put our audience off.'

Anna tried to be annoyed that it was Tim Le Page's presence, rather than her own strength of mind, which made it easy to nod casually to Harry Price, but she was more concerned with what she had suddenly realized she had to say.

'So what is it?' Tim took up, the moment they had settled with brandies far enough from the music for them to be able to hear each other at normal pitch without being heard by any of the people around them.

'I came up to bed last night just after half-past eleven. I know that was the time because I'd looked at my watch before asking the people I was with to excuse me. I wanted to go and see what the view from the lookout was like by night but I must be more impressionable than Olivia because I went upstairs instead and made do with opening my window as wide as it would go with the lights off and the curtains back. I just stood there for five or ten minutes, enjoying the air and listening to the silence, and then there were suddenly footsteps like pistol shots going from right to left on the pavement under my window. They broke the silence so dramatically I remember jumping. I thought of them as men's feet, and now I'm trying to think why. I suppose because although they were regular and sort of brisk, they were spaced for long strides and they didn't clack like women's shoes tend to. They were hard soles, though, and I noticed Charles's . . .'

'That's very good, Anna. Did you by any chance hear a door before you heard the shoes?'

'No, I'm afraid – Yes!' He saw her eyes widen through the gloom as she leaned towards him. 'There were a whole lot of tiny sounds – an owl, a mouse, things like that – and the last

73

one before the shoes was the closing of a door. So softly that I hadn't remembered it. But I definitely heard it. And it was definitely beyond my window.'

'Thanks.'

'I couldn't tell you where it came from, but it must have been from the right, mustn't it, the way the shoes came? The only doors to the left are the swing doors of the Duke and it was too near to have come from the houses facing down the park. Could it be evidence that Charles went the quick way to Candie Gardens?'

'It could. And of the lack of observation of the general public. Will you go down to St James in the morning and say you want to add to your statement? You'll be expected – I'll tell them tonight.'

'I'll go first thing, then I'll go to Olivia.'

'Good. I'm glad you're here, Anna, although I suppose you rue the day you came.'

'Not in the least. I was at home the moment I arrived, and I still am.'

'The individual counts here. I think that's why I never wanted to work anywhere else. The police are the one Guernsey outfit with the same system as the British – we train in England – so I could have opted to work in the UK.'

'Do you feel British?' She was curious.

'We're part of the British Isles,' Tim said slowly, thinking it out as he went. 'But not of Great Britain or the United Kingdom. We don't have to worry about which party gets power in Westminster, we have our own parliament. And there are no political parties, just the man or woman voted right for the job.'

'How blessed you are!'

'I know,' he said smugly, enjoying her envious surprise and the reassurance he was giving himself that the basic structures were still intact.

'It works?'

'Very well. Perhaps because we're small,' he conceded. 'We do share a Queen with you, and you defend us.'

'That doesn't answer my question about whether or not you feel British.'

'No.' He grinned at her. 'All right then, I don't. But if any nation contains my fellow countrymen, it's Britain. There's a muddle for you.'

'Not France? According to the plaque at the end of L'Hyvreuse, you're only forty-two miles from Cherbourg.'

'France? Heavens, no! Oh, we're British – of a kind.'

'A unique sub-species. At least you could buy a house in Britain if you wanted to. It's like Jersey here, isn't it?'

'You don't have to declare a large sum of money, but I suppose in effect it is. Guernsey has two housing markets, local and open. Most of the island's housing stock is local, which means strictly for islanders only. The open is what it says, with prices starting at the level of the dearer properties in the Home Counties stockbroker belt.'

'That would be it for me, then.'

'Not necessarily. Professional people have skills the island might not always be able to supply for itself. If you were offered a permanent job by B, J and C when Barry Jones leaves you'd be given a permit to live here, perhaps even in local market property. And if you worked here for fifteen years and kept your nose clean you'd earn yourself local status – something an incomer rich enough to buy an open market property can never do. An incomer gets local status, too, if he or she marries a local.'

'Like Olivia.'

'Yes and no in Olivia's case. In 1969 a law was passed requiring all householders to opt once and for all for open or local market status. Open was available only to houses over a certain rateable value, and of course Saxon Lodge qualified. Charles decided to turn it into a hot property by putting it on the open market register. By doing that he lost his and his wife's native right to buy on the local market, but the right would have remained with their children, giving them the best of both worlds – they could have sold Saxon Lodge at an open market price and bought locally. There are some small open market properties to be had, of course, if not at small prices, so he and Olivia – Olivia – could always move into an easier-run place. Not that I can imagine her ever wanting to, that house fits her like a shell.'

'What about you?'

'We had a rather nice local house in St Andrew, but my mother left and when my father died I sold it and bought the house you saw off the Amherst Road. It's convenient to where the CID is supposed to hang out, but I don't expect to be there much in the next few days.' The focus shifted back. 'I must get down to St James and catch up with the latest phone-ins.'

He was on his feet, and Harry Price at the next table but one had his hands on the arms of his chair. 'I'll move on, too.' Anna got up. 'I don't suppose Duffy's walk prospects are too promising at the moment. Would he come out with me? I'd love his company, particularly if he'd go in the car.'

Smiling his pleasure Tim Le Page looked young again. 'I might have to encourage him into it the first time. I'll try to look in at Olivia's in the morning between agreeing the day's plans at St James and going out and about. If you're not there I'll look in here. If I find you I'll whip you down to the house and tell Duffy you're *persona grata*, and if he agrees with me I'll give you the key to the side gate.'

'I'll be at one place or the other. I hope when I see you you'll have had a breakthrough.'

This time she brought a chair to the window and sat with her arms on the sill, recalling what she had heard the night before and remaining confident that she had got it right. Tonight the weather was as beautiful, the silence as murmurously profound. And the darkness no doubt still as dangerous.

Chapter Seven

He hadn't brought a radio, and he had been too late when he got in to see the news on the only television set the hotel appeared to own apart from the one constantly bawling out of Mrs O'Malley's private quarters.

He'd be a fool to look too eager to see a paper this morning, but he couldn't wait until after breakfast, have the horror dripped to him bit by bit by his fellow guests.

He managed to hold back until ten minutes before the gong, then walked as slowly as he could manage to the shop round the corner, keeping his mind off what really mattered by cursing the hotel. No newspapers under the bedroom doors, meals on the dot – it was just a glorified boarding-house. Which he should have realized when he saw the price of the holiday. Before the nightmare began he had been dreaming of doing well enough to take another holiday in a five-star outfit, but after the wakeful agonies of the night he couldn't even let himself think about the loot lying on that high narrow shelf alongside the length of piping, nor about the skills that only yesterday he had been so proud of.

When he got to the shop he learned that the local paper didn't come out until mid-morning. The woman serving knew he was a tourist because he had asked for it at the wrong time of day, and she looked surprised that a tourist should want that particular paper at any time. Would she remember him when the police got round to her a second time? He had to hold himself firmly in check not to invent some story about picking up a copy for someone else, which would have been sure to fix him in her mind. He was definitely getting edgy, but murder . . . He settled for a national tabloid and made himself stroll out of the shop and back to the hotel and upstairs, mumbling unnecessarily to a fellow guest going down that he had forgotten his handkerchief, trying not to glare at the hovering chambermaid.

Yes, it was there on page three, under a large headline. A headline even worse than the ones he had conjured up during the night.

FROM MUGGER TO MURDERER!

No! He had only pushed the man away from him. In self-defence! Yes, that was it. The man had reeked of drink and had reacted violently to his request for money and jewellery, trying to rush him and take the piping. He had hardly tapped the fellow, hadn't meant to hurt him, just protect himself, and it must have been his head hitting the ground that had done the damage. When he was taking the watch he had heard and felt strong breathing, had never imagined the man could be really hurt. Murder! It wasn't fair!

The reverberations of the gong were climbing the stairs, and in panic he dropped his eyes to the paragraph under that terrible headline.

The murder on Wednesday night of well-known Guernsey advocate Charles de Garde in Candie Gardens, St Peter Port . . .

Candie Gardens?

He had never set foot there, had never even heard of the place.

Relief surged through him so violently he had to collapse on to the bed before he could carry on reading.

Even confirmation of the girl's bombshell that the murder weapon had been a piece of lead piping couldn't affect his wonderful sense of relief. While that other piece of piping had been crushing a man's skull in Candie Gardens in St Peter Port, his had been raised in self-defence the other side of the island. By the fort between Vazon and Cobo, near enough for him to get back to the hotel on foot and not have to take a taxi like when he had worked the town. Thank heaven his instinct had told him he'd pushed his luck in St Peter Port as far as it would go . . .

Scurrying his eyes quickly through the report he found what he was reluctantly looking for under the sub-heading

Fort Hommet Horror. It brought back a flash of the old pride, which as it ebbed made him feel worse than ever.

Guernsey police are seeking a connection between Mr De Garde's murder and the violent robbery of Mr Terence Smith at Fort Hommet on the west coast earlier the same night. Mr Smith, 45, owner of a £500,000 house above Vazon Bay, was knocked to the ground with a piece of lead piping by a man answering the description of the mugger who for ten days has been terrorising the island. He suffered bruising to the head but was not detained in hospital. Mr Smith told the police he had been attacked at about 11.15 p.m., which would have given the mugger time to cross the island by car to St Peter Port to attack Mr De Garde.

Which the mugger hadn't done. For the first time he had touched a man with the weapon he was carrying, but he wasn't a murderer.

And as the paper made clear, he couldn't have got across the island in time without wheels – that was a sort of an alibi, wasn't it? Like Mrs O'Malley locking her front door behind him at just before midnight. So long as she remembered . . . And he still had his piece of lead piping. He hadn't gone near it since he had heard the news, of course, but it was there in its hiding-place, where he had stowed it after Fort Hommet and before coming back to this dump and finishing the bottle of duty-free in his room to try to take his mind off what had happened. The piece of lead piping found in Candie Gardens was another man's weapon, the murderer had copied him, hoping the police would put the murder down to the man who had done the mugging. Copycatting. He knew all about it – he'd done it himself in London. It was taking a gamble, and the murderer's gamble hadn't paid off. Even the police couldn't believe one murderer would use two identical murder weapons in one night.

But the police didn't know there were two and he couldn't tell them.

His head was aching. Despite his relief he was dreadfully confused. He'd have to have a good think about it on his own, but the thing now was to behave normally, not to attract any attention.

His hands were trembling too much to make the paper look as if it hadn't been violently assaulted. He flung it on to the

79

bed and himself out of the room and down the stairs. To his relief he came up behind old Mr Benjamin, shuffling in his usual slow way through the dining-room doorway.

'Just in time, Mr Ridgeway,' the proprietress of the hotel said sternly, taking Mr Benjamin tenderly by the arm and glaring at his fellow-guest. Mr Benjamin was an annual visitor.

'Yes. Thank you. I'm sorry . . .'

'Prunes or cornflakes?'

The routine was precisely as it had been the day before, and the day before that, except that everyone was eating quietly and politely (save for Mr Benjamin, noisily slurping the juice from his prunes), out of respect for the terrible news.

'There was an incident earlier,' Mrs Dunning said at last, not needing to introduce her choice of topic. He felt a surge of disgust that this so-called hotel seated all its guests at the same table. He didn't want to know that this boring, self-satisfied old woman with the bird's nest hair-do was called Rita Dunning. 'Not all that far from here.' She leered suspiciously round the table. 'That first man was lucky – he only got bruised.'

'Must have a car,' Mr Tate pronounced, wiping a cornflake from his chin with a table napkin that revived the mugger's memory of yesterday's curry. Real hotels changed the table linen every day. But Mr Tate was saying the right thing. 'Couldn't have got across the island in time at that hour of the night unless he had a car or got a lift.'

'That's what the paper said,' Miss Watts timidly interjected.

'Yes!' He heard his own eager voice before he got round to telling himself to keep quiet. But it was all right, total silence could draw as much attention as too much talk. And Mr Tate had made an important point, one he would draw police attention to when he –

When he what, for God's sake? All right, the German bunker was stuck on to the fort nearest to this apology for an hotel, but the island was so small and the bunker such a good hiding place anyone could have come from anywhere to make use of it. And if they found the stuff on that shelf they couldn't connect it with him, not even the lead piping. And it had already occurred to him, hadn't it, that it might be a good thing if they did find the lead piping, because two lengths of the stuff would confuse them, make them at least consider that the mugger and the murderer might be two different people . . . It would be rotten to lose all the stuff, let all his dangerous work go for nothing, but it would mean he could look them in the eye when they searched him and his things, took his fingerprints.

'All right, Mr Ridgeway?'

His spoon had clattered back into his bowl of cornflakes, spattering milk on to the surrounding cloth. It was immediately absorbed by evidences of earlier carelessness, but nevertheless Mrs O'Malley had leaned over his shoulder with a cloth.

'I'm sorry, Mrs O'Malley, the spoon's a bit heavy.'

'The highest quality,' Mrs O'Malley told him severely.

'Yes. Of course.' He had never touched the piping, or any of the money, without gloves, but he hadn't been able to resist holding some of the jewellery in his bare hands, putting a man's ring on his finger . . .

Fool.

'Cooee, Mr Ridgeway!'

Bloody effing fool. He had let Mrs Dunning ask him twice to pass the marmalade.

'A hell of a lot of taxi drivers frightened by their late-night fares just now,' Detective Sergeant Tostevin reported gloomily. 'Must be in the mind, sir.'

'Not with all of them, let's hope.' Tim looked round the busy Incident Room, trying to set its intense, absorbed activity against the sense of frustration that had been only briefly eased by the sight of Duffy wagging his tail on Anna Weston's passenger seat. 'There's a list ready of drivers I ought to see?'

'Coming up any moment. Nothing so far, though, that really fits. The most promising is a motorist who rang in to tell us he gave a lift from Cobo to the north side of town on Wednesday night at what he thinks might have been the significant time although he hadn't looked at his watch . . . I'm sorry, sir.' DS Tostevin's sharp dark eyes had seen Tim's

81

weary reaction to the familiar words. 'Apparently the chap couldn't keep still. Fidgetting about the back seat all the time and muttering to himself.'

'Would our chap still be on the loose if he behaved like that?'

DS Tostevin sighed too. 'I know, sir. Ah, here comes the list. Good luck. And I think DS Mahy –'

Ted was signalling across the room. 'Yes, I can see. Thanks, Reg.' Tim went over to DS Mahy, nodding his approval to the rare beings temporarily detached enough to greet him. 'Any joy, Ted?'

'Maybe. A woman worried about the behaviour of her son. Parading about in black with one of her kitchen knives.'

'As I've just said to DS Tostevin, if our man did that sort of thing, would he still be at large?'

'Probably not. The other one's a bit more promising. A wife worried about the change in her husband, who's started going out on his own at night. She says he's become depressed and withdrawn, but swears it isn't another woman. And this morning she found the burnt remains of his black anorak in the garden incinerator.'

'What are we waiting for, Ted, and where do we have to go?'

Detective Sergeant Mahy looked down at the paper in his hand. 'The Simmonds – that's the husband and wife – are just off the Cobo Road in Castel. Well-placed, wouldn't you say, sir? The mother and son are on the edge of town, near the cemetery at Foulon. Shall we call in there on the way?'

'I suppose so. Then if it's still necessary after the Cobo Road, there are a few drivers I ought to see. Ted, why did no one notice Charles?'

'Because people are so wrapped up in themselves? Because he happened to choose ten minutes when there was no one about?'

'Perhaps. Or because people are so used to seeing him at that time of night? Olivia told me he'd been going into Candie Gardens nearly every evening since the hot weather began.' *So some one could have been waiting . . .* His detective reflex was as unwelcome as it was irrelevant. 'Let's go, Ted.'

The first address was a small solid terrace house in ochre stucco with a very neat front garden. Following DS Mahy's finger on the bell the door was opened immediately by a very neat plain woman in an all-over floral apron.

'Mrs Guillen?' Tim held out his ID. 'I'm Detective Inspector Le Page and this is Detective Sergeant Mahy. We've come in response to your telephone call –'

'The police, are you? I was expecting uniforms.' The anxiety in the thin pale face was if anything keener than when Mrs Guillen had opened her front door, and tinged now with disappointment.

'We're sorry.' DS Mahy got his own ID out and held it as close to her face as he could inoffensively put it. 'But you can see –'

'Oh, I'm not doubting you're who you say you are. It was just that uniforms . . . You'd better come in, anyway. He's in the garden.'

'Your son's still armed?'

'Armed?' A look now of bewilderment. 'Oh, the knife! Yes, he's still got the knife. He put it down for a moment but I've just seen through the window that he's picked it up again.'

'Better stay inside, I think, madam,' DS Mahy advised.

'Oh, there's no need . . . Well, perhaps it *will* have more effect if you go first.' Mrs Guillen led the way into a room at the back of the house and across to a french window. 'There you are.'

A small figure dressed and hooded in black was running about the tiny immaculate lawn, lunging at trees and bushes with a large kitchen knife and uttering loud, shrill cries.

'He saw the news last night,' Mrs Guillen called out as Tim and Ted advanced on to the grass. 'It gave him nightmares, but this morning he seems to be seeing it differently.'

'All right, lad.' Tim went slowly up to the black-clad figure, reaching it as Detective Sergeant Mahy disarmed it from behind, holding it struggling against him and throwing the knife in among some begonias growing in rows near where Mrs Guillen was standing.

'That's enough!' Ted decreed sternly, and the struggling ceased. The suddenly lolling head was the height of Ted's stomach.

'What's all this?' Tim demanded, not daring to catch the detective sergeant's eye.

'I'm the mugger!' the boy muttered. 'I'm the murderer too.'

'Are you, now? Perhaps you'll tell us your name, and how old you are.'

'My name's Ronald Guillen and I'll be eleven next week. And gosh, I'm hot, I think I'll take this thing off.'

'Let me help,' suggested DS Mahy, scrupulous in avoiding Tim's eye.

The stripping of the black revealed a rosy-faced schoolboy with tufty hair and pebble glasses.

'I told you I'd bring the police!' the mother called out. 'They've come to take you away!'

'Oh, ma!' The wailing was as penetrating as the war cries. 'I was just playing a game . . .'

'We haven't come to take you away, Ronald,' Tim said quickly, crouching down and putting his hand very gently on the boy's shoulder as Ted backed off. 'Police don't take people away unless they've done something really wrong, and they come to help people much more often than they come to arrest them. You haven't done anything really wrong, but you shouldn't have taken your mother's knife and you should have given it back to her when she asked you. No one should ever play with a knife, it's dangerous and silly.'

'It's silly, too, to dress up like a really bad man.' Ted Mahy came round in front of the boy. 'You wouldn't want to be a man like that really, would you, Ronald? Keep your anorak for a rainy day, and always remember the police are here to help you. Off you go now, and do what your mother tells you.'

'We're trying to catch a dangerous criminal, Mrs Guillen,' Tim said, as calmly as he could manage, when the boy had run sobbing into the house. 'Every second wasted could jeopardise someone's safety.'

'I'm very sorry, I'm sure.' Having gained her objective Mrs Guillen looked suitably apologetic, but was still, Tim could tell, totally unaware of how outrageously she had behaved.

'Why isn't he at school?' Ted asked.

'He's getting over the measles, isn't he? Still not quite right, I suppose, and his sight's got worse. I think it's frightened him. He'll be better now, though. He's no father, you see. A cup of tea?'

84

'No, thanks,' Tim said. 'We have to get back to work. Please don't make Ronald look on the police as bogeymen, Mrs Guillen. It might just mean he'd run away from one of us when he needed protection. If there's any more trouble have a word with his teachers. And take him back to the eye specialist.'

'The joke is,' he said in the car when they had stopped laughing, 'we did exactly what she wanted, so that even though we told her off she'll be certain she did the right thing.'

'I suppose she did, though, didn't she? We might just have helped her sort the lad out. It may be the best thing we do today.'

'I hope not, Ted, although I agree with you that we probably haven't completely wasted our time with the Guillens. But I rather like the sound of this next one.'

'So where did you go?' Olivia asked, as Duffy collapsed panting in the darkest corner of her sitting-room.

'Cobo Bay. Lots of springy turf, and Tim had told me how much Duffy likes it there. After he'd had his run I had a swim and he came in the water with me. He's dry now –'

'I don't care whether he is or not.' Olivia, relaxed in her chair, was gazing at the dog with an open affection that reminded Anna of their long ago trip to the Animal Shelter and the Zoo. 'Tim was really pleased that you wanted him. I'm glad you've had a seaside trip, Anna, you'll be working soon enough.'

'There'll be days off. I only went because of the dog.'

'Thanks. But being alone doesn't worry me, so don't feel you've got to dance attendance. Although I'm more glad than I can tell you that you're here.'

'So am I.' It was good to feel so positive. 'Shall I stay for lunch?'

'Please. We'll go outside eventually, but I'm waiting for Charles's secretary – she's bringing me the contents of his private safe. Well, the things that aren't obviously office. Knowing our Miss Tomlinson, she'll have a quick nervous peep, then dash the non-office things straight into a plastic bag with face averted. She once nearly had a nervous breakdown because she opened a letter to Charles she hadn't noticed was marked personal.' Olivia's bulk shifted slightly. 'Nothing to do with Charles's little affairs; he made sure they didn't generate anything in writing. It's just Jennifer Tomlinson's upright nature. She's the most scrupulously correct person I've ever known. She's also very clever and reliable, and Charles really depended on her. She's devastated, it was obvious even over the telephone.' So Olivia had control enough of her own devastation to be aware of the suffering of her husband's secretary. Anna's admiration came with a pang, as she remembered how other people had ceased to exist for her in the days following Mickey's death. 'She'll be here in the next five minutes, she's scrupulous about time as well. If you go and stand at the front window . . .'

Miss Tomlinson's small car drew up as one of Olivia's clocks was striking noon. She was thin and dark with hair tight in a french pleat and the face of a sleepwalker, and was carrying a plastic bag.

'Here she is. She's not local, is she, Olivia?'

'Born here to incomers, which gives her local status. But she went to school in England and worked there until she started working for Charles about ten years ago.' The bell pealed. 'Mrs Moleson will let her in.'

'It's all right, I'll go.'

'Oh!' Miss Tomlinson's setback was very temporary. 'You're the cousin. How do you do, I'm Jennifer Tomlinson, Mr De Garde's secretary.' The pale blue eyes were suddenly red with repressed tears.

'Please come in, Mrs De Garde's expecting you. I'm so sorry.'

'Thank you. It can't have been very nice for you, Mrs Weston.'

'No. But its awful for everybody.' Turning to lead the way into the sitting-room, Anna heard the choked breath behind her.

'Jennifer!' Olivia held out her hand, and the thin figure dropped to its knees beside her chair, bizarrely retaining its formality.

Anna went across to the open french window and far enough into the garden for the murmuring voices to be drowned by birdsong.

86

'Would you like to pour us drinks, Anna?' Olivia called after a few moments. 'Jennifer likes a medium dry sherry, you'll find it in the cupboard. I'll have a tomato juice and get what you want for yourself.'

The outline of Miss Tomlinson's carefully lipsticked mouth was on Olivia's cheek. The plastic bag was on her lap, and one of her hands gently caressed it through the awkward twenty minutes it took Miss Tomlinson to sip her way through her sherry.

'I'll go down the garden while you look through the bag,' Anna suggested when she had shown Miss Tomlinson out. 'You won't want to wait and you won't want an audience.'

'Poor Jennifer,' Olivia said. 'She's so upset over Charles I don't think she's started to realize yet that she may have difficulty getting another job. I suppose it just might suit her to work from home. Her father's a widower who's getting on and she's a wonder with complex documents. But I'll have a word with the office . . . There won't be much in here.' Olivia began slowly to draw the small stack of papers out of the bag. When they were halfway visible she started to flip through them. 'As I thought,' she murmured. 'Mostly to do with private finances. The Saxon Lodge deeds . . . The bill for the new roses . . . new guttering . . . Nothing that needed to be locked away, but Charles always liked to think he had a private place, even though neither of us would dream of trespassing on each other's rooms or drawers. Oh, God –' Olivia thrust the papers back and let the bag slide to the floor. 'Forgive me, Anna, I'll be all right. It's just – realizing why I had all that on my knee. You'll know how you can suddenly feel as if you'd only just learned . . .'

'I know.' Olivia had slumped down in her chair, her eyelids fluttering and her breath a sobbing gasp. As Anna ran up to her she saw that her whole body was trembling. 'What can I get for you?'

'Nothing,' Olivia whispered. 'Just – stay where I can see you.'

Anna dropped to her knees and took one of Olivia's hands, holding it until she was still. 'Have you cried?' she asked then.

'Not yet. Could you?'

'Not for a day or two. When it comes you'll feel better.'

'I'm all right now.' Olivia's breathing was back to normal and her eyes were once more wide and staring. 'Did you and Tim decide what you're going to do with Duffy for the rest of the day?' She struggled upright.

'I've got the key of the side gate and I'm to put him back when it suits me. Tim will feed him.'

'Take him out again after lunch. You ought to see as much as you can while the weather's so good, and it looks as if I need a rest. If I can sleep a bit I might be able to keep awake for you, and maybe Tim, for an hour or two after dinner, and then the night won't seem so long.'

'You wouldn't think of coming with me? We needn't see anyone and a walk –'

'The lookout's my limit, Anna, but thank you anyway. If I had any sort of an exercise routine I suppose it might be an idea, but I'm far too lazy.'

'Are you, really?'

Olivia shrugged. 'I move when I have to. When I don't – I'm even going to ask you to go and tell Mrs M we're ready for lunch. Outside, don't you think? I'll just take this upstairs and put it away until I can cope with it.'

Anna retrieved the plastic bag and put it into Olivia's hand when she had helped her to her feet. Olivia walked to the stairs in a languorous swirl of full cotton skirt, and when Anna had seen that she was able to climb them she set out for the kitchen, overtaken *en route* by a suddenly energetic dog.

Chapter Eight

The Simmonds' garden incinerator stood on short rusty legs in the middle of a bald patch of earth just clear of the bottom fence, inadequately screened from the house by some singed and sickly conifers. It was still smouldering, and Tim sought and obtained Mrs Simmonds' permission for Detective Sergeant Mahy to put the fire out. Fortunately her anguished desire to discover whether or not she was married to a murderer had caused her to pull most of the remains of the anorak clear, and they lay on the edge of the small lawn, an untidy stack of dark flakes streaked with tarnished metal.

'It was the toggle,' Mrs Simmonds told them hoarsely. A smoker's voice deepened by fear, Tim thought as he spotted the yellow vee outlining the space between the first two fingers of the gesticulating right hand. 'I recognized the toggle when I went to burn some stuff from the kitchen. I'd seen the smoke and I thought I might as well take advantage. He was down there all last evening, burning branches and so on he'd been cutting back.'

'Not the time of year for cutting back branches,' DS Mahy observed.

'No . . . I told him the bushes was all right, if he wanted something to do he could get down on his knees and pull up a few weeds, but he insisted. Could've wanted an excuse to light the fire . . . Oh, God.'

'Where is your husband now?' Tim asked.

'At work, so far as I know. Forecourt of the garage round the corner. Comes home for his lunch at twelve, if you'd like to hang on.'

89

'Thank you, Mrs Simmonds, we would. How about if you make us all a pot of tea and tell us what's been worrying you?'

'So you don't think there's another woman?' DS Mahy prompted, when the three of them were sitting with their elbows framing steaming mugs on the vinyl-covered table dominating Mrs Simmonds' small kitchen.

'Another woman? No! Not Jack! Never!' Mrs Simmonds lit a cigarette.

'Why are you so sure?' asked Tim.

'Because I know my husband, don't I?' Smoke and steam mingled, making Tim want to cough. 'Never looked at another woman from the day we met at a dance – a blind date, it was – and never would, that's one worry I'm free of. Never goes out on his own at night, neither, even takes me with him when he fancies a drink. Until a month or so ago, and then he was off out two nights out of three. Late. Not home before midnight. Told me he was with some mates . . .' Mrs Simmonds tailed off. 'Did I say I knew him?' Her huge dark eyes were a striking feature in her small pale face, and seemed to take it over completely as she stared imploringly at Tim.

'And that's still going on?'

'That's the funny thing. It all stopped a week or so ago and he was right back to normal.'

'You mean –' The dawning disappointment was the worst Tim had experienced, coming as it did just when he had thought he was close to a breakthrough. 'Your husband was at home with you the night before last?'

'Not that night, no. I wouldn't have brought you here to look at a burned-up anorak, would I, if he'd've been? Said he was going to a party. Took the car at ten. Ten! To start a party! And Jack doesn't go to parties without me anyway, whatever time they start. Came back at one in the morning.'

'How was he?' asked DS Mahy.

'The worse for it. Falling all over the bedroom. Not that I was asleep, I was too bothered.'

'What was he wearing when he went out?' The resurgence of hope in that stuffy, smoky room had brought Tim a splitting headache.

'He looked quite smart,' Mrs Simmonds considered judicially, blowing smoke at the yellow ceiling. 'Had a scarf at his neck and the pullover I gave him for Christmas. Don't know what the point was if he was going to cover it all up with the anorak . . . I didn't see the anorak, but I suppose he could've put it in the car before he said goodbye. I didn't see it was missing from its hook.'

'How did he seem?'

'Sort of jolly, not natural. And he didn't look me in the eye. That was as bad as anything, knowing he wasn't being straight with me.'

'But it isn't a woman?' Ted persisted.

'No. Not Jack! Just – I thought maybe he'd got into something. He's good-natured, Jack, likes to help people. And then I saw the telly last night . . . And found the anorak this morning . . .' Tim saw his DS look sharply away from Mrs Simmonds' dilating eyes, as if afraid of being hypnotised. 'If he did it he wouldn't've meant to. My Jack, he isn't violent . . .'

'Did you ever see a piece of lead piping about the house or garden?'

'Never. When the news and papers were full of the mugger I had to ask him what it'd look like. He described it to me . . .'

'He'll have come across it at work.' And been able to get hold of some. 'Thank you, Mrs Simmonds, you've been very helpful and public-spirited. I know how hard this must have been for you –'

'I'm not really all there at the moment, and that's the truth.' Mrs Simmonds lit another cigarette from the remains of the live one. 'I feel like I'm in a dream, I can't believe it. I can't feel afraid of him, you see. Not even now. But the anorak . . . It was new, he liked it. Why else would he burn it?'

'We don't know yet, Mrs Simmonds. Now, we'll have to take charge of the remains of the anorak, as you'll appreciate, and I'm afraid we'll have to apply for a search warrant and –'

'Here he is now!'

Mrs Simmonds jumped up as the back door opened and a slim, slight man with receding hair and chin came slowly into the kitchen. When he saw the two men he swayed and leaned back against the wall.

'These gentlemen are the police, Jack,' his wife said. She pulled smoke deep into her lungs, letting none of it out. 'I found your anorak and I had to send for them.' She had shopped her husband, and she wasn't afraid of him. No wonder, Tim thought, that she was in a dream, knowing the man she wasn't afraid of could be a murderer.

'Marge!' But there was no real protest. Jack Simmonds moved away from the support of the wall and sat heavily down on the fourth kitchen chair. 'I'd better tell you,' he said, looking from his wife to the detectives. 'Stay here, Marge.'

'You are not obliged to say anything unless you wish to do so, Mr Simmonds,' DS Mahy explained. As always on these mercifully rare occasions, Tim marvelled at the sincerity in his sergeant's voice as he spoke the statutory words. 'But whatever you say may be taken down in writing and given in evidence.' DS Mahy took out his notebook in illustration, and laid it open on the table.

'I do wish to. I'll be glad to. I suppose I might've got away with it if this murder hadn't happened but I wouldn't've been happy. It's a relief, really . . . Give us a fag, love. All right to smoke?' Simmonds asked, turning to Tim.

'All right. Think we might have the back door open, Mrs Simmonds?' But it was the dizzying alternation of hope and disappointment, as much as the smoke, that was orchestrating the hammer strokes in Tim's head.

'What?' Her intense eyes slowly focused, registered surprise. 'Of course. If that's what you want.'

DS Mahy opened it wide. 'When you're ready, Mr Simmonds,' he said as he sat down again, taking out a ballpoint.

'This chap started coming regular for his petrol,' Mr Simmonds hesitantly began. 'We're not self-service, and he used to chat to me. Told me he was an incomer, had a house on Rocquaine Bay. Asked me a few weeks ago if I'd like an extra job. Very well paid. Just a bit of driving, he said, asked me to his house to talk about it. Plan it.' Mr Simmonds' eyes dropped to the table. 'All right, I knew it wasn't straight, although he never said so. He introduced me to another bloke, the same sort as me. We were to work as a team. Pick up a load at St Sampson's –'

'On the second of June?' DS Mahy suggested.

'Yeah, that's right,' Mr Simmonds agreed. 'So you know the rest.'

'The great cigarette heist,' Tim said wearily. 'The end of the mugger's first week.'

'I was driving. The other chap was my mate. And the night before last we went to a party. Given by this bloke at his house to celebrate the success of the job.'

'So why the panic over your anorak?' Tim managed. In a normal world he would be sitting at that kitchen table rejoicing at being on the edge of solving the St Sampson's warehouse robbery, instead of swallowing a disappointment so severe it was a pain in his chest.

'Because it had blood on it and I didn't want the police to notice me.' Mr Simmonds gave a weak snort of laughter.

'Oh, Jack!' his wife said.

'I was worried enough about it when the police was just looking for the mugger – I thought of getting rid of it then. But it wasn't a house-to-house like it will be now, and I just hoped for the best.'

'He always does,' Mrs Simmonds told them.

'Where did the blood come from?' DS Mahy asked.

'My mate caught his thumb in the door when we was leaving the warehouse. He bled on me, didn't he, when I tied it up for him. He was always clumsy.' Mr Simmonds squared his shoulders, making a poor attempt to look defiant. 'But that's all I'm going to tell you about him. Or the boss.'

'If you mean that,' Tim said, 'you'll find yourself in a very difficult position. Even if the blood group doesn't match you'll have tried to dispose of a black anorak and be unable to account for your movements at the very time –'

'I'm scared,' Mr Simmonds said, dropping his head on to his hands. 'The boss,' came his muffled voice. 'Ever so nice all the time, even when he told us what would happen if we didn't get it right. If we ever said anything to anyone . . .' His head came up and he stared in anguish at Tim.

'Even your Mr Big,' DS Mahy pointed out, 'could hardly expect you to keep quiet under threat of a murder rap. I'm afraid it's the lesser of evils for you, Mr Simmonds, and I know which I'd choose.'

'You haven't got a choice, Jack,' his wife said softly.

Mr Simmonds' head went down again, but his hand came out and gripped her wrist.

93

'I'll just use your telephone,' said DS Mahy.

'I'll drive,' Tim said, when they had handed over and the police car was disappearing from view on its way to St James with Mr Simmonds and his smiling wife.

'Pity you can't work your frustration off with a bit of speed,' Ted commented, as his chief nosed round the immediate first bend. 'Even forty –'

'Perhaps just as well, the way I'm feeling.'

'We're about to clear up that warehouse job.'

'I know, I know. But I'm obsessed with the other one.'

'Let's stick with this one for a moment, sir. I can't think Mr Simmonds is either resourceful or unrealistic enough to have invented his alibi, or foolhardy enough to set his so-called boss up – to do that would mean certain death, whereas shopping him under the circumstances wouldn't be more than a maiming for life. I'm only trying to cheer you up, Tim, by putting it in an amusing way. And it could be that Mr Big has been responsible for other crimes of the St Sampson kind – there may be fewer of them in the future. Mrs Simmonds is quite a woman. Rather a good marriage, wouldn't you say?'

'I would, Ted.'

'What are we going to do now?' It was after half-past twelve, and the detective sergeant was hungry.

'We're going to see some taxi drivers, Ted, then some motorists. I don't want to go back to St James as blank as when I left.'

They had to wait for a couple of taxi drivers to finish jobs and come in, and another was on a rest day. Lunchtime came and went without Tim being aware of it as something in which he normally participated, while Ted Mahy's eager stomach sent its protest ever more insistently up to his head. Even when the people who answered doors to them appeared in an aura of cooking smells, shouting instructions over their shoulders to go and see if this or that was boiling or burning, the detective inspector, despite his sergeant's increasingly desperate prayer that his chief's nose, if not his memory, might be jogged, failed to connect it with his own usual mid-day habits.

When the four taxi drivers and the three motorists at the top of their respective lists had been spoken to, DI Le Page at last turned the car towards home. But to his sergeant's despair he drew into the first layby. 'Let's just sum up, Ted. The two taxi drivers who dropped fares in Cobo – the descriptions of the man and his behaviour tally, it was round about the same time – the right time – and one was on the night before the murder. I think that's the area to base the second lot of house-to-houses. The muggings that weren't carried out in Town were carried out north and south of Cobo Bay, after the first one just behind it in Le Guet. That could be significant – the chap trying himself out locally, as it were, then when it worked getting down to proper planning. If he'd had a car I think he'd have gone further afield, but all the non-town jobs were done within sprinting distance of Cobo. And all those small hotels . . . Another thing, Ted. Now he's turned murderer the mugger will know his home or his hotel room's going to be searched, may already be afraid of a public-spirited hotel proprietor or landlord showing a bit of private enterprise.'

'You don't want to think of him as a local, do you, Tim?'

'Whoever he is, he'll be expecting a search. So he'll have to have found a hiding place. The forts and martello towers, Ted –'

'The forts and martello towers have been looked into.'

'Looked into, yes!' Tim said irritably. 'But not exhaustively checked. North and south from Fort Hommet I want them gone over with a fine tooth comb. Which includes an exhaustive check of the Watchtower at Le Guet.' He started the engine. 'Let's get back and set things up here as well as at Cambridge Park.'

'And have ourselves a bite to eat?'

'I'm sorry, Ted.' Tim wondered if his short fuse might be connected to his own empty belly. 'The moment we've got the west coast campaign under way you can chase us up the biggest ham and cheese rolls the canteen can provide, with a mug of coffee apiece. We'll eat and drink in the privacy of my temporary office.'

By the time they got there it was half-past three, and Tim was wondering whether he was hungry after all. And starting reluctantly to think about the likelihood of small hotels and boarding-houses locking their front doors at a godly hour so that the mugger-turned-murderer would have had to ring to be let in or risk the proprietor hearing his key in the lock. If this had happened, they would already have been told. So perhaps the fellow stayed out all night. Or was local . . .

'Excuse me, sir.'

Detective Inspector Le Page came to attention. His sergeant wouldn't be saying that if he was bringing in food. And his hands were empty.

'What is is, sergeant?'

'It's a chap to see you, sir. Says it's important. Says' – an indignant flush flooded DS Mahy's freckled face as he spread his lunchless hands – 'says he's the mugger but not the murderer. Those are his words, sir. I think perhaps you should –'

'Bring him in, sergeant.'

'He's right here, sir.'

DS Mahy looked round the door, beckoned sharply. Then stood aside as a small thin man wearing purple shorts and a boxer vest came hesitantly into the room, a large plastic carrier bag clasped to his chest. He had sharp features and unattractively sun-reddened face and limbs. He looked to Tim to be in his early thirties. 'He resisted anyone else trying to take it,' the DS said as he shut the door. 'Said he'd seen your name and your picture in the paper, so I thought –'

'That's all right, sergeant.' The man was moving slowly towards Tim's desk. 'What have you got there, sir?' Tim asked him. 'Sit down and tell me. You sit down too, sergeant.'

Ted Mahy was the more prompt, but after a few seconds of staring at Tim the man put his bag carefully down on the desk and took the chair facing the detective inspector, his gaze in the continuing silence growing in intensity.

'Well?' prompted Tim, after counting to fifty.

The man grabbed the bag again, to shake its contents on to the desk so abruptly Tim felt himself start.

'Dear Lord,' said Detective Sergeant Mahy.

On Tim's desk there now reposed a jumble of black clothing intermittently agleam with rings, necklaces and watches, and a length of lead piping.

'I did all the muggings,' the man said hoarsely. A bizarre flash of pride entered the straining voice, crossed the pink sweating face. 'But I swear I never did the murder. I never been in them gardens. Not that night nor any other. And I couldn't have got there, where that man came at me was miles the other side of the island and I ain't got wheels. And I didn't hit him neither. I just touched him as he came at me. Self-defence, that was. And I wouldn't've had two pieces of piping, you gotta see I wouldn't've had –'

'All right, sir. Sergeant?' Trying to disregard the sinking of his heart, Tim watched DS Mahy assemble the wherewithal for the taking of a statement. 'Now, if you'll just tell us your name and address we'll start from there.'

'It hasn't been at all convenient,' Mrs O'Malley said peevishly, her eyes snapping round the complement of guests still seated in their customary places at the cleared dining table.

'I'm sorry about that, madam,' Tim responded insincerely. All the proprietress of the Ocean View Hotel had had to do was to ask her clients to remain in their places when they had finished eating their high teas. And he hadn't kept them waiting. He and his sergeant had got back from Grandes Rocques while the waitress was still removing the unattractive remains of the meal. 'I asked your guests to remain at table because I thought it would be the easiest way for them to answer general questions before giving us their individual statements. Nothing to worry about,' he added hastily, as a nervous movement crept round the table like a sudden breeze. He was leaning with DS Mahy against a massive mahogany sideboard while he surveyed the increasingly restive rectangle in the centre of Mrs O'Malley's dining-room and tried not to be aware of the unpleasant stains in varying shades of yellow on the grey-white table cloth.

'Well . . .' He had said enough to mollify the proprietress. 'We like to assist our police force, of course. While we're still in a fit state and not all murdered in our beds.'

An assenting shudder passed round the table.

'We've been lucky,' a fragile-looking old lady asserted, nodding her head more vigorously than it had been nodding of its own accord. 'Sleeping under the same roof as a murderer.'

Tim felt his sergeant's sharp movement, and placed a restraining hand discreetly on his arm. To contradict would

97

be to distract from the clearly defined task in hand, as well as to risk publicity where they were not yet ready for it.

'Mr Ridgeway is in custody,' he said soothingly. 'Not yet proved guilty of anything, but not due to return to the Ocean View Hotel.' He remembered the place's name without fumbling, because of having been struck by the untruthfulness of the notice at the hotel gate and its lack of artistic quality. 'Now, I'm hoping you might be able to help us in a very important area of our investigation.' He was hoping they might not. 'We want to know if Mr Ridgeway did in fact spend the night of the thirteenth of June, the night Charles De Garde was killed, in this hotel. I gather the doors are locked at midnight, Mrs O'Malley.'

The proprietress offered him a self-satisfied smile. 'They are indeed, inspector. I run a very respectable house.'

'I'm sure of it.' But her choice of words had made Tim wonder if she had once run a house of a different sort. 'Do you give keys to those guests who want to return after the door is locked?'

'I do not, sir. Guests who return after midnight have to ring the bell and disturb me. Most of my clientele, I am happy to say, are too considerate and too respectable to cause me such a disturbance.'

Too intimidated, Tim corrected in his head. A sharp movement by the young waitress, drooped against the window, made him probe further.

'It's always you then, Mrs O'Malley, who gets up to answer the door?'

The waitress had the courage to cough, and Mrs O'Malley darted her an exasperated glance. 'It is not always me, Inspector, although I am always awakened.' The waitress pulled a face at her employer's back, then looked at Detective Sergeant Mahy and blushed. 'Sometimes Sharon here will reach the door before me.'

'Thank you, Mrs O'Malley. Now, Sharon.' The girl pulled herself upright as Tim turned to her. 'You live in at the hotel?'

'Yes, sir. Every night of the week, sir.' There was definitely a hint of mockery in her demureness. She would surely be capable of helping a non-conformist client over a window sill.

'Would you remember the night of the thirteenth of June? The night before last. Wednesday. Don't worry if it's blurred in your mind, these things are hard to recall. But don't say you're sure about anything unless you really are.'

'I'm sure nobody's rung the bell at night for the past week,' Sharon said unhesitatingly, no sub-text evident in her eyes or her voice. Unless she was a consummate actress, she was telling him that she had seen no one come in through another door or a window, either. Although when they took the individual statements later they would have to inquire how well she had come to know the accused . . .

'Thank you, Sharon. That is very helpful indeed.' Tim returned his gaze to the proprietress. 'Mrs O'Malley? You agree with Sharon?'

'I've no reason to disagree.' Mrs O'Malley shot a displeased glance at the waitress.

'So Mr Ridgeway was either asleep in his room,' Tim continued on a wave of weariness, his eyes travelling round the attentive group at the table, 'or he stayed out all night and appeared at breakfast time as if he had just come downstairs like the rest of you.' He'd float the possibility of entry during the night other than through the front door on a one to one basis. He didn't want Mrs O'Malley's renewed outrage to unsettle them again.

'The bare-faced cheek of it!' gasped the woman with the bobbing grey head.

'If that *is* what happened,' the sergeant said with slight severity. 'We don't know yet that it did. If any of you saw Mr Ridgeway at any point during the night it would prove his innocence of the murder. So this is very important.'

'Innocence indeed!' Mrs O'Malley sniffed, seating herself showily in the room's one armchair.

'We are all innocent under Guernsey law until proved guilty,' Tim reminded her, keeping his voice as neutral as he could. 'Now if any of you can tell me –'

'I saw him.' The voice wheezed from the man who was clearly the oldest person at the table, ashen-faced with eyes sunk in dark rings, and a big frame that looked too large for what survived inside it. 'Well, I heard him first. His snoring that night was worse than usual, he must've been drinking. Mostly I put up with it or knock on the wall. I mayn't be able to see or walk as well as I could, but me hearing's still good.'

Pride lit up the watering eyes. 'Too good to be sleeping next to a racket like that Ridgeway chap made.'

'I'm sorry, Mr Benjamin,' Mrs O'Malley interposed, leaning fussily towards him. 'I'm having some structural work carried out in the autumn and next year –'

'Not just now, Mrs O'Malley,' DS Mahy said, but with a smile. Tim added a conspiratorial nod, and she subsided.

'Probably drinking off the effects of the Fort Hommet job,' the sergeant murmured to his chief. 'That whisky bottle was empty.'

'It'd fit,' Tim murmured back. 'If it was the right night.' A sudden desperate wish welled up in him that the evidence would be inconclusive, that the investigation of the murder could continue to focus on people who hadn't known Charles. 'So what did you do that night, Mr Benjamin?'

'I went into his room, didn't I?'

'No locks on the bedroom doors, Mrs O'Malley?' the sergeant asked.

'No locks required,' the lady aggressively replied. 'None of my guests has anything to hide, and none of them would go into a room that wasn't their own. Unless they were bothered like poor Mr Benjamin,' she added hastily, as that gentleman's rheumy gaze wandered towards her.

'I see. What did you do when you were in the room, Mr Benjamin?'

'Went up to the bed, of course. Put my hand on the fellow's shoulder and shook it.'

'You could see your way across the room?'

'After I'd put the light on. The switch was by the door.'

'And Mr Ridgeway woke up?'

'Did 'e heck! I told you, he'd been drinking. But he grunted and turned over, and the racket stopped. So I went back to bed.'

'Turning the light off? Had you noticed anything unusual in the room?'

'I hadn't noticed anything except the snoring. I didn't look round the room, I just wanted the noise stopped. Awful noise, so reg'lar you keep listening for the next one. Yes, I turned the light off – though I almost didn't. Would've served him right, but I ain't a vindictive chap.'

'That's very helpful indeed, Mr Benjamin,' DS Mahy said, after an understanding glance at his chief. He knew how the DI must feel. 'The only thing is – can you be certain this happened on the night of the thirteenth of June, the night before last? That it wasn't the eleventh or the twelfth?'

'Course I can be certain.' Mr Benjamin's pale eyes were scornful of police ignorance. 'It was half an hour into me birthday, wasn't it? I thought, that's a fine way to start me eighty-fifth!'

Chapter Nine

'Come in, Tim, I'm glad to see you.' Olivia led the way into her sitting-room, enfolding him in her wake with the unique sultry perfume that always evoked vague imaginings of an exotic world beyond his experience. Impervious to such nuances, Duffy bounded past them and out through the open garden door. 'Anna will be here when she's had her dinner at the Duke.'

The high summer arc of the sun had carried it out of sight, but its last rays were a dazzling, sharply-angled yellow knife across the soft green carpet, making the elegantly cluttered corners of the room seem already dusky.

'I have some news,' he said reluctantly, flopping into the second largest armchair – Charles's armchair, he thought on a pang – as she crossed to the drinks cupboard. 'Yes, I'll have a whisky. Thanks.'

She came silently with his drink, and in silence set it down beside him, unquestioning, prepared to listen to what he had to tell her: an attractive Olivia trait.

He waited until she was sitting in her chair, half smiling at him, her face showing nothing of her ordeal save for the tic at work under one of her serene brown eyes. Through his reluctance he was aware, as always, of how satisfying he found her to look at, in the way that he found certain women in portraits. But nothing more personal than that, although he was so fond of her. 'We've got the mugger, Olivia.' He was glad to see the glass in her hand. 'He isn't the murderer.'

She took a drink, slowly put the glass down. 'So there are two people.'

'Yes. The mugger was so anxious for us to believe he isn't the murderer that he came into St James this afternoon and gave himself up. Brought his gear, including a length of lead piping, and what looks to be every last bit of the stuff he stole.'

'Why should he think proving he was the mugger would prove he didn't kill Charles?' Olivia picked up her glass again and drank.

He was glad she hadn't been watching the news, reading the papers, glad above all that the media had obviously stuck to their bargain with Anna – but at least they might have prepared her. 'Because he was mugging a man at Fort Hommet – the other side of the island from Candie Gardens, as I don't have to tell you – somewhere round about a quarter past eleven the night Charles was killed. The booty he spilled out on my desk included the victim's watch and wallet, and a piece of lead piping.'

'And he told you he didn't have transport?'

'Yes.' As usual she had gone to the heart of it.

'He could have hitched a lift, hailed a taxi.' Her face was still calm, but he knew that her statement was an entreaty.

'Of course. But the boarding house where he was staying in Cobo has a midnight curfew superintended by a gorgon, and a fellow guest went into his room at half past to try and stop him snoring. Which really doesn't give him time to have taken a return trip to Candie Gardens, even if he had organised someone inside to let him in at the back door or through a downstairs window.'

'Obviously not.' Olivia looked away from him, to put her glass carefully down. 'But Tim – it's so strange.' She raised her head to engage his eyes again. 'Why didn't he just do nothing? Stash his gear and his takings if he hadn't already done so, and write them off?'

He couldn't tell her anything to help her, but he could allow her the short time even Olivia must need to be able to face the new probability. 'He hadn't been able to resist trying on a couple of the rings. He knew he ran the risk of being fingerprinted, on his way home if not in his hotel.'

'But if he wiped the stuff . . .'

'He'd already hidden it on a barely accessible ledge in the German bunker built onto the fort at Grandes Rocques. He'd obviously been as pleased as Punch with himself for finding such a hiding place when it was only a matter of mugging, but with twice as many police being twice as determined after the murder, not to mention an islandful of outraged and suddenly eagle-eyed locals, he knew how risky it would be to carry on going in and out of the bunker. So he decided to cut his losses and bring it all to us with a confession, reduce the risk to the possibility of being stopped between picking the stuff up and getting it to St James. If he'd left it there and taken us to it he'd have cut out that risk too, of course, but he was so anxious to be seen to be handing it over of his own accord that he panicked. He was in a terrible state when he got to my desk and poured his spoils all over it, hardly able to get a word out at first then babbling his relief that he'd pre-empted us. But I don't think it was entirely panic. I have an idea his sub-conscious wanted to make a dramatic gesture, show me as impressively as possible how he'd dictated my working life for the past ten days. And it made us believe him right away.'

'So he's innocent of murder.' Uncharacteristically when there was no need for it, Olivia prised herself from her chair and went to stand at the open garden door, looking out. Tim noticed that she had interrupted the weakening sunshaft, jack-knifing it to climb her unexpectedly slender legs. 'You have to start looking for a different kind of murderer now, Tim.'

'Yes.' He had half expected she would say it for him; there was nothing slow about her mind.

'Someone taking advantage of the mugger's activities to start a rival industry and hope it will be credited to the first man. But not having the first man's restraint.'

Tim felt his throat tightening. She had brought them to the crux. 'I think we can assume that whoever killed Charles took advantage of the mugger's activities and hoped the murder would be put down to him. But anyone ruthless enough to kill a stranger for gain would be ruthless enough to rifle his victim's body. Nothing was taken from Charles, Olivia, as you know. Not even his money. Or the little dagger.'

The splendid statue didn't move, but he thought he heard a catch of breath. 'What if he lost his nerve?' There was no tremor in the voice. 'He could have been so appalled by what he'd done he couldn't take advantage of it.'

'Olivia –'

'Oh, Tim!' Speedy reactions from Olivia were so rare they had enormous effect. She spun round to face him. 'I know what you're going to say. That Charles's killer was someone who wanted him dead.'

'Yes.' He got to his feet and went over to her, taking her hands from her sides and bringing them together between his. 'I'm sorry, Olivia, it's so much worse –'

'Charles is dead; nothing could be worse. It's all right, Tim, I have to face it. Even the fact that I shall be a suspect myself.'

Since Mr Benjamin's revelation he had been thinking of Charles's women – one in particular – but not of his wife, whom his women had never threatened. For the first time in his working life, Tim felt a surge of hostility against his calling. There was, though, something else separating Olivia from further ordeal as yet. The unhealable sores of Occupation resentments unto the latest generation. 'Joly Duguy,' he said. 'The suspect now is Joly Duguy.'

'Oh, God, Tim . . .'

He had to help her back to her chair, where she lay with closed eyes and panting breath. He knelt beside her. 'Olivia –'

'I'm all right.' To his relief her eyes opened. 'It's just that there seems no end . . . Joly!'

'We both know how he behaved on Tuesday night.' Tim, too, was shocked by the idea of Joly as a killer. But who could predict the sticking point of an angry Peter Pan? 'Has there been anything since?'

'No. But I suppose I ought to tell you, now . . . It must have been Monday night although it seems such a long time ago. Charles went into Candie Gardens that night, too. Before he went I thought something was bothering him, and when I asked he told me he'd come across Joly Duguy in town and that Joly had looked at him with utter hatred. Those were the exact words he used, Tim. They stuck in my mind because they sounded so – so extreme. Joly really seemed to have got to him. Charles even fancied he could be draining his strength.'

'So we'd better find out what Joly was doing on Wednesday night.' Despite the jolt to his instinct that Joly was a child in need of care and protection, Tim felt a flash of his old relish, the possibility of regaining his impersonal sense of belief in detection as a fine art. 'And not just Joly. I'm bound to ask you now if you believe Charles had any other enemies.'

'Enemies?' she echoed, with an ironic lift of an eyebrow. 'There could be several, I suppose, depending on how amenable certain women were to Charles's loss of interest in them. Will you pour us another drink, Tim?'

'Sure.' He crossed to the cupboard, marvelling at her realism. 'It wasn't even loss of interest really, was it? I mean, you can't lose something you didn't have in the first place. I'm not trying to cheer you up,' he said as he put her glass down beside her. 'I'm talking facts. Charles always belonged to you. An emotionally involved woman who was forced to realize she was in the category of a fillet steak could suffer something of a trauma.'

'Yes . . . The dish that wasn't cooked for him at home. You knew that, didn't you, Tim?'

He had to meet her calm gaze. 'Charles never spoke of it, but I thought it was possible. Perhaps because I could see you weren't jealous. It isn't evident, Olivia.'

'No. And that might be to my disadvantage on the mainland. A gossip columnist, Tim, once labelled me voluptuous. People could think I had other lovers, too, and wanted my freedom. Fortunately on an island the size of Guernsey it's virtually impossible to lead a secret life – witness the general knowledge of Charles's regime. If I'd had lovers I couldn't have kept them secret. But I never have had. Appearances can be deceptive. In fact my strongest instincts are maternal.' There was a sparkle in her eyes, but no tears fell.

He felt painfully moved. 'I had no idea. You could have adopted –'

Olivia shrugged, her half smile restored. 'Strongest doesn't necessarily mean strong. The blood tie could have overcome my indolence, the idea of going to an adoption agency didn't. We're straying from our subject, Tim.'

'Yes. Olivia, I want you to start thinking. About possible enemies. Including the women.'

'I can't help you over the women, Tim. I didn't take any interest in them. They didn't affect my life or my relationship with Charles.'

106

'Not even when one of them –'

'Talking of what people were doing that night' – Olivia spoke so calmly, so much at her own pace, that if he hadn't known her he might not have realized she was interrupting him – 'Janet and Douglas Chapman were having dinner with the Brightwells. They told us on Tuesday night, I think you were here. They'd be unlikely to have left before midnight, and they would have been together.'

'Thank you for reminding me. I hadn't taken it in.' His disappointment showed him that since his visit to the Ocean View Hotel he had been holding Janet and Douglas Chapman at the back of his mind as a last resort. Chapman the other night hadn't known of the affair, he was sure of it. He couldn't have sat at a dinner table eating so heartily with the woman who had dealt such a blow to his pride. But if he had learned since – or if Janet had been made to see herself as the equivalent of a fillet steak . . . Forcing his mind away from what was now academic speculation, Tim found himself wondering how Olivia had got to know of the affair. Had Charles or Janet told her, or had she heard it from some busybody who claimed to have her welfare at heart? *I didn't take much interest in them*. But Janet was her friend . . .

'I'm afraid that's as far as I can go with Charles's women.' She could have told him one thing more, but she didn't want to involve even a trollop unless she had to, and she would wait until Tim had investigated Joly. Poor Joly . . . Olivia shivered. 'The funeral, Tim? The inquest? I'm sorry, I should have put them the other way round.'

He got up and walked over to the window. The sun had flared a last defiance of the dusk, and in the spaces between the green and gold spread of climbing roses the bricks of the west wall glowed crimson. Duffy came galloping up to him, stopping so abruptly in the doorway Tim imagined the squealing of brakes. 'The inquest's on Monday,' he said, fondling the dog's head. 'It'll be adjourned for further police inquiries, but establishment of the cause of death will be straightforward and the coroner's bound to release Charles's body, which means we can arrange the funeral. Tuesday if possible? The Town Church?' He turned back to her as Duffy staggered indoors and collapsed panting in his favourite corner. 'Perhaps you'd like me to –'

'You're busy, Tim, and it ought to be me.' Olivia struggled upright in her chair. 'And I ought to be thinking about making you a sandwich.'

'Have you had anything?'

'Mrs M left me a salad. I ate most of it.'

'I'm all right, Olivia. Really, I had something in the canteen.'

'I don't think Anna took Duffy home till late afternoon. They were going on another expedition this afternoon. But she'll tell you, she should be here any moment. I hope neither of you will mind if I leave you to entertain one another. I'm a bit weary.'

When Olivia said goodbye the shock of her revelation kept Janet leaning against the wall, the telephone receiver still in her hand. She had behaved so strangely since Charles's death that it was several moments before Douglas turned round to ask her if she'd been turned into a pillar of salt.

'I'm all right.' She hung up and crossed the room back to the sofa. 'That was Olivia,' she told him as she sank down.

Douglas had returned to his paper. 'So I gathered,' he said, without looking up.

'The mugger went into St James and confessed.'

'The murderer, you mean.' He was looking at her now, warily.

'No. The mugger and the murderer are two different people.' Douglas's paper slid to the floor. 'The mugger confessed to knocking that man Jones – Smith – down at Fort Hommet. He brought the man's watch and wallet to Tim to prove it.'

'Which proves he didn't kill Charles De Garde?'

'I'll have a whisky, if you'll pour me one,' Janet said. Making tetchy noises Douglas heaved himself to his feet. 'There wouldn't have been time without transport, which he doesn't have. But that's academic. The police have proof that he was in bed in his hotel in Cobo at half-past midnight.'

Janet saw that her husband, standing with his back to her by the drinks cupboard, was rigidly immobile. 'Douglas?' She had to say it twice before he turned slowly round.

'The mugger didn't just steal a watch and a wallet at Fort Hommet. What about all the other stuff?'

'This man brought it in. Everything that's been stolen.'

Douglas cleared his throat, pulling on his moustache. 'Perhaps Olivia didn't get it quite right.'

'Olivia always gets it right. It's extraordinary, isn't it, Douglas?'

'Extraordinary? I wouldn't call it extraordinary,' he said as he set a very small scotch on the table beside her, in the irritated tone of voice which was now customary when he addressed his wife. 'If this chap's been able to prove he isn't the murderer, obviously the murder was a copycat crime that went wrong.'

Janet took a long swallow, almost emptying the glass. 'The man at Fort Hommet lost his watch and his wallet while he was unconscious, dead for all his attacker knew. Whoever killed Charles left his belongings intact.'

'So?' The drink Douglas had poured for himself was at least three times as big as Janet's. The glass rocked in his hand as he sat down again, spilling a few drops on to his lapel.

'So the police believe,' Janet said, forcing herself along, 'that the person who took advantage of the mugger must have been someone who knew Charles and wanted him dead.'

The silence was total. In it Janet heard the shriek of a night creature in the dusk beyond the window, a car starting up nearby. Since learning of her affair with Charles, Douglas had moved his chair slightly so that he no longer faced her, and she was able to watch him without the risk of meeting his eyes as his plodding thought processes brought him the significance of what she had said. They brought, too, an unhealthy mottling of his face which by the time he spoke was beginning to affect Janet with a queasy mixture of elation and alarm.

'That means . . .' he began, in a strange deep voice. 'That means . . .'

'It means that Mary Brightwell cancelling her dinner-party could be a very unfortunate thing for you and me.'

'You and me!' he repeated indignantly, swivelling round to glare at her. Seizing the opportunity, she could see, to turn his alarm into anger.

'You and me,' she said again, realizing on a wave of triumph that the totality of her wretchedness had shrivelled Douglas's effect on her to nothing. Except for the beginnings of fear. 'You haven't got an alibi either, Douglas.'

His mouth opened and closed, but no sound came out of it. 'Well?' she challenged. 'You went out.'

His eyes left her face as he swivelled his chair back to its new position. 'I went to the Club.' Janet's sense of triumph deepened as she heard the defensive note in his voice. 'Played a couple of frames of snooker, had a couple of drinks. I told you.'

'You may be asked to tell the police. They'd want a statement a bit more detailed than a couple of frames of snooker and a couple of drinks. You weren't very far from Candie Gardens.'

'Nor were you, Janet. Fort George to Cambridge Park? Ten minutes in the car.' On the offensive now. 'You'll have to tell the police what TV programmes you were watching, and if you went out, too. All these expensive empty acres, nobody need have seen you.'

'I'm sure you're right, Douglas. Actually I didn't go out. And I didn't watch TV apart from the news.'

'That's unfortunate,' he said, not disguising his glee.

'It's the truth.' How they were exhausting each other, so constantly at war! Did they really hate one another enough to try and make a murder charge stick without reference to the facts? At least now that Douglas had ceased to matter to her there was a chance of disengagement.

She had succeeded in breaching his self-satisfaction; it was time to tell him the rest of Olivia's news. 'Anyway,' she said. 'There's Joly Duguy. You were at Saxon Lodge on Tuesday, it's a wonder you haven't thought of him yourself.'

'Of course. Joly Duguy.' Douglas was instantly restored. 'Practically announcing his murderous intentions.'

'Perhaps.'

'Perhaps?' he echoed sharply, turning to glare at her. 'Is Le Page saying perhaps?'

'He's investigating Joly's movements on Wednesday night.'

'There you are then. I don't know why you gave me all that rigmarole about having to worry about not being at the Brightwells. I didn't hear you tell Olivia the dinner-party was cancelled.'

'There'll probably be no need to tell anyone.'

'Of course there'll be no need. It was obviously Duguy.'

She met his angry glare with a smile, a movement so unfamiliar she had to force the stretch of her mouth. 'I'm glad you've settled things to your satisfaction, Douglas.' Janet held out her glass, and as he pulled it roughly from her hand she allowed herself the faint hope that she might not have entirely lost her sense of humour.

Dear Jane,

I was going to start off by apologizing for not having written for so long – then realized it was only yesterday. And only yesterday that I found Charles's body. Time seems to be playing funny tricks just now, as if the horror has exploded through it and destroyed its sequence.

I couldn't have imagined yesterday that the first thing I'd be telling you in my next letter would be that I've had the companionship of a splendid dog all day. I don't suppose many people would see it as important under the circumstances, but for me it's the best thing that could have happened, apart from waking up and finding it's all been a dream.

As far as you're concerned, though, I ought to be starting where I left off. When I'd posted yesterday's letter I went to see my new employers and warn them –

That's where I was up to when you rang. I should have had the sense to realize that you were bound to hear about it from one part or another of the media before you got my letter. It must be one of those tricks time's playing on me. I'm sorry for being so stupid and not ringing rather than writing, but I'm glad you told me to go straight back to this letter!

Yes, my new employers were super, no worries there. But Jane . . . I didn't say anything on the telephone, and I don't know what Tim and Co will say to the media, so keep it to yourself, please, for the moment. The mugger gave himself up this afternoon, and it's been proved beyond any doubt that he couldn't have killed Charles.

Tim Le Page told me an hour ago in Olivia's garden. He'd already told Olivia, and she went to bed soon after I arrived. She said she was just tired, but this further blow

111

*must have been devastating. My first thought when Tim told
me was that another would-be mugger had staged a copycat
robbery that went wrong, but he said nothing was taken
from Charles's body and the police can't believe a man who
would kill in the course of robbery would leave empty-
handed. So – the motive must have been the death of Charles
rather than the theft of his belongings.*

*At least there's an obvious suspect: Joly Duguy, the chap
who made all that fuss outside Olivia's house the night of the
dinner-party. Olivia told Tim that he and Charles met by
chance on Monday, and Joly gave him a look of 'utter
hatred'. So the situation at present is that Tim and his team
are investigating Joly's movements the night of the murder.
It looks cut and dried, but of course one has started thinking
about other people who knew Charles. If Joly Duguy has an
alibi, I expect the Guernsey police will even have to look
into the possibility that I could have met Charles in London,
perhaps came to the island as a woman scorned, and
couldn't wait to take my revenge.*

*The awful thing, Jane, is that there is nothing far-fetched
about that scenario.*

*And the women who really did have affairs with Charles
. . . If Joly's no go, will they all have to be chased up and
their movements that night accounted for? I let Tim know
Olivia had told me about Charles's women, and about Janet
Chapman, and he told me Janet and her husband were out
to dinner together on Wednesday night. I thought there was
a trace of disappointment in his voice about that. But I
suspect he has more sympathy for Joly Duguy than for the
Chapmans, particularly Janet. Am I making him sound self-
righteous? He isn't. But he's obviously worried and
unhappy. Neither of us spoke of the bizarre fact that Olivia
herself has to be a suspect. Knowing her just the little that I
do, I'm sure she'll have been the first to realize it.*

*But life goes on I suppose, and let me finish up with the
dog.*

*He's Tim's Duffy. I met him first with Tim in Candie
Gardens that morning. He's a rough-coated gingery Heinz
of just the right size, with ears that work like semaphores
and gleaming brown nose and eyes. Very intelligent, but not*

112

sufficiently to realize I'm a vet – I hope I don't have to treat him at any point and reveal myself a Judas. Tim of course doesn't have much time to spend with him just now, so it's one of those rare arrangements that suit all parties equally. When Tim opened my passenger door this morning Duffy jumped straight in, and went on wagging his tail even when Tim walked off.

I took him to Cobo Bay on the west coast – where the mugger was staying, Tim just told me – because that's where he particularly likes to run around, and then we went two bays down to Rocquaine, where Tim had also told me the bathing was particularly good. It was, and Duffy came in too. We went to Olivia for lunch, before which Charles's Miss Jennifer Tomlinson, prototype of the devoted secretary, arrived with the papers from his office safe and drank a demure sherry. Will this surely-virgin spinster be required to provide an alibi, too, if it turns out that Joly Duguy has one? The papers upset Olivia, when Miss Tomlinson had left she started going through them and had to give it up. If only she could cry.

She went to lie down after lunch, and Duffy and I drove to Bordeaux Harbour, a lovely natural inlet on the north east coast. As many birds as tourists, and Duffy respected both. I put him back in his garden very reluctantly at five o'clock, when Tim or some emissary was due to come and feed him, and we had a rapturous reunion at Olivia's just now.

Jane, it has to be Joly Duguy.

What will life be like for Olivia, if it can't be proved it was anybody?

So Jimmy says he's glad I like Guernsey. If I thought that was emotional blackmail it wouldn't get to me, but I know from him it isn't. Oh, hell!

But I also know I'm doing the right thing, and I'm just about sure already that I'll never go back to him.

Much love as always,
Anna.

Chapter Ten

'Hi there, Joly.'

Joly Duguy looked up from the piece of wood he was whittling. 'If it isn't Detective Inspector Le Page,' he said, when he had looked down again.

'As large as life,' Tim agreed. There was a rough-grained stool to match the one on which Joly was crouched outside the open door of the shed that was his office building, and Tim sat down. 'How's business?'

'Steady.' Joly glanced at the cloudless sky and then round his yard, untidily stacked with the materials he used to make and repair small boats. Beyond the open gates was a narrow view of the blue sea across the road, separated from the paler blue sky by a faint grey horizon.

Tim sat a few moments in silence before stating the obvious. 'Good weather for you.' A Guernseyman, he didn't have to make an effort to lead gently towards the matter in hand.

'It's all right.'

Joly was of a type, Tim reflected, that would be unlikely to admit to satisfaction with any aspect of its lot. Although he had lived all his life in the family home where he was now alone, he had a rootless air and a gipsyish look to him, with his dark curly hair and brown sharp-featured face, and would have been a figure to note even without the drama of the Duguy family reputation. Guernsey people didn't visit the sins of the fathers on the children, and Joly, born in the mid nineteen-fifties, held a unique position in St Peter Port as an object of mingled embarrassment and compassion. A position, Tim thought now for the first time and with a pang of pity, which was probably responsible for his air of automatic mistrust. Especially noticeable at this moment because Tim, as a half De Garde, belonged in Joly's eyes to the enemy camp.

'Good,' Tim said. 'But you'll know I'm not here just to inquire about the health of your business.'

'So?' Joly was still busy on his piece of wood, which Tim, despite his absorption by professional thoughts, was fascinated to see was changing steadily into a boat.

'So the island's first and, I hope, last mugger is safely in custody.'

'So what's new?' This time Joly didn't even look up.

'He's in custody for mugging. Not for murdering Charles De Garde. He has a watertight alibi for that.'

There was no doubt that Joly had received a shock. The sure fingers jerked, then began to nurse an unplanned concavity on the ship's hull. 'Jesus,' he said, but it could have been for his wounded craft.

'So we have to start thinking differently,' Tim went on, when it was clear the shock hadn't been strong enough to tip Joly into one of his violent swings of mood. But there was still time. 'And looking elsewhere. At first we thought someone must be taking advantage of the mugger's activities to start a business of his own. But although Charles De Garde was carrying money, credit cards, an expensive watch and a jewelled dagger, nothing was taken from his body. What does that suggest to you, Joly?'

'It doesn't have to suggest anything to me. You're the police.'

'I'm glad you're remembering that, Joly. What it suggests to me as the police, and to the Chief Inspector of Crime' – Joly made a gesture of mock obeisance – 'is that Charles De Garde was killed because someone wanted him dead. Someone took advantage of the mugger's notoriety, attacking in a remote place in the dark, using the same sort of weapon. Probably intending to make it look like a robbery, then losing his nerve when he saw what he'd done.'

'Even a mugger could lose his nerve.' Joly seemed to have made good his slip of the hand, and was delicately smoothing the completed shape. 'The copycat had the wrong temperament. He never should have taken up mugging. First too violent. Then too soft. Result nix all round.'

For a moment Tim couldn't speak, his longing was so keen for Joly's slick suggestion to be the right one. It was a possibility – he and his Chief had voiced it, if less succinctly than Joly – but although another would-be mugger could be called on to save sanity if they were ultimately unable to charge anyone on their list of suspects, they had agreed that he was unlikely to exist.

'You could just be right, Joly, and we're still on the lookout for him.' They were, of course, but the fire had gone out of the search. 'I'm afraid, though, that we're also having to look at the much more likely possibility – the probability, I'd call it – which I mentioned. That Charles De Garde died because someone wanted him dead. Did you want him dead, Joly?'

Tim waited warily, but the shock tactics didn't seem to have worked. Joly looked up almost lazily as he put his completed artefact carefully into the safe hollow of his crotch. 'Dead, Mr Le Page? I wished him to perdition, everyone knows that, but that's not the same thing as helping him on his way. So if you're set on asking me a question you'd better put it a bit differently.'

'All right, Joly. Did you kill Charles De Garde?'

'No.' Joly's dark eyes glittered at Tim, unwavering.

'You saw him a couple of days before he died, didn't you? In town round about mid-day? He was so struck with the look you gave him he told his wife. Told her you looked at him with "utter hatred". Mrs De Garde was pretty sure those were the words he used. He even suggested you were ill-wishing him, drawing his strength out of him.'

'That's rubbish, Mr Le Page, and you know it.' Joly sneered, but the fear in his eyes didn't go with the curl of his lip. 'And Mrs De Garde can say anything she feels like, with nobody to contradict her.'

'She was lying, then? I can tell you, Joly, she didn't want to say what she did, it made her very unhappy.'

'Too bad.' Joly sneered again, then stared expressionlessly into Tim's eyes. 'All right, it's true. Oh, only that I saw him and didn't exactly wish him the time of day. There's no crime in that, Mr Le Page. I'm not a fool and most of the time I

116

remember what the judge said. But I'm not a hypocrite either. Charles De Garde insulted the memory of my father.'

Tim realized how relaxed Joly had been apart from his one sharp move, because as he spoke his whole body started to tremble and his carved ship pitched in its protective surround.

They had moved on to tricky ground. This was Joly's vulnerable area, the place that could turn him into a shrieking, sobbing child even though he couldn't be ignorant of his father's wartime behaviour. Following the Liberation there had been some nasty scenes – Tim's father had told him about Duguy père having to be rescued from a hostile crowd – and many of them were on photographic record to give substance to the Cecil Duguy legend.

'Certain things happened during and after the war, Joly,' Tim said carefully. 'They're known facts. Charles De Garde didn't invent them. And he didn't name names.'

'He didn't have to, with all my father's come in for. The De Garde family leading the way. They killed my father, he was only fifty when he died. So what was the point of starting it all up again? My father's dead. I'm alive. I hated Charles De Garde.'

The danger signal was a sobbing growl. Tim heard it now, but as he waited it subsided and Joly dropped his head, his shoulders shaking.

'I can understand that, Joly,' Tim said gently. He could. He had thought Charles was over-confident and perhaps insensitive in his certainty that time would have healed all the wounds.

'But I didn't kill him!' Joly's head shot up, the eyes wide and wet. 'Haven't you overlooked something, Mr Le Page?'

'Joly?'

'Whoever killed De Garde, if it wasn't a mugger, they knew where he'd be and when. Maybe had an appointment with him. You should be talking to those women, if you can find them all. How would I know Charles De Garde was going walkabout in Candie Gardens at midnight?'

'By hanging about his house like you did the night before, then following him.' No point in asking what he meant about the women; Joly had to be aware he already knew.

'I didn't follow him. I didn't kill him.'

117

'I don't suppose you planned to kill him, Joly. But when the mugger and his lead piping got into the news . . . Had you found a piece, too? All of a sudden there was a scapegoat, who was probably a visitor and who would probably get away with his mugging. So why not with a murder, too? An open verdict, no one harmed except Charles De Garde. It was a gamble, though, wasn't it, for anyone who tried to take advantage of the mugger's activities? A gamble that didn't come off now the mugger's in the clear. What were you doing on Wednesday night?'

'What do I do every night of the week, Mr Le Page? I closed the yard about six. Went home. Cooked up a meal. Went along to my local. Went home.'

'Didn't go along to L'Hyvreuse?'

'On Tuesday. Not on Wednesday.'

'The landlord of the Happy Fisherman tells me you were in there on Wednesday night. But he calls time at eleven, and he doesn't know what you did after you left.'

'So you've talked to my landlord.' A change had come over Joly. He was alert now, wary, no longer pretending to be indifferent.

'Yes. Who can I talk to about what you did when you left the pub, Joly?'

'I didn't do anything when I left the pub. It was like most nights, I've just told you. I walked home. Got a sandwich. Went to bed.'

'You walked home alone?'

'What's new?'

'When you got in did you watch television. Make or receive any telephone calls?'

'Do me a favour. There was a late movie. I could tell you a bit about it, it wasn't bad. But it might have been Monday or Tuesday.'

'Try to remember, Joly, it could be important.' Tim looked towards the gate. 'I've arranged for a visit here by a couple of my men, they'll be arriving any minute. Just to have a look round. Then they'll take you home and have a look round there, too.'

'If I say I'd rather not?'

'I have a warrant. I'm sorry, Joly.'

'Are you, Mr Le Page?'

'When they've had a look round your house they'll bring you to St James to make a statement.'

'Got it all sewn up, haven't you?'

'Not yet, Joly.' Joly rose as Tim rose, clenching the carved boat in his fist. 'May I see that?'

'Sure. It's bound to have my fingerprints on it.' Joly opened his hand and brought it up to Tim's face. The curl of his lip this time was a token, and the suffering in his eyes made Tim drop his to the object held so aggressively close to them.

'It's very good,' he said. 'Will you give it to me?'

Joly's astonishment dissolved in a snort of unamused laughter. 'The disposal of my goods, eh? Have we got to that, Mr Le Page?'

'I'm sorry, Joly,' Tim said again. He had to make an effort to conceal how sorry he really was. 'I just like what you've done, and I know you do it easily, make lots of models. I thought you might spare one.'

'Oh, sure. Take it. Put it in your display cabinet alongside the De Garde silver.'

'I'll put it on display.' Tim took the boat, aware from the feel of it as he put it into a pocket that Joly's palm was sweating. 'If there's no evidence you had anything to do with my cousin's death, Joly, that will be the end of it.'

'You think so, Mr Le Page? Like it was the end of my father's persecution at the end of the war?'

'It isn't at all the same thing. And I'm not enjoying this.'

'Only doing your duty. Yes, I know. Go and order your men in, then.'

'Thanks for the carving.'

Joly made a sweeping bow, then turned and went slowly into his office. He picked up the telephone receiver and dialled a number, seeing Detective Inspector Le Page's car go past the gap beyond the gates as he waited for the dialling tone to cut out. Le Page had his telephone at his ear – he had only pretended that his men had already been summoned – but there wouldn't be much time.

'Hello?' The familiar seductive drawl.

'Are you alone?'

'Joly! Oh, darling, I didn't expect – after last night –'

119

'You're alone. Good. Look, Helen, could I see you later today? Say five o'clock?'

'Darling, you know Geoffrey's coming home, he'll be here by lunchtime. I'm so sorry.'

'Leave him.'

'Joly darling, you know I couldn't do that. You know he'd kill me. You too, probably. I don't like the way you're laughing, darling.'

'I'm sorry.'

'I can't leave him, Joly. And I shan't be able to see you for a while, I'm afraid, he isn't going away again for ages. Well, you know that, I told you last night. If I get any kind of a chance I'll ring you, but I daren't take any risks. Even without knowing anything Geoffrey's so terribly suspicious. It's being away such a lot, I suppose, on top of a jealous nature. If he didn't kill me he'd do something to my face. I told you what he said when we got married.'

'Yes.' He dashed away a tear.

'Joly?'

'I've got to go.'

'All right, darling. Thank you for last night.'

'My pleasure.'

'Oh, and mine. Take care. I'll be in touch when I can.'

'Sure you will.' Joly's eyes were staring anxiously through his dirty window, surveying the yard. 'Goodbye.'

'Au revoir, darling.'

Joly slammed the phone down and ran outside to the spot where his eyes had last rested. With a grunt of relief he found what he was looking for, and pulled it from its hiding-place. Then went back to his stool and sat down in the sunshine, as ready for Tim Le Page's mob as he would ever be.

Janet had once been grateful to golf for taking Douglas out of the house at weekends, but so many uneasy thoughts had started crowding in on her unhappiness she had begun to dread solitude. By Saturday afternoon she even found herself looking forward to his return, and the irritation that would come with it, to distract her from her inner turmoil.

She could hardly bear the office, now, and yesterday she had decided to take herself out to the Apartment for lunch. A colleague of Douglas's, Desmond Baker, had been there and had asked her to join him. His relaxed commiseration over the death of a friend indicated that neither Douglas nor the grapevine had told him about her affair with Charles, and after the first wary moments she had been able to make an apparently jokey comment about their snooker match on Wednesday night keeping Douglas out beyond his bedtime. But Desmond had looked at her with surprise and said, 'Half eleven? Not that late, is it, Janet?' It had taken all her self-control to nod and smile and say that time could hang heavy when you were on your own.

Douglas had arrived home on the evening of the murder at half-past midnight. A ten-minute journey had taken nearly an hour. Had he been hanging round Cambridge Park, round the entrance to Candie Gardens, watching to see if she was meeting Charles? Had he actually gone in?

Janet slumped off the sofa and across to the patio doors, pushing them wide. The weather was still set fair, and the slight heat haze gave the windless garden a pastel look under the pale blue sky, a water colour where the brightly coloured, windy days of spring when she had first slept with Charles had been painted in oils. It matched how she felt; it looked scarcely real.

She had overhead Tim Le Page, during dinner at Olivia's, call Fort George a rich man's fantasy. Fortunately Douglas hadn't caught the comment, but Janet had understood Tim, and agreed. She had never said anything uncomplimentary about the place to Douglas, of course – he had seen the company's choice for him of so expensive a temporary home as a tacit endorsement of his indispensability, which it no doubt was. And he uncritically liked it, no point in making things even worse between them by disparaging it. But from the start of their time in Guernsey Janet had wished herself among Guernseymen in an organically grown community, seeing Fort George, with its lack of local people, as rootless and artificial, depressed by the spaced series of self-consciously expensive open market houses in their large orderly gardens, the open-plan fronts fading together in featureless lawn. The grass was barbered, unrelieved by buttercup or daisy; carefully set urns of geraniums, petunias

121

and fuschias could be seen through carefully sited arches. It couldn't mellow because mellowness had been built in. It was as sterile as she was.

Janet ran out into the garden. Better to lie on the grass than the sofa, and she had successfully fought the gardener's attempts to put down weedkiller at the back. And still there were no weeds.

She didn't want to lie down, after all, and wandered aimlessly about, feeling the sun on her shoulders but unable to summon up her old joyous response to it. If she could get involved in some task . . . But the garden was immaculate, and in Fort George she had no home-making instincts. Reading? She was unable to concentrate.

There was only one thing she could do, and she had known it all day.

In a sudden anguish of hurry Janet sped back into the sitting-room. Then paused with her hand outstretched to the telephone. Joly Duguy was helping the police with their inquiries. She might never need to say anything. Wouldn't it after all be better to wait?

No. Tim Le Page must know about her and Charles, and if Joly Duguy turned out to have an alibi the police wouldn't tell her, they would just start investigating her and Douglas's movements that night. Better to volunteer the information than to have the police discover it for themselves and think she had been trying to keep secret the fact that Mary Brightwell had cancelled her dinner-party. And they would discover it, they could have done so already. Even now it could be tricky explaining to Tim Le Page that there was no significance in the fact that she hadn't even told Olivia.

Janet looked up the St James number, then punched it out.

The darkness was warm, and Olivia, Anna and Tim had coffee and brandy on the terrace, laughing rather too extravagantly at Anna's account of the man who had come to her table during dinner at the Duke in an attempt to book her for the ballroom.

But when they at last let themselves fall silent they were almost relaxed, aware of companionship and the rose-scented beauty of the garden. It was a quarter to eleven when Olivia pulled herself to her feet and said she was ready for bed.

122

'Don't hurry off,' she told them. 'Sit here as long as you want.'

'I think I'll give Duffy a last walk.' The dog's tail thudded against stone. 'Anna?'

'Yes. I'd like a walk. You won't come, Olivia?'

'Goodness, no!'

'If you wanted me to stay –' Tim and Anna began in unison. They all laughed again.

'If I wanted you to stay, if I wanted you in the night or any other time' – the moon-pallid round of Olivia's face turned from one to the other – 'I'd let you know. I promise. Now I just want to take a pill and go to sleep.' Too deep for the new dreams to trouble her a third time. 'Sunday tomorrow.' Sunday would be the cruellest day. 'Will I see either of you?'

'Coffee?' Anna suggested.

'Half-past ten. Then you'll have time to go somewhere afterwards.'

'Will you come with me?'

'Not tomorrow. After the funeral.' Since hearing from Tim that Charles was dead she hadn't crossed the threshold, or wanted to.

'We'll see to it,' Tim said.

'Thank you.' She hoped they would. If they didn't she might turn into a recluse.

'I'll come tomorrow, too,' Tim said. 'When I can.'

'Which way?' Anna asked him on the step.

'It's a bit earlier than it was when Charles took his last walk to Candie Gardens, but I'd like to retrace it. See if anyone appears to notice us, and how many people are about in Cambridge Park.'

'Right.' Anna started up L'Hyvreuse.

'Hold on. I also want to walk it the other way, see if we meet anyone at all. The murderer' – Joly? – 'could have been watching for Charles to leave, then decided to take the other route and meet him at his destination. Oh, it's academic now, but I've found from experience that it's possible to create a good climate for one's instincts. Thanks to you we're sure about Charles taking the short way, so we'll save that until nearer the right time.'

'Fine.' They turned the long way, and Duffy lifted his leg in exasperation against Saxon Lodge's doorpost before surging ahead of them.

'You didn't tire him out.'

'I can't think why not.' Anna and Duffy had spent the afternoon back at Cobo and Rocquaine, where they had stayed until she had managed to dismiss shallow sentimental thoughts of how Jimmy would have enjoyed the dog's company.

'Not many lights.'

There was one in the area basement of the first of the grand detached houses, outlining the pots of African violets on a window sill, and a glow from the dark stuccoed turret of the castellated mansion beyond them.

'No one in the road.'

And no one at the lookout during the ten minutes they stood there.

'No holiday makers whooping it up in Cambridge Park,' Tim said as they gazed across the descending complex of lights. 'Not even on a Saturday.'

'Not even now the mugger's in custody. It's beautiful.' The small islands on the horizon were pinpricks of light, and Castle Cornet shone its way out into the water.

'It's darker farther on.' But no point, now, in considering an encounter between Charles and a thief in the narrow blackness of Beauregard Lane.

They reached the green gates without seeing anyone. Tim looked up and down the deserted road. 'So the murderer could have come this way and been a hundred per cent lucky.'

'Yes. I was surprised the Gardens aren't closed at night.'

'They always were. Then this year, with the weather being so good and the Gardens used mainly by local people, there was an experimental round-the-clock summer opening. Since yesterday, you won't be surprised to hear, they've gone back to opening at sunrise and closing at dusk. Charles's father was given a key by the parish of St Peter Port when he retired as a Deputy. He did a lot for the island and he loved the Gardens. Charles inherited both, the love and the key.' *The key to his death.* 'All right, dog, we're not stopping. Let's go the short way back to L'Hyvreuse and then retrace our steps. Have two

124

tries at being noticed.' The focus shifted and Tim grinned. 'I'm sorry, Anna, you don't have to go along with my obsession, you have the option of going into the Duke.'

'And encountering Harry Price? Anyway, I'm interested in your experiment.'

In Cambridge Park Road two young men in hotel livery were chatting in the doorway of a house opposite the Duke of Richmond. A man and a woman came out of the external door of the Victoriana Bar as they reached it, turning in front of them without making eye contact. The young man lounging in the entrance to the hotel kitchens was gazing at the sky.

Saxon Lodge was in darkness and they turned just short of its front door and started back, Duffy venting his frustration on the same spot.

The young men were saying goodnight, and the one leaving ran across the road in front of them, his attention on the possibility of traffic. The youth in the kitchen doorway was still in his reverie, and a girl with earphones and a blank face was coming down past the houses.

Vauxlaurens was still deserted.

'So even Duffy didn't make any impact,' Tim said as they stopped again by the gates. 'A man, a woman, and a dog, and all those people would have said we none of us were there.' The focus of his attention switched back again to Anna and her consoling smile. 'Thanks for being so patient. Look, I've got a key and I rather want to go into Candie Gardens. I've never been there in the dark and I just might pick up some vibes. Perhaps you'd rather not, though?'

'It's such a wonderful night I don't feel like going indoors, so I'll stick it out. Unless you feel you'll be a better detective on your own.'

'Don't be silly.'

He let them in, locked the gates behind them.

'How about Joly Duguy?' she asked, as they started down the slope. 'If you can tell me.'

'Not officially, but neither you nor Olivia's going to pass it on and it helps to talk to intelligent laity. Anyway, you're family, aren't you?'

She had forgotten that Tim Le Page was the one who had lost the blood tie. 'That's why I offered to drive you home the other morning.'

125

'I didn't mention Joly in front of Olivia tonight because I'd brought her up to date before you arrived and she's unhappy about him. We didn't find anything at his yard, or his house, to connect him with Charles's murder, but we weren't necessarily expecting to. The soil on his boots matches the soil at Candie, but it also matches the soil in his own garden. The killer didn't have to have blood on him, and the lead piping was in the pool. And if Joly had decided to kill Charles there was no need for him to dress up in black. I'm afraid it'll have to be sustained pressure. My Chief and I are going to see him in the morning. At least he doesn't seem to have an alibi.'

'While you're waiting it'll be tricky with the Press, won't it?' She was as quick as her cousin.

'It will. So far we're managing to keep them at bay with the old chestnut of the man helping the police with their inquiries. Hoping we can hold them off long enough to give the man a pair of identities before it's rumbled that there are two of him.'

Or one of him and one of her. Behind Joly there were, after all, Janet and Douglas Chapman. Tim's Chief had caught him on his car phone in mid afternoon and sent him to take statements from them, an inevitable follow-up of Janet's telephone call despite Joly Duguy. When he had asked her why she assumed the police would be interested in her and her husband's activities the night of Charles's death she had told him not to play games with her, told him he already knew. He had answered that a policeman does not 'know' rumour and gossip. Janet had said then, in so many words, that she had been having an affair with Charles and that her husband was aware of it.

Chapman of course had hummed and hawed, but in the end he hadn't denied his knowledge and Tim had been content for the time being with that, keeping in reserve the question to which he was confident he already knew the answer – the question of how long he had known. After Chapman's discovery that the police hadn't yet picked up Joly Duguy there had been righteous indignation and injured dignity to overcome – as well as a tongue lashing of his wife for what Chapman called her 'insane behaviour' that made Tim almost sorry for her – before he could secure an account of the Wednesday evening, which Chapman appeared to have spent at his club. That was something that could be easily checked, unlike his wife's solitary evening at home, but he would leave the Chapmans alone while Joly was centre-stage, content to know they were in the wings.

Which meant out of sight of the audience, and the audience at the moment had to include everyone who wasn't the police. It was up to Janet to tell Olivia what she had told him, if she wanted Olivia to know.

'We'll go as far as the first pond, where it happened. You probably don't know there are three more beyond it. Or the story of the Gardens?'

'Not yet.'

'They were the grounds of Candie House, the big old place on Cambridge Park Road which is now the Priaulx Library and contains just about every book that's been written about Guernsey. Osmond Priaulx gave his house and his four acres to the people in the 1880s, and a few years later the States voted £300 for laying out the Gardens with exotic trees and shrubs. For me it's always been an enchanted place.' The gleam of water showed ahead of them. 'Ducks come to the ponds. I've taught Duffy to respect them. I always wonder what they do at night, whether –'

He heard the thud, and her scream, a few seconds before something hit him in the face. Something heavy and hairy, with a thin bitter smell, which rested against him, butting gently at his nose, until he stumbled backwards away from it, pulling her with him.

She was shuddering the length of her body, and he held her with one arm while he advanced the other.

The hairy substance was a jacket; he found the lapels. His eyes had got used to the darkness, and as he looked down-wards he could see the slight separation of the legs. And the boots, on a level with his waist and still swaying.

Duffy arrived snarling and hurled himself at the boots, snapping wildly. Anna freed herself from Tim's arm to pull the dog away and kneel beside him until the noise he was making had subsided to a whimper. She knew it would, of course – she had been through this nightmare before.

127

Looking up Tim saw the stout straight branch supporting the rope. It belonged to the fancy holly growing just inside the railings beside the place where Charles had fallen.

'History repeats itself.' She heard her voice loud and harsh, the renewed shock had made her angry. 'D'you know who this one is, too?'

He knew before his torch found the face, probably from a mingling of instinct and a recent memory of the clothes. Joly's head hung sideways and down, reminding Tim of the angle of the Christhead in paintings of the Crucifixion. His wild curls were a serrated edge to his silhouette against the paler sky, and his eyes, shining in the torchlight, stared angrily at the ground.

'It's Joly Duguy. I'm sorry, Joly.' He said that aloud, too. 'Dramatic, isn't it?' He was thinking and talking like a drunk. 'Our chief suspect has confessed.' By completing the end of the Duguy-De Garde feud in the place where he had begun it. 'We'll have to go back to the Dunnings' cottage.'

'Like we always do.'

Abruptly he was sober, aware as he should have been right away that the Gardens had assaulted her poise with a second shock even more gruesome than the first.

He took her hand. 'This time you'll have your tea sitting down. Come on, dog.'

Chapter Eleven

Olivia had dreamed again. Terrible dreams of Charles being struck down, but now it was daylight and she could see the familiar beloved landmarks. She moved slowly about her house, touching furniture and ornaments, looking at pictures, trying to console herself with what her life still held. She had lost her husband, but not the home to which he had brought her, the refuge of her island.

Sunday. A day she had relished when Charles was there, with its raised drawbridges and people absorbed in their families, offering a surer prospect than the week of leaving her undisturbed. Now, though, a day to be afraid of, with so much space for uneasy thoughts. The cruellest day.

Olivia lagged her way down the stars, drawing a finger along the row of topographical prints that descended with her. Two clocks were chiming the half hour in attractive disharmony. It was time for Anna to arrive.

In the sitting-room the coffee tray was ready beside her chair, the Thermos filled. She wouldn't sit down, she would only have to struggle up again as soon as she was comfortable, to answer the door.

Olivia took a biscuit from the tray and sailed slowly over to the front window. Nibbling the biscuit she stood looking out across the green of Cambridge Park. A man and two women had stopped to chat on the sandy path, their dogs frisking round them. She knew them; if she went to her front door and called they would come hurrying across to her. That was Guernsey, and the friendliness it uniquely offered would always be there if her sense of isolation ever grew strong enough to overcome her indolence.

And there were Anna and Tim.

Tim, though, had begun to worry her. She didn't want to help him, she didn't want anyone she could name to be accused of Charles's murder. She had hated adding to the evidence against Joly, even though she had only told the truth.

And if Joly turned out to have an alibi? She would have to tell Tim then about the impudent creature who had come to her house just before Charles noticed Janet. She could still see her, strong young legs planted self-consciously firm on the threshold, saying she was the woman Charles loved.

Olivia laughed, as she always did, at the ludicrous memory. But now only on a reflex. She had said 'You'd better come in and tell me more,' and had received a small reward in the way the girl had sagged as if she had been punctured. She had followed Olivia reluctantly into the sitting-room, then suddenly blazed, throwing back her head and displaying her slender youthfulness in triumph.

A triumph that was short-lived. Olivia had gently told Linda Parrish just where she stood in Charles's fleeting hierarchy, comfortable in her knowledge that Charles would have told her himself and that the girl's belief that she was important enough to alter his life arose solely out of her own over-confidence.

Olivia laughed again at the grotesque misjudgment. She hadn't managed to reverse it entirely, but she had sent the girl away in a very different mood from the one in which she had so aggressively arrived. She had even offered coffee, and seen the hesitation before the refusal. That had been the last she had heard of Linda Parrish, of course, and Charles's next conquest had been Janet . . .

She had never told him of that visit. There was no need and he would have been aghast. He had not been aghast when she had told him she was aware of his affair with Janet; mingled with his regret and concern had been relief that she had said it for him, admiration that she had agreed on their friendship with the Chapmans continuing as before. Once she had let Janet know, obliquely, that she was aware of the situation, even the relationship between the wives had proceeded in its established, uninspiring way. It had just been a matter of waiting until Charles moved on and she got her old, comfortable ignorance back.

At least Janet and Douglas had alibis. Tim couldn't suspect either of them of murdering Charles.

Olivia turned away from the window, trying to turn away too from her thoughts, from how much she was missing Charles, his presence in the house, their mutual understanding. She was self-sufficient – her need for distraction and outside stimulus was small – but her husband had been her friend and she had loved him.

She gave a little moan at the shock of the bell, then moved with untypical speed to the front door, smiling at her reactions. Feeling the smile fade as she saw Tim's wary face.

'Something's happened.'

'Yes. Coffee?'

'It's ready.' She led the way into the sitting-room, noticing that his hands were clenched at his sides. 'Anna should be here by now.'

'She's coming when I've talked to you. Sit down, dear.'

'Tim! What is it?' The sense of foreboding was making her feel faint and she fell backwards into her chair.

'Joly Duguy has hanged himself. I'm sorry, Olivia, there's no nice way – hold on!' He was across the room and back on his knees. 'You've been too strong, you should have let yourself . . .'

Tears were pouring down her face. When he put his arms round her they wet his cheek.

'Oh, no!' She said it over and over.

'It's true, Olivia.'

'You accused him . . .'

'No.' He drew away, and was glad to see that she was still weeping. 'I went to see him, talked to him. He denied it, but we had to search the yard and his house. We didn't find anything to connect him with Charles's death, but perhaps he was as much afraid of living with what he'd done as being found out. That's the end of it all now, Olivia.'

'The end? You think Joly Duguy killed Charles?'

'He must have done. Why else would he take his own life?' What other reason could there have been? 'And in that place? He hanged himself from the holly tree by the first pond in Candie Gardens. Where we found Charles.'

131

Horror was animating her face into the face of a stranger. 'You and Anna – when you left last night –'

'Yes. She walked into him. He'd kicked away one of those light aluminium step-ladders. He hadn't had to carry it far, we found his car down the bottom of the hill, in the layby at the main gates. We also found signs that he threw the ladder over the gates, then climbed after it. The wrought-iron would be easy enough to scale.'

'You're sure he did it himself?'

'We're sure. He must have had a very strong sense of drama. I suppose it was the one satisfaction left to him. Let's have some coffee.' He scrambled to his feet, stumbling with cramp. 'I'll pour.' He had never before presumed to take that office from her, but she made no protest. He filled two cups and limped back with one of them to his chair.

Olivia gave a shuddering sigh. 'Poor Joly.'

'Poor Joly! Even you, Olivia, can't be as magnanimous as that.'

'He's dead, isn't he? And when he was alive he didn't have much of a time. I think he was terribly unhappy.'

'I think he was a little bit mad.' He hoped so. A normal mind, pushed to such despair –

On the table next to Olivia the telephone rang, and she stretched out a hand.

'Janet! Good morning.' Tim started getting to his feet, but Olivia waved him down. 'Yes, of course, go ahead.'

Olivia listened in silence until the voice Tim could just hear stopped speaking.

'I see. Thank you for telling me, Janet. A pity you didn't tell me at the time, yes. You'd have found it easier. Just a moment.' Olivia covered the receiver. 'Tim, can I tell Janet about Joly?'

'Yes. The Press will.'

She took her hand away. 'It doesn't matter, Janet. Joly Duguy hanged himself last night. In Candie Gardens, by where Charles was killed. Tim and Anna found him. Yes, terrible . . . Tim says that's the end of it. Yes, of course, I can see how it was never quite the right time . . . Don't worry, Janet, there's nothing to worry about. I'll hope to see you soon.'

Olivia replaced the receiver and looked across at Tim. 'It's reassuring to discover that our Detective Inspector can keep his counsel. If you haven't already realized, that was to tell me that Wednesday's dinner party at the Brightwells was cancelled, and that Janet rang you yesterday to tell you rather than have you find out for yourself and wonder if she had something to hide.'

'I've realized.'

'I don't think there was anything significant about it, Tim. We've both had other things to think about. Anyway, from what you've said about Joly's suicide I assume it's now academic.'

'Yes.' Why wasn't he feeling the usual happy relief that came with the closing of a difficult case? 'I'll be glad to be simply Charles's cousin and closest relative at the funeral rather than an investigating officer. What time did you say it was?'

'Twelve noon. Town Church, and then Candie Cemetery.' She didn't falter, although her only child lay there. The last De Garde, now, for certain.

'Private interment?'

'Yes. I've been promised a notice in tomorrow's Press, saying that.'

'The Town Church will be full. Official cars?'

'Only for you and me and Anna. Oh, unless . . . Did you get hold of your mother?'

'She's left Paris for Brazil, I got hold of her eventually. She told me over a very bad line that she didn't think she could make it.' He was glad Olivia laughed as well. 'No one from England?'

'Your two old aunts won't travel, and there's no one so far as I'm concerned.'

As he had thought. 'Afterwards – No one will expect anything.'

'They will. And I owe it to Charles to have something ready for his friends and colleagues. Don't worry, Mrs M will help me cope.' She leaned towards him. 'As you will, Tim. I don't know what I'd do without you.'

'You won't have to, so long as you're here. D'you think you'll stay in Guernsey, Olivia?'

133

He saw her surprise. 'Of course I'll stay in Guernsey, it's my home. I'm not a local, but I don't anticipate being asked to leave.'

'We may be strict, but we do recognize the naturalized islander. Of course you won't be asked to leave.'

'I was happy enough in England before I met Charles, Tim, but I wouldn't want to live there now.'

'I'm glad that's how you feel. Aren't you due to go to London?'

'Next week.'

'You'll go?'

'I'll force myself. I don't want to contract agoraphobia, and I'd like to expand my work a bit, now I've only myself to look after.'

He saw the involuntary shudder ripple under her loose dress, but her eyes now were dry. 'That sounds like a good idea.' He longed to help her, but the only ways he could think of were ludicrously trivial. 'Let me provide the drinks on Tuesday.'

'Don't be silly, Tim, they'll come out of Charles's estate with the funeral expenses. But I'll be grateful if you'll help serve them.'

'You know I will.'

'Thank you. And if you'll stand by me – literally – when we come out of church? There'll be people who won't come back to the house and I'd like to greet them.'

'Olivia! You don't have to –'

'I've just told you I'm staying here, Tim. I'd like to get all the embarrassment over in one ordeal.'

'Yes, I can see. Of course I'll stand by you.'

'And come with me to my advocate some time tomorrow afternoon? You're in Charles's will.'

'Oh, no.'

'Don't worry, it isn't a lot. Three o'clock? I'll meet you there.'

'Thanks.' The front door bell rang. 'I'll go.'

Anna was on the step. She was her usual cool self, but shock had done something to her eyes and her mouth that made him more than usually aware of them.

'Come in. Thank you for giving me this bit of time. She's all right, and she's wept at last. Are you all right?'

'Yes.'

Following the precedent created by Charles's death, Anna embraced Olivia before taking the cup of coffee her cousin had poured for her. 'I've received my invitation to the inquest,' she told them as she sat down. 'Will Joly's suicide make it any easier?'

'It will when the inquest's resumed,' Tim said, 'but it won't affect the opening of it tomorrow – after you and Olivia and the doctors and I have said what we can about the circumstances of Charles's death it'll still be adjourned for further police inquiries. Everyone will be aware of what Joly's suicide means, but don't expect to hear his name at this stage. Officially in fact you may never hear it. If we don't find forensic evidence that he murdered Charles – and it doesn't look as though we're going to – the verdict will have to be unlawful killing by person or persons unknown. But the outcome will be the same either way. The case will be closed.'

'What happens to the mugger?' Anna asked.

'The police request for his remand in custody comes up in the morning. The Crown Officers have asked for a trial in the Royal Court as he terrorized the island for ten days and caused an injury. He'll go to gaol.'

'Then there'll be the inquest on Joly Duguy.'

'Yes. Nine-fifteen on Wednesday. You'll be invited to that too, Anna, as of course you realize, and expected to say another few words. I'm sorry. At least that inquest won't be adjourned, it will be over in one go.'

'Don't you start work on Wednesday?' Olivia asked Anna.

'Nine o'clock. I'll just have to be late. I'll go and see them tomorrow after the inquest and offer to put in some extra time.' And assure them that despite appearances their temporary partner wasn't in the habit of discovering dead bodies. 'On Tuesday I'm moving to Brian Bradshaw's.'

'So you have to vacate your room at the Duke by noon. Bring your things here before the funeral.'

'Thanks. That would help.'

'I'm sorry, Anna,' Olivia said. 'Your holiday's been messed up, and the start of your job.'

'I'm sorry, too,' Tim said.

'I'm not, I'm glad I was here.'

135

'Thank you,' Olivia said. 'So am I.'

Tim got to his feet. 'You'll go down to the coroner's court together in the morning, won't you? I'll see you both there, unless you'd like to come for a swim now with me and Duffy. I'm going to give myself a couple of hours off.'

'Not me.' Olivia settled more deeply into her chair. 'I think Anna would like to.'

'But –'

'I'll expect you back for lunch.'

'Right. Thanks.'

As he felt in his pocket for his car keys, Tim's pleasure was checked by his discovery of Joly's little boat. Poor Joly, who had never had a chance. Perhaps it was the wretchedness of his villain that was denying him his usual sense of job satisfaction.

'Hey! Where are you off to? It's Sunday morning and it's only half-past ten. We didn't get to bed till three.'

Geoffrey Falla's lazily outstretched hand was too slack to keep hold of his wife's silk nightdress as she slid out of bed.

'Sorry, Geoff. It's another lovely day and I'm going for a drive.'

'Shall I come with you?'

'Not this morning, darling.' She turned at the bathroom door to smile at him, her tousled curly hair and small slim body making her look like the mischievous girl child he hoped she'd give birth to when she had stopped making gestures and he could be sure it was his. 'I feel like an hour or two on my own.'

He had the key to her code. 'All right, Helen. Just as long as you come back.'

She came back to the bed, bent down and lightly kissed the relaxed face on the pillow, searching for signs of distress and as usual not finding them. 'I'll always come back, Geoff.' Not just because she appreciated her amazing good fortune in having married a man who had agreed to her retaining her pre-marital lifestyle and was abiding cheerfully by the agreement, but because, too, she loved him. To an extent that made her suspect the time was near when she would begin to honour her marriage vows. Her increasing anxiety that un-

136

happiness might lie behind Geoffrey's apparently effortless acceptance of her behaviour was making the exercise of her sexual independence less and less vital.

She certainly wished she hadn't got involved with Joly Duguy. The affair had begun in his boatyard a couple of months ago, when he had started making her a boat and she was regularly calling in. The attraction had been there between them right away, and she had resisted it for two or three visits only to prolong the delicious period of anticipation. When she adjudged the time was ripe she had needed to make only the very slightest of moves. Despite her increasing regret at what she had done, the memory of Joly's powerful response still made her feel faint.

Helen Falla didn't expect to regret her affairs – they just passed amicably into history. Her lovers didn't usually become dependent on her. Aware of Joly's eccentric reputation – it had, of course, been part of the excitement – she had been prepared for something rather more intense than her usual liaisons, and had at least been prudent enough to insist from the start on an unnecessary secrecy and caution. But she had not been prepared for the extent of her effect on Joly, and in a sort of panic self-defence had built poor Geoffrey into a monster of aggressive jealousy.

Ironically, it was Joly she had begun to be afraid of. When he asked her to leave Geoffrey and live with him she didn't dare tell him she didn't want to, and said Geoffrey had threatened her with physical violence if he ever found out that she had been unfaithful. But in her dreams it was Joly who held a knife to her cheek . . .

She hated herself for her cruel distortion of Geoffrey's tolerant and gentle nature as much as for the sexual greed that had got her into this mess. Joly had turned out to be a man who needed commitment before he could unleash his skills, and in her eagerness to experience them she had gone through the motions of offering it. But when the chemistry that worked so explosively between them ceased for her, as it inevitably had to, she wouldn't be able to go on pretending he was as important to her as she was to him.

On the telephone yesterday he had given her anxiety spiral another twist – he had sounded so wild and strange. After his call she began to worry that he might come to the house to confront Geoffrey, and find himself squaring up to a smile. At which point it would become evident to Geoffrey that she had betrayed him outside the terms of their agreement, to say nothing of perhaps putting him in danger. Joly's reputation included a tendency to sudden violent changes of mood, and although they were said to be linked with hypersensitivity about his father's disgrace following the Liberation – a subject she had always avoided – stress might turn them elsewhere. So she had decided to go and see Joly, offer him the devastating risk she was running, with Geoffrey home from his latest London visit, as proof of her devotion. Getting in deeper wasn't of course going to solve her problem, but she would have to make do with it until she could think of something better.

She drove first to the yard. It was nearer, and Joly made no distinction between the working week and Sunday. And he was an early riser, restless at dawn even when she was with him.

She had almost touched the yellow tape across the yard entrance, and there was reproach in the round flushed face of the helmeted young police constable who was waving her back. He followed her out into the road as she reversed against the kerb, and stood beside her window until she opened it.

'Perhaps you would be good enough to give me your name and address, madam.' He was in short sleeves but sweat was trickling down his temple. His expression was a mingling of solemnity and excitement and Helen's heart had shot up into her throat. She had to cough before she could speak.

The police constable wrote down what she told him. 'All right, Mrs Falla. Thank you. Would you care to tell me now the purpose of your visit to Duguy's Boatyard on a Sunday morning?'

Thank heaven Joly was still working on the boat. 'To see how Mr Duguy is getting on with my new boat. Sunday or Monday, it's all the same to him. Is there something wrong?'

The triumph of uncertainty over the other emotions in the young man's face told her he was about to pass the buck. 'Perhaps you could have a word with Detective Sergeant Guilbert.'

'Perhaps I could, constable. Will you let me in?'

'I think it would be better if you stayed where you are, Mrs Falla. I'll go and see if DS Guilbert is able to come out to you. Excuse me.'

The constable ducked under the tape and Helen sat rigid, her hands clenched on the wheel. Mrs Falla, Mr Duguy, and the police. A public connection established between her and Joly. Her promise to Geoffrey broken.

But it wasn't; she was being panicked by her fear of Joly and her increasingly uncomfortable conscience. It was no secret that she was Joly's client, and she hadn't broken her rule not to put anything in writing. She was confident that Joly picked up a pen only in the way of business, and the police wouldn't find anything in the yard beyond the specification for the boat. But what were they doing there?

'Mrs Falla? Perhaps I could get into your car for a moment?'

Detective Sergeant Guilbert was a good-looking man, and her type, but Helen to her surprise was admiring him objectively, as a contentedly married woman. If she could only be free of Joly she'd stay that way . . . 'Yes. Yes, of course.' She opened the door for him. 'Is there something wrong, sergeant?'

'I'm afraid there is, Mrs Falla. Joly Duguy is dead.'

'Dead . . .' Detective Sergeant Guilbert's blue eyes were looking keenly into her face and it had never been more necessary to hide how she was feeling, the mingled intensity of her shock and her relief. 'That's terrible. How did it happen?' She thought she made it sound like a conventional reaction to someone else's tragedy, but she wasn't quite in charge of her breathing and her face could be unnaturally red or white.

'Well . . .' The detective sergeant hesitated. 'It will be on the news later, so . . . It's not very nice, Mrs Falla, I'm afraid. Mr Duguy got into Candie Gardens last night and – well, he hanged himself from a tree.'

She knew now she was unnaturally pale, she could feel the blood draining from her head. She had to put her face against the wheel, but a woman didn't need to be Joly's mistress to have a squeamish reaction to news like that about him.

139

'In Candie Gardens . . .' With her head down she didn't feel so dizzy. 'Why –'

'We don't know why, Mrs Falla. That is . . . The tree he – chose – is just by the railings where Charles De Garde's body was found.'

'No!' Helen thundered the word, but mercifully only in her head. 'You're trying to say . . .' she whispered.

'I'm not trying to say anything, Mrs Falla, I'm just describing the place where Mr Duguy died the way the media will be describing it as the day goes on.'

Yes, the media would make a meal of the proximity of the two deaths. And then they would interpret it, to solve the murder of Charles De Garde. Joly's last phone call . . .

Not yet. Not until she was alone.

'I'm sorry, sergeant.' Helen forced herself to offer him a rueful smile. 'But it is rather awful.'

'Very tragic and distressing, Mrs Falla,' the detective sergeant contributed. 'I'm sorry to be the bearer of such news, but before the day's out everyone in Guernsey –'

'I appreciate your telling me. It can't have been easy. I'll go home now.'

'That's the best thing, Mrs Falla.' Detective Sergeant Guilbert opened the passenger door. 'So far as your boat's concerned – well, you'll realize that at the moment . . .'

'That's the last thing on my mind, sergeant, at the moment.'

'That's very understanding of you, Mrs Falla. The people Mr Duguy was doing work for' – anguish was searing through her, but she was aware of relief, again, at being restored to public anonymity – 'will be contacted in due course by his advocate. Now, if you'll excuse me . . .'

The extra anxiety on her behalf had left his attractively sunburned face; his thoughts were back on the investigation of Joly's yard. She was as free as she had been when she arrived. And free of Joly.

Oh, but no. Helen sped on up the north coast through St Sampson's and turned down to the sea just north of Bordeaux Harbour. One of the few spaces between holiday-makers' cars was as private as being alone: the cars that weren't empty contained tourists dozing beside open windows, and no one

140

was going to notice the agonized white face she saw when she pulled the driving mirror towards her.

Helen saw, too, the insistence in her reflected eyes that she must be honest. Joly had rung her that last time to ask for an alibi for the time of Charles De Garde's murder. And she had talked so convincingly about the murderous jealousy of her husband that he hadn't even bothered to mention it. Then, instead of trying to clear himself at her expense, he had taken a rope into Candie Gardens and solved everyone's problems.

A sense of honour? Of insupportable despair?

She could never know, but at least she could save his memory. Staring unseeingly at the varied evidences of enjoyment going on around her, Helen sat a long time trying to subdue the agony of knowing that she could have saved his life.

Chapter Twelve

He oughtn't to be wearing running gear in the witness box, and he shouldn't have Duffy with him, only guide dogs were allowed into the Coroner's Court. The Magistrate was leaning towards him.

'Detective Inspector Le Page,' the Magistrate said solemnly, 'to find one body in Candie Gardens was a misfortune. To find two was sheer carelessness.'

'Sheer carelessness! Sheer carelessness! It really was sheer carelessness!' sang the Inspector, the Deputy Greffier and the Court Usher in chorus, cheerfully repetitive in the Gilbert and Sullivan mode.

'If I could just explain, sir . . .'

But the singing wouldn't give him a chance. It was getting louder and louder and less and less like Trial By Jury.

It came from a ghetto blaster being carried past his window.

Tim groaned and sat up. The dream had scarcely been the half of it. Not only was he to be in the witness box at two inquests in one week, but he was to be there in both cases as the discoverer of the body, each time in the company of the same female incomer. Thank heaven that Anna Weston was Olivia's cousin.

Groaning more loudly Tim slumped out of bed. It was already hot but he put on a tie. At eight-thirty he sent a reproachful Duffy into the back garden and drove down to town, a jacket on the seat beside him. When he had been into St James and had a word with DS Mahy he put on the jacket and walked round the corner into the Rue du Manoir, the narrow lawyers' street dominated by the imposing raised facade of the Royal and Magistrates Courts.

142

Tim's years in the police had taught him the wisdom of gauging all crime-related assembles for elements of the unexpected, and inside the Magistrates Court he looked keenly round as he chose a seat towards the back of the gallery, from which he would be able to see as much as possible of any unforeseen faces. Not that they were likely; a few alert crime buffs might be tempted into court, but it was when inquests into the deaths of murder victims were resumed that they tended to become interesting.

'Morning, Tim.'

The police doctor in the row in front of him, waiting to tell the Coroner's Court about Charles's body. Sitting with Charles's own doctor, who would tell the court that Charles had had a weak heart but even the stoutest . . .

The court reporter was taking her place; there were two reporters in the press box where there was usually only one. Olivia and Anna were arriving together, Anna under the protection of the deference being shown to Olivia by everyone, bar the younger of the two reporters, whom Tim hadn't seen before and who was being literally held back by his colleague from his threat to break the consensus. At least one national newspaper had made what Tim hoped would be the unrewarding effort.

Olivia and Anna were turning into the gallery, sitting down on the other side a little further forward, gazing ahead of them like people who see an acquaintance in the street and aim to get past without signs of recognition.

The Deputy Greffier was in his place. John Rowe, nearing the end of his year's term as Prosecuting Inspector, was in his, looking through a file. The Magistrate was arriving and the Court Usher in his imposing dark uniform was telling everyone to be upstanding.

Interested parties were sworn in at the bar between the witness box and the dock. *Swear upon the faith and truth you owe to God . . . So help you God*. Only a hand raised, no Bible like in England. Making people less wary, Tim always thought, about answering questions.

He and Olivia and Anna and the doctors had gone back to their seats to await their calls. Tim was noting his mingled relief and disappointment at the absence of the unexpected when the door closed by the Court Usher burst open and a young woman swept in and up the step to the first row of the gallery. The Court Usher shook his head in disapproval as she settled herself into her seat with what seemed to Tim to be the maximum of fuss.

He felt the rare prickle of professional excitement along his spine. Why would Helen Falla, glamorous young incomer wife of banker Geoffrey Falla, have taken the trouble to find out when the inquest on Charles De Garde was to be opened if she wasn't, or hadn't been, his mistress? He had heard her described at a dinner party recently as a highclass tart, and had come to the rescue of her personality, if not her reputation. Not that he really knew her, but he had met her socially a few times and rather liked her, even though he had been aware at the first meeting that she was assessing his sexual potential. He had let her see that so far as she was concerned he had none, but that hadn't stopped her being friendly and easy to talk to the next time they found themselves at the same dinner table. If she did have affairs he was sorry for her husband, Geoffrey Falla deserved better, but he didn't know the real situation between them any more than most people knew the real situation between Charles and Olivia.

Had Janet Chapman been superseded?

Tim turned his attention to the body of the court, but he held Helen Falla in the corner of his eye.

The doctors spoke briefly. Charles's said that despite a heart condition his patient had met his death in generally good health. The police doctor told the court that no human head could have withstood the blow received by Charles De Garde's.

Even at that point Olivia sat motionless, continuing to watch and to listen calmly and without visible reaction. As she made her way slowly to the witness box Tim saw the sympathy of the court in the surrounding faces. The Inspector asked her about the circumstances of her husband's departure for Candie Gardens, her own subsequent walk to the lookout, and her discovery that her husband had failed to come home, and she answered each question in the same quiet, steady way. When she was told she could stand down the sympathy culminated in a collective sigh.

144

Anna too spoke quietly and without stumbling, her neat dark head and narrow navy-blue shift in dramatic contrast to Olivia's golden-brown swirl of hair and skirt. She spoke as clearly about her thought processes as about what they had prompted her to do, and made a good impression. Tim, to his slight shame, found he was glad for himself as well: the witness from England was so evidently a serious person the risibility factor in his own position vis-à-vis his colleagues would be substantially reduced.

When his turn came he found himself disconcerted to be at the public's end of police interrogation. But the sensation was overlaid before he was out of the witness box by the sight of the hostility in Helen Falla's face.

It was soon over. When the Prosecuting Inspector had read out the forensic report that the piece of lead piping recovered from the relevant pond was undoubtedly the murder weapon, he requested an adjournment to enable further police inquiries to be carried out, and the Magistrate granted it and brought the proceedings to a close.

Tim's eyes went to Helen Falla, and he was intrigued to see that she looked disappointed. And that before making an exit as obtrusive as her entry she turned and stared at him.

He had to hurry to catch up with Olivia and Anna. 'You both did well. I'm glad it's over for you. What are you going to do now?'

'I'm going home,' Olivia told him, 'and Anna's going to work.'

'I'm going to try. As compensation for being late on my first day, and because I want to.'

'Did you come down by car?'

'We walked,' Olivia said. 'Even I can see the advantage of that sometimes.'

'I'll walk a little way back with you.' He was wary of the young reporter, who at that moment slid past and turned to face them before they were round the corner into James Street.

'Mrs De Garde, if I could just ask you –'

'I'm sorry . . .'

'Mrs De Garde has said all she intends to say today,' Tim told him, and the smiling gaze moved to Anna. 'Mrs Weston,

145

too. The police will be giving a press conference.' He had to be glad that his Chief had announced his intention of presiding over it.

'Everyone knows the nutter who hanged himself killed Charles De Garde,' the reporter gabbled in desperation. 'Because of a family feud going back to the Occupation.'

'Everyone knows there was no love lost between De Garde and Duguy,' Tim amended. He was acting professionally, but he ought to be feeling more glad than sad that the young man had so unambiguously stated the reason why the most distressing case he had ever had to investigate could now be closed. 'Excuse us.'

He swept them in through the door of St James, and stood watching the reporter until he was reluctantly out of sight round the corner back into the Rue de Manoir.

'I thought that would happen.' He hesitated. 'There could be more of it now, Olivia. On your doorstep.'

'I'm ready, Tim.'

'I thought you would be. But I'll walk you home.'

'Thank you, we can cope. The two of us.'

'All right. I'll see you later, then.' He watched them walk away, unlike each other in every way but their strength.

By the time Tim reached his desk he was convinced that Helen Falla's presence in court had been a gesture to connect herself publicly with Charles, and that she had looked at him as the one person who would be bound to take note. He was also sure that she was offering him more than that: her hard gaze had been either an invitation or a declaration of intent. If she didn't come to him, he could go to her. She certainly had something to tell him.

But he must give her a chance. At least waiting would be less frustrating thanks to the motions he must continue to go through in the unhopeful search for more evidence against Joly. Last evening he and DS Mahy had visited the landlord of Joly's local, where they had obtained a list of his regular cronies, and made appointments with the ones who were there. The utopian attempt to obtain a sworn connection between Joly and Candie Gardens on the night of Charles's death had its first date at eleven.

146

As they set off Tim handed a note to the duty sergeant, suggesting that any member of the public who asked for him be invited to wait, or return later. When they got back from a fascinating but fruitless three hours, the sergeant told him there were no messages.

He had a sandwich at his desk, glad at least that a chunk of waiting time had been surmounted. His hopes remained high, and by the time he left for his meeting with Olivia and her advocate he had decided that if there was still no message when he got back to St James he would go out again and call on Helen Falla.

His mood was at total variance with all that was going on around him. The Incident Room was being run down, and already the everyday concerns that a war overlays were on their way back to the surface – as he went out the duty sergeant was giving his relaxed attention to a woman reporting the loss of her canary.

When he and Olivia were facing her advocate across his desk, Tim had to discipline his thoughts to keep them from straying.

'"To my dear and only cousin Timothy John Le Page I leave the sum of five thousand pounds and my silver tankard."'

The advocate laid the sheaf of papers back on his desk, and Tim, brought abruptly to attention, turned sharply to his cousin's widow. To his relief she had turned to him and was smiling her approval.

'So that is it, Mr Le Page.' The advocate removed his spectacles and laid them on the paper. 'Entirely straightforward. It is merely a matter of awaiting the valuation of the movables and the proving of the will.'

'Yes. Thank you,' Tim said hurriedly, embarrassed because he always found it harder to receive than to give, and because the words 'my dear and only cousin' had made it necessary for him to blow his nose. When he had returned his handkerchief to his pocket Olivia took his hand.

'I'm very glad, Tim,' she said.

'It's an awful lot.'

'He had it to give. I won't feel the lack of it.'

On behalf of them both she declined the advocate's offer of tea. She had come down to town this time by taxi, and asked

147

Tim to drive her back to Saxon Lodge, where tea awaited them.

'I suppose you've started to pack up,' she said as she poured out.

'Yes, although we'll be looking for evidence against Joly until the inquest resumes. Everyone prefers a verdict with a name.' For the first time since the words *dear and only cousin* he remembered Helen Falla. Reluctantly, now. Things were best as they were.

'I shall be glad when the funeral's over.'

'Yes. Funerals are ordeals – they put people on stage just when they ought to be in private.'

'Other people would feel deprived.' Olivia smiled at him, struggling to her feet. 'I'd like you to take the tankard, Tim. The only other bequests are small legacies here and there: everything else is left to me. The money will have to wait for the will to be proved, as Peter said, but I don't think I shall be doing anything seriously illegal by letting you have the tankard now.'

'I don't think you will. Thank you, Olivia.'

While she was out of the room finding a carrier bag Tim began to fidget. 'I shall have to go now,' he said when he had declined a second cup of tea and thanked her again. 'I've a few things to clear up personally.'

He could tell she was at comparative peace and regretted his earlier excitement. By the time he was back at St James he had almost persuaded himself that he was hoping Helen Falla wouldn't come to him, and that if she didn't, he wouldn't go to her.

She was sitting in the lobby. When he saw Tim the desk sergeant made a gesture towards her, but she had seen him too and was already on her feet.

'Detective Inspector Le Page.' From Helen Falla the words were formal, but although her anger had gone cold he could see that it was still there.

'Come through, Mrs Falla.' Tim led the way into an interview room. 'We'll just have a chat to begin with.' He didn't want a third party present until he knew for sure why she was angry. 'Please sit down,' he said across the narrow table. 'So you knew Charles De Garde.'

148

'Of course I knew him.' He saw surprise in her face. 'I know Olivia. Oh, for God's sake, you're thinking . . . Tim Le Page, I gave you more credit.'

'For what?' He was already uneasy.

'For perception. Observation. Oh, I don't know. Anyway, there isn't any significance in my knowing Charles. I knew Joly.'

'Knew . . . Joly?'

'Biblically. Got it, Inspector? I was having an affair with Joly Duguy.'

'*Joly*!'

'Feeling a bit snobbish about it, are we? The Duguy family background is every bit as good as the Falla, Inspector. As good as the De Garde, even: there's a Duguy family vault in Candie Cemetery, too. Because Joly chose to live in his own way didn't put him beyond the pale.'

'Of course not. Forgive me, Mrs Falla, it was just that I was thinking –'

'That I was at the inquest into Charles De Garde's death because I had been one of his mistresses. Well, it was a fair assumption, I suppose. But the reason I was there is because I was so furious at the way people are linking his death with Joly's. It was even on TV last night. That Joly – hanged himself' – for the first time she faltered – 'because he had murdered Charles.'

He had been right that she'd been disappointed in court, hoping to fuel her anger but not reckoning on the essential circumspection of the law and the police.

'Why else would he hang himself, Mrs Falla? And in that particular place?'

'Out of despair, Inspector.' She was all at once so quiet he could only just hear her. 'Because he couldn't use his alibi for that Wednesday night.'

'Alibi? Joly?'

'Joly!' She shouted the word and Tim felt himself jump. 'Joly Duguy had an alibi for the time Charles De Garde was killed. He was with me. All that night from when he left the pub. He rang me on Saturday morning, and I know now that he was going to ask me to support him. Only before he got round to it I gave him another burst of fantasy about my

149

husband's jealousy. I even told him Geoff had threatened to cut my face up if I looked at another man. Geoff! So Joly hung up without bothering to ask for something I had apparently made it very clear he wouldn't get, and took his piece of rope and went to Candie Gardens and . . . and . . . Oh, God, I could have saved his life and I didn't know!'

'Of course you didn't know – no one could have known that.' Tim was shocked by what he was hearing, and had to force the meagre comfort. 'I suppose Joly was getting too demanding and you were trying to back off.' Knowing even the little he did of them both, it was easy to work it out. 'Not a very good way of doing it, Mrs Falla.'

'You *are* perceptive after all, Inspector. Yes, that was it. And no, it wasn't a very good way of dong it.'

'Joly might have been fine as a bit on the side so far as you were concerned, but he had a code of honour. He wasn't the man for a casual affair.' The alibi was nothing, yet, beyond one woman's unsubstantiated word, but already Joly Duguy was being restored to Tim as an eccentrically honourable figure.

'You're right again, but you're cruel, Tim.' He saw with a sense of satisfaction he was a little ashamed of that she really did look anguished. 'As if I didn't know! It was Joly's code of honour that made him despairing enough to tie himself to that tree. Most people, even if they realized they weren't going to get any help with establishing an alibi, would have a go at it on their own. Not Joly. Not at someone else's expense.'

'Because he believed what you told him, and was prepared to die rather than put you in peril of your life or even your looks.'

She stared at him, tears starting to run down her cheeks. 'Thank you, Tim.'

'I'm sorry, Helen.' *Let him who is without sin* . . .

'No, I mean it. That's it in the most terrible nutshell, and it's the worst thing I'll ever have to face. Believe me, I know what I've done. I'll have to live with it. And with the knowledge that I turned my gentle Geoffrey into a monster for my own convenience.'

'I think we can assume that Joly carried that picture to the grave without showing it to anyone.'

'I'm sure he did, but I gave it to him. I want to do what I can now, Tim.'

'With a dramatic gesture like your entry into court this morning? Letting everyone know about your affair with Joly? I don't doubt it will make you feel better, Helen, but it won't be very good for your marriage.'

Her eyes flashed. 'Tim Le Page, you're a prig. I thought it would have to come out, and that I might as well face it with my head up. Joly has to be cleared.'

'Of course.' His uneasiness now was almost overpowering. 'And he will be if you can produce someone willing to swear that he spent last Wednesday night with you from the time he left the Happy Fisherman.'

'I can produce two. My friend and neighbour Mary Crawford was with me when Joly arrived. Well, an unfaithful wife has to have one confidante. And my daily arrived in the morning before he left.'

'Thank you.' A terrible lassitude had fallen on him and it was an effort to speak.

'So won't it have to come out?'

'It will come out that Joly Duguy has an alibi for the murder of Charles De Garde. Not necessarily that you provided it.'

'Thank you, Tim.' Helen Falla sighed, relaxing back into her chair. 'I don't really want to put myself right at the expense of Geoffrey. I won't make any more gestures.'

'I'm sure that's wise. We'll do our best to keep your name out of it.' He found it an effort to get to his feet. 'I'll ask a constable to join us now and you can make your statement.'

Anna was watching the lights from the lookout when Duffy came bounding up to her.

'What a relief!' Tim strolled up as the dog started licking her hands. 'I've been working all afternoon and even though I've had a bath I was afraid he might sniff the dreaded smells of the surgery. Poor innocent!'

'He's due for his jabs. You'll have to take a chance or keep out of sight when I take him in.' He could smell her perfume, fresh and sharp. 'I've just said goodnight to Olivia, and looked in at the hotel. When I didn't find you I thought you might be here now the mugger's in custody. How did you get on?'

151

'It was wonderful. I feel transformed. And I like the attitude of people here. You?'

'Something's happened. I'd like to talk about it.'

'Come to the Duke for a drink?'

'Come to my house. You know how close it is.'

'Fine.'

'Fine. On foot you can cross the park and then the edge of the football pitch and you don't have to get on to the road till you're past the Leisure Centre.'

They walked in silence, Duffy leading the way, until they came out on to the Amherst Road.

'Behold Police Headquarters,' Tim said then. 'Out of which I normally operate.'

'It looks like a private house. Except for the not exactly sensitive addition.' Police Headquarters was Victorian gothic, bisected by an upended off-white rectangle.

'I suppose it was once.'

'You won't be glad to get back there.'

'St James is where things happen. I always spend more time there, even when there hasn't been a murder.' Tim turned down the hill towards his home. Abandoning distractions, Duffy made purposefully for the gate and sat down outside it, wagging his tail and looking back at them.

'I like these solid houses, they're reassuring.'

'Yes. Duffy's welcoming you.' Tim opened the small iron gate. 'He's discriminating; it isn't automatic.'

'I appreciate that.' Making conversation was like ploughing through sand.

Tim unlocked his solid front door. 'Come in.'

'Thanks.'

He stood aside, close against the wall so that she wouldn't be forced to touch him. He had left the lamp on in the hall and the light was soft and welcoming.

'Nice.'

'Come into the sitting-room.'

Again he left her space to pass him. The room was crowded with friendly furniture, ornaments and pictures, pleasing Anna the far side of her agitation.

Tim had stopped in the doorway. 'Coffee or brandy? Or both? Or of course you can have tea . . .'

He tailed off and they stared helplessly at one another. Then began to laugh as Anna held out her arms.

'Tim!'

He sprang across the room and closed against her as if she was a magnet. 'Anna!' He wanted to tell her it was serious and he was a single man, but he didn't know what she wanted and he couldn't risk it. 'Upstairs?' he whispered against her lips, astonished to hear himself sabotage his theory of the importance of a proper foundation. Was the De Garde in him coming out at last?

'Yes.'

They fell over Duffy on the stairs as he tried to race past them. Tim put his basket out on the landing and closed the door on his reproachful face.

Still laughing at their delighted surprise, they took a long approach to the crowning, uncontrollable moments. Marvelling their way up the hill to heaven, Tim thought lazily when they were side by side again and smiling at one another.

'Coffee or brandy? Or both?'

'I think I'd like tea. Only I don't want you to go and get it.'

'It won't take a moment. And I can leave you Duffy. He'll be feeling neglected out there. Unless you're one of those severely hygiene-conscious –'

'I'm not. Bring me Duffy and don't be long.'

Her body was so comfortable that without Tim to remind her of its existence it yielded place to her mind, soaring in an unfamiliar way towards the future. A future of no more than imagination and conjecture – all she wanted or could cope with as yet – but one she was going to be able to think about with interest rather than indifference or dread.

Duffy had curled into the warm place left by Tim, who pushed him resisting to the floor when he had put the tray down.

She was touched to see a matching china tea service. 'I think this goes with your sitting-room, but I wasn't really taking it in.'

'I suppose it does. Family stuff. My mother's the only one still alive and she isn't bothered about it. I like it.' He handed her a cup and got back into the bed which had demonstrated for the first time his good judgement in choosing a small

153

double to replace his old single. 'Anna, Joly Duguy didn't kill Charles.'

Tea slopped over the roses on her saucer. 'You were so sure!'

He told her about Helen's visit, and what had come out of it. 'Geoffrey Falla was away on Wednesday night, and Joly spent it with his wife from the time his local closed until half past eight the next morning. Her story's been corroborated by a friend who was at the house when Joly arrived, and by her daily who is also in her confidence and saw him leave. You see what it means.'

'Yes. You have to go on looking.' She stroked the hair back off his forehead. It didn't hurt too much that it grew like Mickey's.

'In my heart I don't think I was ever really convinced about Joly.'

'The Chapmans? Olivia? Don't let my relationship to her stop you saying what you think.'

She felt his shudder. 'I could as soon believe it was me. She loved him, and her life as it was suited her absolutely. I know she walked to the lookout and could have walked on to Candie Gardens, but one of the Chapmans could have got there without being seen, too. Lots of dark places to park round about at night, and the dinner party they were invited to was cancelled at the last minute. Janet actually rang me on Saturday to tell me about the cancellation in case I might think she was trying to conceal the fact that she and her husband didn't have alibis for the time of Charles's death. That meant I had to take statements from them even though we were concentrating then on Joly. Now . . . They can't even give alibis to one another. He went to his club and she stayed at home.'

'What time did Douglas get back?'

'That's the crucial question. Janet said twelve-thirty, and despite a lot of huffing and puffing he didn't deny it. So Janet could have gone to Candie Gardens at midnight, and so could he if he left his club in time. At least that's something we can check.'

'Can you see either of them as a killer?'

'I don't know them well enough to say. Douglas seems to be on a short fuse, easily irritated by small things, but I can't

154

imagine . . . He's so self-absorbed, but I suppose jealousy could have brought him to exploding point – I'm convinced he'd only just got to know about the affair.'

'But your instincts go for Janet.'

He jerked against her. 'I hadn't faced it, but they do.'

'Why?'

'I suppose because I feel it was a crime of passion.'

'Douglas's *amour propre* could be his passion.'

'And you could be the devil's advocate. I'm also convinced that Janet Chapman's hiding something. And a woman scorned . . . If not yet, it was only a matter of time.'

'Would she have had the strength?'

'Two hands and implacable hatred? Yes. And perhaps I feel that telling me about her lack of alibi was a sort of Christie-type double bluff. Her husband was furious.'

'There could still be another mugger.'

'Yes. He'll be there, thank heaven, if we can't ultimately charge anyone who knew Charles. But if we can't, life here for Olivia will never be comfortable again and there's no-where else she wants to live. Anyway, after the funeral I'll be inviting Douglas Chapman to be a lot less vague.'

'After the funeral?'

'My Chief agrees we keep Joly's innocence quiet until then. It'll keep the Press quiet too and there isn't any hurry, with the poor chap being in the mortuary rather than a prison cell.' He didn't feel flippant about Joly, but he wanted to keep his pity within bounds. 'And it'll make for a better atmosphere at the funeral.'

'And perhaps someone who thinks he or she's in the clear will do or say something careless and Detective Inspector Le Page will be looking and listening.'

He rolled over on to her, pummelling her shoulders in mock rage. 'You're right, you horribly perceptive woman. But it does seem the most sensible thing to do.' His hands slid down her body.

'I ought to get back to the Duke.'

'Soon but not just yet. The Duke doesn't lock its doors like Ocean View. Have some more tea.'

'Thanks. Tim . . .' She sat up. 'You said ages ago your mother left. What did you mean?'

155

'Just that.' He put the cup into her hand, hardly believing his luck. He had never been able to talk about his mother, but he had been waiting all his life to tell the right person, and now that person was actually inviting the story. 'There's a rackety streak running through the De Gardes. Some of them have been – well, one-off jobs. Some are reliable and conventional, like me.' He grinned at her. 'Charles mixed the two strains. My mother . . . she was wonderfully glamorous. I suppose it's a bit of an autobiographer's cliché to have childhood memories of a sultry-scented lady in a floating dress and dangly earrings coming to kiss you goodnight before being driven off by some handsome escort. But that's how it was. I suspect I was a rather boringly well behaved only child, and I think my mother had moods of wanting to jolly me up. Sometimes she was a marvellous playmate. But I'm afraid the escorts weren't always my father, and one day she didn't come back.' He had sometimes wondered about the tone in which it would come out, but hadn't thought of irony.

'Did you miss her as children are supposed to miss their mothers?'

'I don't think I did, really, because we hadn't had the usual relationship. I missed the excitement of her: that occasional splendid companionship. I think I would have missed my father more.'

'You stayed with him?'

'Yes. My grandmother – my mother's mother – moved in. She was wonderful. And my mother hadn't abandoned us – nothing so dramatic. Highly coloured postcards used to arrive from all over the world. Still do. And she still sometimes descends on me for the odd few days. I love that.'

'It sounds a lot more successful than a lot of mother-son relationships in later life. Is she descending for the funeral?'

'From Brazil? No.' He put their cups down and leaned over her. 'Anna . . . Oh, Lord, here's the cat, now.'

'He's gorgeous.'

'He's not staying *there*!'

'Only for a moment while I get to know him.'

'All right.' But the cat had made a space, as well, for Tim's habitual reserve to attempt to reassert itself. 'Anna, I don't usually behave like this.'

'Good. I don't, either. You could have fooled me, by the way.'

'I was taken in hand at a very early age,' Tim said reluctantly, 'by a friend of my mother's. Against the grain, but there it was.'

'I see.' The shaft of jealousy was as sharp as a knife thrust, punishment for having thrown off the protection of her mourning. But a sign, too, that she was still alive.

Chapter Thirteen

When Tim walked into St James the next morning there was a mild-looking elderly lady sitting on the bench by the desk. Another bereaved canary owner, he was drearily certain, but the desk sergeant asked if he could spare a moment.

'This is Mrs Protheroe, Inspector. She'd like a word.'

Mrs Protheroe got to her feet, smiling uncertainly. She was short, with untidy grey hair and a pleasant face, and reminded Tim of the art mistress at Elizabeth College when he had been a pupil there. 'I'm sorry to trouble you, Detective Inspector Le Page – I know how busy you must be, but I've just sorted something out that's been bothering me and I think you may be interested.'

'Of course, Mrs Protheroe. We'll find an interview room. Come with me.'

He hadn't been looking forward to the morning: the decision not to tell Olivia and the Chapmans about Joly until after the funeral had turned the coming three hours into a vacuum in which no action could take place. So, interesting or otherwise, Mrs Protheroe was a timely diversion.

'Now,' he said, when they were seated each side of a table whose surface bore witness to smoking, tea-drinking, and Kilroy-style attempts to make an impression on its surface by the ineffectual but damaging means of keys and coins. 'What is it you want to tell me?'

'I don't believe in telling tales,' Mrs Protheroe began earnestly, her small hands agitating together on the table edge. 'But in this case . . . I'd have told you earlier if I'd worked it out, but it was only after seeing another picture on

158

television last night of the murdered man – what a terrible thing, Inspector! – that I realized why I'd been thinking I knew him. I didn't know him, in fact, but I used to see him quite regularly, visiting my young neighbour. There wouldn't have been anything particular about that, of course, even if I'd known then that he was a married man . . . Oh, dear . . .'

'Just take your time,' Tim said reassuringly. At least, in Guernsey, he didn't have to ask which murdered man. 'How about a cup of tea?'

He could have been offering the crown jewels. 'That would be lovely!'

He went out and ordered tea for two. 'Now, Mrs Protheroe. Just take your time.'

'Thank you, Inspector. I knew when I saw you on television that you were a kind man . . . Where was I? Oh, yes, Mr De Garde visiting Linda. As I've said, I don't believe in telling tales. Or passing judgment on what people do if it doesn't affect others. But this was something I couldn't help noticing . . . It was last Tuesday, later on the day that I'd seen Mr De Garde leaving Linda's house, the day before he was killed. I'd been sitting in my front window and just happened to see him going down the path. I took note of it, really, because I hadn't seen him there for quite some time. A month or so ago he used to visit her regularly, but then that stopped. Anyway, I just thought, well, perhaps they've made it up. That was in the afternoon, Inspector, and then that evening – it was very hot, but every evening's very hot at the moment, isn't it? – that evening I was in the front garden watering my poor roses when I heard some banging noises from over Linda's hedge, and then a whole lot of screaming. Well, if I'm honest it was more like screeching, hardly like a human voice at all.'

'And did you see anything, Mrs Protheroe?'

'Well, yes . . . The hedge isn't high and it was obvious something was wrong. I went over to the boundary and I saw . . . well, I saw Linda standing in her doorway and . . . and . . . just making that terrible noise. I called to her but she didn't seem to hear me, and then she picked up a garden chair she has by the front door – the houses are the wrong way for the sun, Inspector, the fronts face south – and broke her own window. I rushed round into her garden, then, and so did Mrs

159

Roberts from the other side. Neither of us could do anything with her and she went indoors and started throwing more furniture about so I rang the police from the telephone in her hall. I think she must have been having a brainstorm, Inspector. She was shouting out a lot of awful words' – Mrs Protheroe went faintly pink at the memory – 'such as – well, such as . . .'

Tim saw the relief in her face at the distraction of the tap on the door. 'Come in.'

'Sugar for the lady's in the saucer.'

'Thank you, Constable.'

'Thank *you*, Inspector.' Mrs Protheroe put the unopened packet of sugar carefully on the table. 'Where was I?' She took a sip of tea.

'Awful words,' Tim prompted. 'We'll take them as said.'

'Thank you . . . A uniformed policeman arrived very quickly – I suppose he must have been nearby – and so Mrs Roberts and I went back home. Anyway, Mrs Roberts had slapped Linda's face and she was crying by then rather than screaming and we could tell she wasn't going to break anything else. I wondered at the time if her behaviour had anything to do with the visit she'd had that afternoon, but more often than not I'd seen Mr De Garde's back rather than his face, going rather than coming, you know, and when I saw the first photographs of him after he was murdered I just had this vague feeling I'd seen him before. I didn't connect him with the man who visited Linda. It wasn't until the photograph on TV last night . . . I'm sorry to have been so slow on the uptake, Inspector.'

'You've been wonderful, Mrs Protheroe.' Restoring his professional relish almost to the level of his personal. 'Now, I'll ask a constable to come in and perhaps you'll tell him what you've told me and he'll write it down as a statement for you to sign.'

The realization of what she had told the Detective Inspector dawned in Mrs Protheroe's faded blue eyes. She leaned pleadingly across the table. 'Inspector, Linda's not a bad girl. I'm not trying to tell you that she . . . that she did this terrible thing. I just thought you ought to know what happened to her so soon after she'd seen – Mr De Garde.'

160

'You were absolutely right, Mrs Protheroe.' Why hadn't he heard from that uniformed PC? 'And I can assure you there's no way Linda Parrish can be accused of the murder of Charles De Garde if she didn't commit it. You've done no more than your civic duty.'

'Thank you, Inspector.'

Tim called for a constable and the statement was duly completed.

'You could probably catch Linda at home this morning,' Mrs Protheroe told them as she handed back the pen. 'She works as a croupier at the Magali Club – she told me that in one of our little chats over the hedge – and she doesn't start till the afternoon. She gets home very late and so she usually sleeps in for most of the morning. Obviously she didn't go to work that Tuesday night, and I don't think she went on the Wednesday night, either.'

'Thank you, Mrs Protheroe.' It felt like a long time since he had been so professionally elated. 'If you don't mind waiting just a minute my sergeant and I will run you home.'

Having looked in the duty register under Tuesday, Tim went into the resurrected Incident Room, assigned DS Tostevin to PC Guilbert, and collected DS Mahy.

Mrs Protheroe lived in a road of terraced villas just behind St Sampson's Harbour. Ted Mahy escorted her up the path, and as the two policemen walked next door to Linda Parrish's house Mrs Protheroe's front curtain was already twitching.

Ted rang and knocked several times alternately before they heard the drag of slippered feet.

'You're persistent, aren't you?' Miss Parrish had pulled a short white towelling robe round what Tim's instincts told him was her nakedness, but hadn't brushed the cloud of dark hair above her small pale face. Her wide eyes narrowed as she took them in. 'What d'you want?'

'I'm Detective Inspector Le Page and this is Detective Sergeant Mahy.' They showed their IDs. 'We're inquiring into the murder of Charles De Garde on Wednesday of last week. May we come in?'

'I didn't know Joly Duguy,' she said languidly. 'So how can I help you?'

'Joly Duguy didn't kill Charles De Garde, Miss Parrish.' He had to take the chance. Whoever she spoke to it could

161

hardly reach Olivia and the Chapmans before the funeral, and he was going to tell them immediately afterwards.

He had given her a shock. He saw it in the stiffening of her languor into alertness. She stood aside in silence, then led the way into a room off the hall: bland and tidy, with an aggressive abstract over the low mantelshelf making the only statement, reproduction oak furniture, and a small bar. A corner of the Magali Club, perhaps.

'Sit down if you want.'

Linda Parrish took the armchair opposite the sofa, the towelling robe falling open to each side of her knees as she crossed her legs. Tim was amused to see his uxorious sergeant, in the process of seating himself on the extreme edge of the sofa, avert his eyes until Miss Parrish was settled. Tim took the chair between them.

'Charles De Garde came to see you the day before he died, Miss Parrish. And that evening the police were called to your house after you had what could be called a brainstorm.'

'La Protheroe's description, I suppose. Yes, you could call it that. I've seen the faraway look in her eye when we've met lately over the hedge, and I knew she was trying to put two and two together. She took so long I was beginning to think she'd given up, but then when Joly Duguy . . . I didn't kill Charles De Garde, Inspector.'

Linda Parrish lit a cigarette, her blue eyes wide as she stared at him.

'You can prove it?'

'I'd rather not.'

'That puts you in a tricky position,' Ted observed. 'While you're thinking it over perhaps you'd care to tell us about last Tuesday.'

'Sure. As far as Charles was concerned we'd finished. He'd gone on to the next one – a prissy cow called Janet Chapman who works in his office. She'll be feeling as sore as I was. It was always his wife, she provided him with everything except what he came to us for. All right, I'd thought I was an exception, I'd thought I'd spoiled the pattern and that it was as good for him as it was for me. I was wrong. He came round on Tuesday, Inspector, because he was afraid of how public I was getting trying to hold on to him. He stayed just long enough to make me finally understand that I was wasting my time.'

'And that whatever else you did could only be spite?'

'Oh, yes, and I thought of a whole lot of spiteful things. I never told him but I'd already been to see his wife' – through his shock Tim saw the flash of concern across Ted's eyes – 'and she'd put me down. Very kindly and confidently, but until that Tuesday afternoon I suppose I was still hoping . . . After he'd gone I rang the club to say I was ill and wouldn't be in, and then I started drinking. Sometime in the early evening it all exploded. I don't remember much, except that I think the Roberts woman slapped my face. La Protheroe rang you lot on *my* telephone – rich, that, wasn't it? – and a nice young uniformed policeman arrived and told me to behave myself. He also fixed up with a glazier to come and mend the window I'd broken. He came right away; I was impressed.'

'PC Guilbert. He managed on his own, I gather.'

'There was nothing to manage. I was over the worst. He made me some black coffee and watched me drink it at the kitchen table.'

'Did you tell him what all the fuss was about?'

'I told him I'd broken up with my boyfriend. I didn't name names.' Just as well for PC Guilbert. 'Then he told me to go straight to bed, and left. I did like he said.'

'Thank you, Miss Parrish. Now we'd like to know about Wednesday. I believe you didn't go to the club that night, either?'

'She doesn't miss a trick, does she? My boss came to see me at lunchtime, looked at me, and told me to take another night off. Not as considerate as it sounds, Inspector – he'd taken someone else on.'

'So you've left the Magali?' Ted asked.

'No, I've just been put at a teeny weeny disadvantage. If I'd known what he was up to I'd have gone in on my knees on Wednesday night. As it was I said thank you very much and went back to bed.'

'And stayed there the rest of the day?'

'No. I was in the kitchen getting myself a bit of supper when a visitor arrived – it must have been about ten o'clock. I'm surprised La Protheroe didn't tell you. Ah, but she was having supper that night with her niece in Vale.'

'A man or a woman?' Ted asked.

'A man, and I wasn't expecting him. He left about two o'clock. On foot; he doesn't live very far away.'

'And you're not prepared to tell us who he is.'

'I'd prefer not to. For his sake rather than mine. That's why I've been hoping you wouldn't get on to me, not because I killed Charles. I liked the thought of it, but I'd never have done it. Anyway, as I said, I was at home with this bloke. What will happen if I don't tell you his name?'

'After you've given us a statement – which we'll need anyway – you'll probably be held for questioning.' Ted was exaggerating, but Tim was happy. 'Then your house will be searched, your garden, your dustbins. If we don't find anything we'll obviously let you go, but the Press will make sure people know about your quarrel with the murdered man, and they'll establish a connection between you and his death that'll go down in history.'

'I haven't any connection with Charles's death!'

'That won't make any difference, Miss Parrish.'

'You could keep it quiet, Inspector.'

Tim shrugged. 'When they learn that Joly Duguy's in the clear the media will be starving. Even if we tried to keep you out of it we'd be unlikely to succeed.' It was going to be hard enough with Helen Falla.

'Joly Duguy has an alibi,' Ted took up in the face of her silence, 'and it's cleared him. If you give us yours you won't need clearing. You'll never have been associated with Charles De Garde.'

'Joly Duguy's alibi wasn't much use to him, was it?' She gave them a pert smile, but her hands were twisting together on the white towelling and Tim was confident she was playing for time.

'No, but for you an alibi would be very useful indeed. If you don't give it a name, Miss Parrish, I'm afraid we'll be inclined to believe that you don't have one.'

'Oh, I have one, Inspector.' Linda Parrish lit another cigarette. In the silence that followed the rasp of the match Tim heard a bluebottle buzzing angrily at the window behind him. 'All right, but don't say I didn't warn you. PC Guilbert called in on Wednesday night to see if I was still OK. Nice of

164

him, wasn't it, to take the trouble when he was off duty, even though he does happen to live in the next road? It took me about four hours to reassure him.' She got to her feet. 'If the police force is as fair as it always says it is, Inspector Le Page, there's no way PC Guilbert should get into trouble. He'd reported Tuesday's incident, and it was closed. So I was just a woman he'd met. And if he hadn't come back to me you'd be on a wild goose chase now, wouldn't you?'

Tim's colleagues had been generous with the traffic cones they'd placed along the edge of the road outside Saxon Lodge, reserving enough space for his car as well as the hearse and the car ordered for the family. He was just in time to park before the two long black limousines drove slowly past the house on their way to the end of L'Hyvreuse, where they would reverse in the space beyond the children's playground before drawing up at Olivia's front door.

Anna opened it to him, her brief but immediate smile justifying his rainbow-coloured recollections of the night before.

They clasped hands. 'Sorry I'm late. Business. Not important, as it turned out. You've managed to find the right clothes.'

'I already had the jacket; I always have navy.' Anna stood aside as Olivia came out of the sitting-room.

'Tim.' It was a shock to see her in black even though she had told him she was going to wear it. It had drained her of the colour her usual clothes enhanced. Everything in his life had become so unprecedented he was starting to feel like an actor in a feature film, with Olivia's scenes shot in black and white as a directorial device to represent her suffering. How was the director coping with the waves of aversion that swamped him each time he thought about telling her that Charles's murderer was still at large?

'Olivia.' He bent to kiss her, still holding Anna's hand and wondering how much prominence the director would accord the contact.

Olivia looked from one to the other. 'Good. I hoped . . . Anna didn't say anything.'

'I knew when Tim came . . . They're here.'

They followed the hearse down Candie Road in silence, Olivia in the centre, past the recessed main gates of Candie Gardens where always, now, Tim would see Joly climbing, into the width of St Julian's Avenue and down to the port, where they turned right on to the North Esplanade and travelled slowly along by the sea to the Town Church. There were just three sheaves of summer flowers on the coffin lid – his and hers and Anna's as Olivia had wanted.

Friends and colleagues were already seated in the church, but two other groups were standing about outside, identifiable to Tim through their different expressions as well as what they were wearing: the locals looking sadly interested and showing less flesh than the holiday-makers, who looked surprised by their discovery that the familiar rituals of death were to be encountered in fairyland.

As always before his infrequent entrances into his parish church, Tim glanced up at his favourite fraud: the imposing building looming above it, severe and greyly gothic with its stepped gables, but no more than a facade to the vegetable market bustling at this moment behind it. Today it failed to amuse him.

A couple of flash bulbs exploded as they walked the path cut for them by the professional mourners. In the deep recess of the north porch they were greeted by the rector, and the small procession assembled. There had been volunteers to shoulder the coffin, but Olivia had preferred the less obtrusive movement of wheels. It was a mercifully short walk to the centre of the spacious tower-crossing where the coffin was halted in front of the choir stalls, giving the rector time for no more than a couple of scriptural sentences. *He that believeth in me* . . . Had Charles believed? Tim didn't know. *We brought nothing into this world, and it is certain we can carry nothing out*. He was glad Olivia had chosen the old words. One didn't have to be conventionally religious to feel their impact.

There were a lot people, but the front pews on both sides of the nave had been kept empty: no doubt the invariable policy of funeral directors loth to see family members jostling for position, but offering too stark an indication today of the near extinction of the De Gardes. Tim saw it as an act of instinctive

166

self-protection that he and Anna and Olivia were settling themselves as expansively as possible without giving rise to rumours that there was a falling out between them.

The ushers had directed people into the first few rows of the south transept, probably in preference to the back of the nave. At the end of the week, when he came to the Town Church for Joly's funeral – solely as a mourner, not in the dual role he was, after all, playing today – the south transept would be empty and so would most of the nave. His mind's eye saw Helen Falla alone in the near-emptiness, but if he had really persuaded her that her final gesture had been made, the picture would remain in his imagination.

The majority of the people in the Town Church today were there for official reasons – legal, governmental, parochial, business. Now he thought about it, Charles didn't have many more real friends than Joly, but his busy varied lifestyle, in constant contact with other people, had disguised the fact that he in his way had been as personally reclusive as his wife, ultimately needing only her just as she had needed only him. When he turned towards her Tim saw that her face was calm and dry, her hands motionless in her lap. Out of the corner of his eye he was aware of a handkerchief at work across the nave and wondered on a twinge of exasperation if it was Janet Chapman's; he had seen her and Douglas go into the second row. But weeping wasn't Janet's style any more than it was Olivia's.

The film director must be having a field day. The choir had turned out in full, looking and sounding as fine as their reputation, and the music tingled in Tim's spine. He hadn't asked Anna yet if she liked music, told her there was a concert on Friday night in St James the Less . . .

The rector was offering an admirable review of Charles's life and achievements, extolling the quality of his marriage with a sudden severity which Tim interpreted as a request that the memory of his amatory activities be allowed to die with him. As the singing soared for the final hymn he read the last words on the funeral sheet: *Olivia De Garde asks that the interment be private to her and her family, but on her return from the cemetery she will be pleased to receive at home anyone who has shared this service with her and would like to come.*

She had asked his advice and he had been right to tell her to follow her instincts. For a moment he had a pleasant mental picture of the young reporter getting hold of a copy of the funeral sheet, seeing the simple word *cemetery*, and haring off to the burial ground at Foulon. But if he had got as far as the Town Church he would know about Candie . . . Remembering the flash bulbs, Tim knew he would be openly angry if they followed him and Anna and Olivia to the grave.

When it was time for them to lead the exodus he turned as he got up and tried to look over the congregation, but they remained a sea of faces and all he really noticed was the sweat on Douglas Chapman's temple where it caught the light.

'Do you really want to greet people now?' he murmured to Olivia in the porch.

'Yes. A lot of them won't come to the house, and I want an end of it.'

They stood just outside, Olivia ready to shake hands and introduce Anna. Tim saw more flash bulbs, more unfamiliar reporters. Then his sergeant and a constable, as he had requested, waiting to clear a path for them. Some members of the congregation made for Olivia, some found themselves in front of her and tried to make the best of it. Tim noticed others deciding to avoid her. She thanked those whose hands she shook for their embarrassed mumbles, and sent some of them away articulate.

'We'd better get into the car,' Tim said, when most people had passed by.

She put her weight for an instant on his arm. 'Yes. It's enough.'

Sergeant Mahy led the way. In the car Olivia shuddered, but her eyes stayed dry. Tim's and Anna's fingers met across her meshed hands.

They stopped in Upland Road, outside the lower gates of the high-walled square of Candie Cemetery: opened in 1831, closed now to all except those whose family graves awaited them. As a child Tim had read the dates carved on each gatepost aloud to his grandmother. Then, his hand in hers, had climbed the steps where now the coffin was leading. Ten steps, four strides on the flat, ten more steps, four more strides, twelve steps. He could still walk them blind.

All his memories of Candie Cemetery were dark, and even in the bright June sunshine it looked sombre. He had thought as a child that it was the top of the world, looking down as it did on the towers of his school, and Herm and Jethou out to sea. His De Garde grandmother had come regularly to her husband's grave, bringing him for company and to prompt a proper sense of awe for holy ground. Despite his long agnosticism, Tim found as he walked between the graves that it was with him still.

They were turning left at the central crossover, coming to the south path above Monument Road with its wonderful view of the port and the De Garde plot a dozen steps to the left. A modestly furnished space with few headstones. The Duguy graves on the north side overlooking L'Hyvreuse – next time he would turn right at the crossover – were far more elaborately marked. If he remembered rightly, Joly would join his father under an angel with an open book.

The tiny grave had no headstone. The freshly dug space beside it made it look pathetically small and he gripped Olivia's hand as he heard Anna's sharp intake of breath.

Man that is born of woman hath but a short time to live, and is full of misery. The rector looked up from his book and smiled at them in kindly concern. Olivia was weeping.

L'Hyvreuse was a snarl of manoeuvring traffic, but only about thirty people followed the family into Saxon Lodge. Tim was hardly surprised. The usual anodyne phrases – *The will of God. Spared any suffering. It was so peaceful.* – were so grotesquely inappropriate to Charles's death that they could none of them be spoken, and without them people would be at a loss to know what to say. For the majority of the congregation, to partake of the funeral baked meats would have been unacceptably embarrassing.

At least it meant that those who came did so out of a genuine concern. Or a desire for human contact, Tim thought wearily, after a harangue in the hall from the elderly widow of Charles's deceased senior partner on some ancient office politics.

Even with Anna to distract him he could hardly wait to tell Olivia the truth about Joly, but those who had ventured and surmounted the semantic difficulties were inclined to reward themselves by settling in to enjoy her excellent buffet and the liberal drink that enabled him to free himself from the elderly widow in order to carry it round.

Having a role to play at least helped the afternoon along and offered regular opportunities to observe the Chapmans. Janet didn't move from the single severe chair in the corner by the french window. Her husband, pulling fretfully on his moustache, brought her food which she strewed about her plate, and she accepted a fill-up of wine whenever Tim offered it. He was intrigued to notice that each time he approached her and she laid down her fork, she put her hand in a protective gesture above her breast before holding out her glass. Close to, he could see the puffy white under her eyes and the gaunt lines defining her cheeks. But he could also see that the tension had gone out of her, and made a feeble effort not to feel pleased that he was soon to restore it.

Olivia as usual wasn't drinking much, she put her hand over her glass with a smile most of the times he went up to her with a bottle. Ever since the murder he had been reassured to see Olivia's smile, but now it smote him.

The third or fourth time he went to Janet he found Anna with her, kneeling on the floor by her chair. Tim was a modest man, but he had to believe himself responsible for his love's new aura of warmth and relaxation. Once he had spoken to Olivia he would be able to start enjoying it.

'Could I ask you and your husband to stay on when everyone else has gone?' he asked Janet. 'You'll probably be doing so anyway, but I'd like a word with you both.' He couldn't make his face reassuring, but he spoke lightly and hers didn't change.

'Of course, Tim. I'll tell Douglas.'

'Thanks.' He really meant it; Chapman had refused all his offers of wine, but Tim had noticed regular visits to the corner cupboard with a whisky glass, and his reaction to the request if it came from DI Le Page could have disturbed the quiet gathering. 'Excuse me now.' He touched Anna's hair. 'I'm on duty.'

His impatience was growing painful, and after one more turn of the room he was in no mood to encourage people to

170

linger. Leave-taking was at last under way, although one stout man he didn't know had just come through from the dining-room with a freshly piled plate. And beyond the open french window he could see people still admiring the garden and relaxing on the various outdoor seats.

Abandoning his latest bottle, Tim wandered out. After they had learned there would be no children, Charles and Olivia had told him he was to be made heir to Saxon Lodge, but it was only in the garden that he ever thought of it. The house was Olivia's carapace. It couldn't exist in his imagination without her at its heart, but beyond the french window he sometimes tentatively tried on the mantle of ownership, saw himself in the dusk strolling his bounds.

'Ah, Timothy! Forgive me, but I didn't quite explain . . .'

The elderly widow, too, had gone out into the garden. By the time she declared that she really must go nearly everyone else had left, and the stout man with the piled plate was putting it gleaming on to a table before trying unsuccessfully to stifle a belch as he got to his feet.

Janet Chapman was still in her corner, her husband pacing nearby. Tim nodded to them as Olivia left the sitting-room with the last of her guests, then followed her out.

'Oh! I'm glad it's over, Tim.' She leaned against the front door, smiling at him.

'You did it so well, like everything you do.'

'You exaggerate, but thank you.'

'I asked Janet and Douglas to hang on. Olivia –'

'So did I. Mrs M will have a teatray ready.'

'Come into the dining-room with me a moment.'

'If you insist.' She led the way. There was enough food left for the spread still to look attractive, but as he saw it he felt his gorge rising. 'I must cover all this up,' Olivia murmured. She turned to face him. 'Tim?'

'Please sit down.'

'Janet and Douglas. Anna . . .'

'In a minute. Please.'

When she was settled into one of the eighteenth century chairs he put his hand on her shoulder from behind and told her about Joly and Helen Falla.

There was no reaction from the shoulder, and when he went round to pick up her hands they were inert. She was staring ahead of her, making him think of the morning a lifetime ago when he had told her Charles was dead.

'I didn't want to tell you,' she said at last, to the wall. 'I hoped there wouldn't be any need. But one of Charles's affairs came to see me. Linda Parrish.'

'I know. We caught up with her. At midnight on Wednesday night she was in bed with a police constable.'

'I see.' She turned to look through him. 'You've asked Janet and Douglas not to leave. There was no need, Tim. I know them and they couldn't –'

'Janet was at home that night on her own. Douglas got back from the club at half-past midnight.'

'And I walked to the lookout. Yes, of course.'

'Olivia . . .'

'D'you want to see them on your own?'

'Not yet. I only want to tell them. Please come with me.' She had made her usual swift surface recovery and she would observe the Chapmans' reactions as perceptively as he would. 'The Chief agrees with me, by the way, that we should do our best not to make the nature of Joly's alibi public.'

'I hope you manage that,' Olivia murmured as they crossed the hall. 'Geoffrey Falla's a nice man.' Short of the sitting-room doorway she turned to face him. 'Tim. It was a mugger who lost his nerve.'

'I hope so.'

Janet Chapman was on her feet. Her husband was still pacing about, and Anna was in the garden studying a border. He would have liked her reactions but he had to approve her sense of fitness.

'There you are!' Douglas Chapman said irritably. 'Janet tells me there's something you want to say to us. Perhaps we can get on with it.'

'We can. Perhaps you'd all like to sit down.'

Janet went back to the severe chair, and Douglas dropped with a grunt on to the sofa. Tim remained standing, waiting until Olivia was settled in her chair before he began to speak.

'I have to tell you that Joly Duguy didn't kill Charles,' he said. 'He has a watertight alibi. So we're going to have to – Oh, my God!'

Douglas Chapman had fallen sideways, and Tim was across the room and tearing at his tie as Janet got up. Although he moved so quickly, Tim had time to register that the shock of what he had just said had been replaced in her face by curiosity rather than concern.

'What we could all do with,' Janet said, 'is a pot of tea.'

'A good idea,' Olivia agreed. 'And Mrs M is standing by to make it. Perhaps you'd care to tell her we're ready, Janet. I'm going into the garden, if you'll all excuse me.'

'I'll bring you a cup out. How are you now, Douglas?'

'I'm perfectly all right,' Douglas Chapman said testily. 'Heat and people, what can you expect? All that fuss!'

Tim's announcement that he was going to call a doctor had brought Chapman to his feet to demonstrate his recovery, and his ashen face was restored to its normal putty colour.

The panic was over but Tim thought he could still see the effect of his revelation on the Chapmans: Douglas's eyes uncharacteristically uncertain, Janet's manner uncharacteristically brisk.

When she and Olivia had gone their separate ways Tim sat down at the other end of the sofa.

'You're sure you're all right?'

'Of course I'm sure. I get these turns sometimes, especially if I have to stand about. Low blood pressure.'

And visits to Olivia's drinks cupboard. 'I'm afraid we'll need a more detailed statement from you,' Tim said, as casually as he could manage. 'Just to get it clear about what time you left your club last Wednesday night.'

Chapman stared at him suspiciously. 'Leaping at everyone else in sight, now Duguy's out of the running?'

'No. Ten o'clock tomorrow morning at your house? I don't want to interfere too much with your working day, but there's the inquest on Joly Duguy at nine-fifteen, and I'm afraid that's the earliest I can make it. We shall need a bit more detail from your wife as well.'

'As far as I know she'll be there.' Janet appeared in the doorway with a tray. 'But you can ask her yourself.'

'I'd like to talk to you in the morning, Janet. If I come to your house at ten o'clock?'

'Of course, Tim. I'll pour for you and Douglas and take the tray outside.'

173

'I don't want any tea,' Chapman said childishly.

'You'll have some. It'll be good for you.' She poured two cups.

'Thanks,' Tim said. He sat down again on the sofa as Janet manoeuvred the tray through the french window with a rattle of crockery.

'Marriage,' Douglas Chapman said as she disappeared. 'It's no good.'

'I can't agree with you.' Up till that moment Tim had thought of marriage as something for other people, and was intrigued to discover that, associated with Anna Weston, the institution had begun to have personal appeal. 'But I suppose that's an easy thing to say when you aren't married.'

'Keep it that way.'

'Why?' Tim had no wish to learn Chapman's views on matrimony, but in so far as they might throw some light on his relationship with his wife he was bound to encourage them.

'You can't trust them – you take my word for it. 'Scuse me now.' Chapman laboured to his feet and crossed the room to the hall door, his hands already at his trousers.

Tim decided to take advantage of the opportunity. He would be in dialogue again with Douglas Chapman soon enough. He got up and went out into the garden to look for Anna.

She was round the first corner, alone on a seat with her cup of tea beside her. He sat down and kissed her, his sudden happiness as dazzling as the sunshine.

'Janet's taken the teatray to the enclave. Olivia had a word with me on her way down. She told me about Douglas and said she was sure I already knew about Joly. I felt she wanted to be on her own and I didn't suggest going with her. Janet seemed quite jaunty, she wasn't worried about disturbing Olivia . . . Tim!'

'We'd better walk.' He drew away, grinning at her mock displeasure. 'Yes,' he said as hand in hand they strolled down the garden, 'Janet didn't show much reaction to my news and none at all to her husband's collapse. Unless . . . No.'

'Go on.'

'Just for a moment I had a feeling she was hoping it might be fatal.'

'But he's recovered.'

'He seems to have done. I've made appointments with them both for the morning.'

'And with Olivia.'

'Not yet, but yes, I'll have to go through the motions.'

The natural barriers were so effective they were almost at Olivia's enclave before they heard the women's voices. When they did they stopped short, frozen by the intensity of Janet Chapman's.

'I can't tell you now but I must talk to you. It's very important. Will you come over tomorrow afternoon? Say three o'clock? I've been given another day off and we can sit by the pool and be absolutely private.'

'We can be absolutely private here.'

'I'd rather you came to me. I don't want any chance of our being interrupted, and if we're down by the pool anyone who calls will think I'm out. Olivia, I have to talk to you before I talk to the police. They're coming in the morning but I can stall them until I've spoken to you. Please say you'll come.'

'All right, Janet, I'll come.' Olivia's voice was calm. 'Three o'clock tomorrow.'

'Thank you.'

Tim in dumb show suggested they return to the house. Douglas Chapman was unconscious on the sofa, and remained undisturbed by Anna's investigation of his pulse and breathing. When she was satisfied that these were compatible with sleep they went back down the garden. This time, as they approached the enclave, Tim called out.

175

Chapter Fourteen

The inquest on Joly Duguy opened and closed in twenty minutes, with Tim and Anna the sole witnesses and a verdict of suicide whilst of unsound mind.

When it was over Tim spent a few moments learning about the second half of Anna's first night at the Bradshaws and wishing her luck in regular employment, then went round the corner to the Incident Room to collect DS Mahy. They drove to the Chapmans' house at Fort George, where Douglas Chapman, in his study, told them he had left his club on the night of Charles's murder at half past eleven.

This was the piece of information DS Tostevin would be acquiring, perhaps at that very moment, from the club barman, so Tim welcomed Chapman's common sense rather than his honesty. And his saving of time.

But Chapman went on to squander it on repeated attempts to fudge the vital hour away. In the end Tim asked him if he had spent part of it killing his wife's lover.

'I beg your pardon?' The surprise and outrage were very well done, but Tim couldn't believe them. 'What did you say?'

Tim repeated his question.

'You can't be serious, Inspector. The idea is preposterous!' It took Tim a few seconds to realize that the sharp sound following Chapman's comment was laughter.

'I'm afraid I am, Sir.' He had no doubt Chapman's use of his title was derisive, but it solved his problem of what to call a suspect first met at a dinner table. 'Surely you can see that if you persist in refusing to tell us your movements after you left your club we have to consider the possibility that they took you to Candie Gardens and a meeting with the man your wife was having an affair with?'

Chapman laughed again, without any visible evidence of mirth. When he wasn't registering righteous indignation he had the sort of inexpressive face that made interrogation difficult. 'When a man knows he isn't a murderer' – Chapman's voice now registered injured dignity – 'it doesn't occur to him that other people are considering the possibility.'

'Isn't that attitude a little naive, Sir?' suggested DS Mahy. 'However, now that you know the way our thoughts are tending, you'll be prepared to let us have a full account of how you spent the time last Wednesday night between leaving your club and arriving home.'

Chapman got to his feet and started pacing the carpet, tugging on his moustache. 'If that is the police approach, so be it. When I left the club last Wednesday night I walked to my car, which was parked by the Albert Marina. When I got to the marina I decided to – to continue walking. It was a fine night, and I was restless.'

'Restless?'

'Yes! I wanted to think . . . Oh, yes, Inspector.' Chapman sat down again and looked fiercely at his adversary. It took Tim several moments to realize that the righteous indignation was crumbling into entreaty. 'I had plenty to think about.'

'Having just learned of your wife's affair with Charles De Garde.'

'Yes!' Chapman's fists clenched on the arms of his chair, which turned an arc on its revolving base under the impact. 'I had ample reason for wishing him dead, but that's a very different thing from killing him.'

'True, Sir.' With the usual unhappy pang, Tim thought of Joly. 'So you saw your friends drive off?'

Chapman leaned back, his hands relaxing. 'You're trying to catch me out, aren't you, Tim? My friends weren't parked by Albert Marina. I said goodnight to them when I left the club.'

'Did anyone see you while you were walking?'

'Not that I was aware of.'

'Did you stay all the time at the marina, or did you go on somewhere else?'

Chapman hesitated, his face flooding pink. Tim felt a prickle in his spine, although Janet Chapman, lying in bed somewhere overhead and having asked him to excuse her on the grounds of a migraine, was still in the centre of his unfinished picture. 'I walked I suppose for almost half an hour, then suddenly thought . . . My wife had said she was staying at home, but I wondered if she'd decided to take advantage of the cancelled dinner party.'

'So?'

'I went back to the car and drove to De Garde's office building. There's what they call an executive suite on the top floor; I've been there for parties. The building's not very high but the suite has a good view over the sea, and you can see it from the Esplanade. It has a bedroom, too, Inspector. I – I wondered if there would be a light. I parked where I could see, but there wasn't. Then . . .'

'Go on, please.'

'Then I got out and went to the building and tried the outer doors. They were locked.'

'So you'd learned nothing.'

'Nothing.' Chapman's head drooped, and for the first time Tim felt sorry for him.

'What did you do then?' he asked gently.

Chapman looked up at him, less fiercely. 'I drove back to Fort George.'

'Via Candie Gardens?'

'No!' But the outrage was blunted. 'I – I parked up a side street from where I could see if Janet drove home without being seen myself.'

Tim had the feeling Chapman was all at once glad to talk. Perhaps for the first time; it was hard to imagine him with a confidante. 'What time did you reach Fort George?'

'I looked at my watch to see if it was worth waiting. It was a quarter past twelve.' Giving Janet time to have got back from Candie Gardens. Tim didn't have to be afraid of his next question.

'Did you see her?'

'No. Just before half past twelve I drove into the garage.'

178

Where was your wife when you went into the house?'

'In bed. I put my head round her door. She seemed to be half asleep, but she asked me the time and I told her.'

'You didn't go all the way into her room?' And see if she was properly undressed, for instance.

'No. I didn't want to go all the way into her room.'

'I understand. Thank you, Douglas.' Having heard Chapman's story, Tim also understood his reluctance to offer it. And was inclined to find its feebleness in his favour. 'Perhaps you'll be good enough to tell your wife that we shall be here to see her at the same time tomorrow morning.' If things went as he hoped, they would be there to see her later that day.

Tim dropped Ted Mahy at St James, and went on up the hill to L'Hyvreuse and Olivia.

'Come in, Tim.' Her flowing dress was golden, but it had failed to restore the colour the mourning black had taken away.

'Are you all right?' Tim asked anxiously, as he followed her into the sitting-room.

'I didn't sleep well. Does it show? Reaction, I suppose. But I'm all right. Have you time for coffee? I was expecting your sergeant too.' On the tray by her chair there were three cups. Her realism filled him with admiration.

'We'll have to go through the motions at some point, but not today.' He hoped it would be never. 'Yes, I'd love a coffee.'

Olivia picked up the Thermos by her chair. 'It's ready.' She poured two cups.

'Thanks.' He couldn't broach so bizarre a plea without preliminaries. Even with the distraction of the coffee it was difficult, although every task, now, had the silver lining of his memory and anticipation of Anna. 'Janet Chapman isn't well,' he said as he collected his cup. 'I went to see them this morning but Janet excused herself and Douglas said she had a migraine.'

'That's strange. I'm seeing her myself this afternoon and she hasn't rung to cancel. But she gets headaches rather often and I know they can clear by lunchtime. What are you going to do now, Tim?'

'I'm going to report to my Chief on my conversation with Douglas Chapman.' It was absurd to be avoiding her eyes. 'I

179

want you to be careful, Olivia,' he said in a rush. 'We haven't found Charles's killer: he or she is still around. I want you to be careful even – even in the most ordinary situations. It needn't be another piece of lead piping.'

They stared at one another. 'Thank you, Tim,' Olivia said eventually.

'I must go now.'

He helped her to her feet and she leaned up to kiss his cheek. 'What would I do without you? Have you made another appointment with Janet?'

'In the morning.' It was true, but he hoped it would be earlier. 'As you haven't heard from her it looks as though she must be better. Have a nice afternoon. And take care.' He would have to leave her to take the specific inference, and they understood each other well enough.

'You don't look at all well, Janet. Are you sure your head-ache's gone?'

'Quite sure.' Janet gestured towards the chairs beside the pool, her eyes not meeting Olivia's. 'You know how quickly I can get over them. Thank you for coming, Olivia. Would you like some homemade lemonade? I've got it in the fridge and this afternoon feels hotter than ever.'

'It's going to storm, they say.' As she settled herself into one of the two chairs Olivia thought affectionately of Tim and his ridiculous warning. 'Thank you, Janet, I'd love some of your homemade lemonade.'

Janet disappeared up the garden under a blue sky darken-ing to slate, and was quickly back with a pale green tray holding a pale green jug and matching glasses. The glasses were sparkling clean and Janet poured pale yellow liquid from the jug into both of them. Tim, Olivia reflected, would have been reassured.

'What is is, Janet? You were very insistent about wanting to see me.'

Janet sipped lemonade, then set her glass down on the long low table that spanned the two chairs. 'Olivia, there's some-thing I have to tell you. I don't want to; I've never in my life wanted to do anything less, and if Joly Duguy hadn't turned out to have an alibi . . . Olivia, the police must think now that

180

either Douglas or I killed Charles, and I'm not prepared to go on protecting Douglas.'

'Protecting Douglas?' Olivia sat upright in her astonishment.

'By being a suspect myself. If they suspect us both we're both protected in a sense, aren't we? I mean, no one could think we were working as a team.'

'Well, no.'

'So they don't know which of us to go for, do they?'

'I suppose –'

'I can't bear it any longer, Olivia.'

'And there's something you can do about it?'

'Yes. That's why I asked you to come. More lemonade? It's so very hot.'

'You can feel the storm on its way.' Under the blue-grey featureless sky the flowers in Janet's garden were garishly bright, the shapes of the bushes sharply defined. 'Thank you.' Janet didn't pour any more into her own glass. 'Well, Janet?'

Janet sat forward, turning her glass between her hands. 'Olivia, believe me, I'd give anything not to say what I'm going to say.'

'Please say it.'

'Yes.' Janet put her glass down and her hand above her left breast, a gesture that at their last few meetings Olivia had regularly noted. 'There's no easy way. Olivia, you and Charles were the best of friends. You understood one another, you were happy living together, it suited you both. But Charles and I were *in love*.'

'Charles – and you?'

'Yes. We weren't having an affair – I wasn't one of his women. It started months ago. In the office. We were both working late, we met by chance at the coffee machine, started to talk. It was probably the first time we were ever on our own. We talked for a long time before . . . before anything else. It all happened gradually. We gradually realized we wanted to be together openly, permanently. Neither of us had ever known anything like it. Thinking of you – you and Douglas – we tried for a while to persuade ourselves it wasn't like it was, that it was just a pleasant diversion, but that didn't work because it wasn't. We were getting ready to tell you, tell

181

Douglas, when someone saw us. *We* had to be the ones to tell you as and when *we* felt was best – Charles had decided it should be when you were in England – and so we pretended to have an affair. I had my hair styled, and Charles pretended to notice me in his – in his usual way – when we were out to dinner one night.'

'I saw it.'

'I know you did. Oh, Olivia, we didn't want to do it that way!'

'Do what, Janet? Why should I believe what you're telling me?' Olivia still spoke calmly, and was leaning back relaxed in her chair.

'Because I have proof that it's the truth. Olivia, you must believe that I didn't take Charles away from you. He felt the same fondness for you that he's always felt. It was just that . . . this extra thing happened to him. And to me. Something neither of us had felt for anyone before. I haven't ever really felt anything for Douglas – he was my attempt to escape from myself and of course it didn't work. Charles cared for you deeply, he hoped that eventually –'

'What proof do you have, Janet?'

'I'm sorry. We decided – Charles decided – to write you a letter and send it to you in London. You were going next week, weren't you?'

'I still am.'

'Good. Charles thought – he thought that if you received the letter in England you might find it easier to stay there for a while, perhaps look for a new home. I suppose in a way it was the moral cowardice of the male –'

'I suppose it was. Tell me the rest of it, Janet.'

'Charles sent me a draft of the letter.' Janet's hand started towards her breast, wavered, and returned to the arm of her chair. 'I told him, that afternoon, that I thought he'd got it right, and I was going to give it back to him the next morning . . . Olivia, I would have spared you all this if Joly Duguy hadn't had an alibi. I would just have gone away. That's what I'll do now, I'll leave Douglas and go back to England. After I've shown the letter to the police. To prove I didn't kill Charles.'

'And make the police believe I did?'

'No!' Janet leaned forward eagerly. 'Don't you see? They couldn't believe that. The letter was never sent to you. But Douglas will be on his own in the spotlight and if they can't break him down they'll go back to the theory of a mugger.'

'Douglas? You believe –'

'I believe he could have done. But I don't know.' Janet spread her arms in a gesture of helplessness. 'I don't *know* him.'

'As I apparently didn't know Charles.'

'You did know him. And he knew you. You knew one another well, it was part of what made you so comfortable together. It was only when this other thing . . . It could just as easily have happened to you instead of Charles, Olivia. There's nothing in the world so strong.'

'Isn't there, Janet? I'm not in a position to judge.'

'Neither was I, until . . . I hadn't dreamed.'

'The letter, Janet. May I see it?'

'I've put it in the bank. And anyway I have to let the police have it, now I've told you. Perhaps eventually they'll let you . . . Although –'

'Although you'd rather keep it yourself, to remind you of how Charles felt about you. You really think the police won't start suspecting me of killing Charles if you give them the letter?'

'Of course they won't. You haven't seen it!'

'Having seen it themselves, you think they'll be prepared to believe that I was unaware of a basic change in my husband's feelings? You believe that yourself, Janet?'

'Olivia – I knew you believed we were having an affair. But the rest of it . . .'

'Charles's affairs didn't change him. They didn't touch our relationship. But as you've just said, I knew my husband. You played the victim swept beyond all loyalty and decent behaviour by his charms very well indeed, but do you really believe it was only at that point that I knew something had happened?'

'Olivia . . .'

'You both underestimated my perceptiveness, Janet. That hurts as much as anything.' There was no evidence of hurt in Olivia's calm face. Janet wished Olivia would lose her calm: it was unnerving. 'I knew – of course I knew – that Charles had moved away from me. And when he apparently started an affair with you after having known you for so long – his affairs always started on first meeting, or not at all – I knew why.'

'Oh, Olivia. Oh, my dear . . .'

'Don't, Janet.'

'I'm sorry. Oh, I am. But the police won't know any of this, and you didn't see the letter.'

'I did see it, Janet. I found the draft in Charles's drawer.'

In the cramped back of the van parked on the driveway of the Chapmans' holidaying neighbours, the euphoria engendered by the discovery that the new surveillance equipment worked was short-lived. It turned to a frowning concentration by the four men crouched in the small space: on sound quality by the boffins, and on the content of the dialogue by Detective Inspector Le Page and Detective Sergeant Mahy. The DS, uneasy, began by trying not to think about the personal element of the eavesdropping so far as his Chief was concerned. But as the disembodied conversation went on he was uncomfortably reminded of it by the DI's stricken face and had to turn away from him. Private grief! thought DS Mahy, outraged by the fact that his superior was having to suffer in front of him.

Tim saw and understood the gesture, and put a hand out to press his sergeant's shoulder. It enabled Ted Mahy to look round briefly and smile his condolences. The boffins continued to twiddle knobs.

'Charles and I have always respected each other's privacy,' Olivia went on. 'We both knew without saying that neither of us would so much as open a drawer in the other's piece of furniture. But when I became aware that my way of life was threatened the unwritten rules ceased to apply.'

'Olivia! You seemed . . .'

'You don't have a monopoly on deception, Janet. I knew that I'd lost Charles's confidence, and I began to look for evidence of what I had to be afraid of. The night Peter Jopling had his accident his wife rang to ask Charles to go over. I knew the call was genuine because I took it, so I knew Charles

184

wouldn't have time to cover his tracks properly – he was in his study when Ena Jopling rang. After he'd left I found the draft underneath some other papers in a drawer of his desk. Yes, that's the worst thing, Janet.' Olivia's voice at last trembled, lengthening and sharpening the electronic jags on the equipment in the van, making Tim catch his breath and Janet's eyes fill with tears. 'That Charles could believe I was so lacking in perception, so sunk in myself, he didn't have to be careful . . . I read the letter, I even copied parts of it. Not that I needed to – I learned it straight off by heart. I put it back as I'd found it and hid what I'd copied, even though I knew there would never, ever, be any danger of Charles looking through my drawers.'

'You didn't say anything. Charles would have . . .'

'He would have told you. Of course. No, I didn't say anything.'

'You didn't show anything, either. Olivia, how did you manage?'

'It was vital for me, Janet. No one knew I'd seen the letter, that I had anything new to worry about.'

'Of course not! That's what I was telling you. The police aren't going to think you killed Charles because of a letter you never saw – Olivia!' Janet shrank back into the recesses of her chair. 'You did see it . . .'

'That's right, Janet. And I did kill him.'

185

Chapter Fifteen

Even Inspector Robilliard took it in, and told the electronically-obsessed Constable Ozanne in dumb show to start listening to the words rather than the tone. Tim, with the economy and precision of a robot, and no more feeling, gestured to Ted Mahy to put into operation the contingency plan they had devised against the possibility of a confession by Janet Chapman on her own or her husband's behalf: to leave the van and then radio for the car they had managed to line up without giving a reason for needing it. Tim indicated that although it was to be brought close to the Chapman house its occupants were to await his signal.

Ted gripped Tim's arm as he shuffled past, threatening the instant rigid clamp Tim had placed on his personal reactions. Police sergeants weren't sorry for their superior officers during the course of their duties, and if he was to carry his out, superior officer was what he must be.

The silence from the machine created a miasma of unease in the cramped space. When Janet Chapman at last spoke, the three men still in the van each visibly relaxed.

'Olivia – I can't –'

'I killed him, Janet. I killed Charles. "You have been of all people the most understanding, Olivia, and you will understand now that feeling as I do I have to live with Janet." No. I *didn't* understand.'

'The letter . . .' The worst part of Janet's nightmare was that Olivia looked the same as always, calm and half smiling.

'I told you I knew it by heart. But I have my copy here.' The paper crackled through the van. '"You wouldn't want to stay at Saxon Lodge under those circumstances, Olivia." He was right there, Janet, I wouldn't. Which doesn't meant I wouldn't want to stay on the island. However: "Had I not put Saxon Lodge on the open market I would be in a position, both legally and financially, to buy you a local market home in Guernsey. But you know that by opting for the open market I forfeited my right, on your behalf as well, ever to buy a local market property here, and you will realize that although I shall of course ensure that you live according to your present standards, I lack the resources to buy another open market property. This means that you will have to do what I assume you will prefer to do anyway: go back to England. Or, of course, anywhere else in the world." Anywhere but my island, Janet. "My financial inability to buy another open market property will of course be recognized by the Matrimonial Causes Division of the Royal Court." Parts of the letter are very businesslike, aren't they? But there's a thoughtful note struck farther on, where Charles tells me he's posting the letter to England. "We can let it be believed – even more effectively if you don't come back to the island – that you've left me and I've turned to Janet for consolation. Janet is agreeable.'" The paper crackled sharply. 'Thank you, Janet.'

'Olivia . . . You're saying if Charles had opted for local market status for Saxon Lodge he would still be alive?'

Olivia's face was suddenly a face Janet had never seen, tense and angry. 'Is that all you think there is to it, Janet? You may have considered yourself free to fall in love, but Charles wasn't. He was committed to his marriage, to me – we belonged to one another. The betrayal was monstrous. It killed me before I killed him.'

'But you were still concerned about your precious way of life,' Janet welcomed her own sudden fury. It crowded out her fear.

'What else was there for me to be concerned about? I was as good as dead, but I still had to go through the motions of living, and I preferred to be widowed in Guernsey than divorced in England. I had more reason than ever to make the best of the trappings – they were all I had left.'

'You're saying your marriage was as good as that, Olivia?'

187

'I'm saying it was the one happiness I've known.' Olivia closed her eyes on a gasp of breath that had Inspector Robilliard's equipment dancing. 'Except for the baby.'

Janet winced. 'Charles's feelings for you didn't change. It was just that he found something – more. If you'd been the one to find it, he would have understood.'

'Would he, Janet?'

'Eventually. He would have sulked and so on, but he wouldn't have bashed your skull in . . . Oh, God. Oh, no.' Janet leaned forward, her arms outstretched in entreaty. The equipment picked up her agitated breathing. 'Olivia, tell me at least that you didn't do it yourself, that you – what do they call it? – took out a contract.'

'I did it myself, Janet. It asked to be done. There was a piece of lead piping in my greenhouse and a night that met the essential conditions. The weather was still hot enough to take Charles into Candie Gardens. You were out of the way, I thought, and having read the letter I knew he wouldn't be meeting anyone else. And my trip to London was still in the future. You remember how the letter ends? "No one but Janet and I will know of this until you know; until you have received this letter." So it had to be done before I went to England, and there might not be another night with all the qualifications.'

'Tell me about it.'

'Are you sure, Janet?'

'Tell me.'

'I'd had a migraine earlier. I was over it, but I was still in bed. As soon as Charles went out I got up and dressed and put on a pair of rubber gloves. I prised the lead piping out of its channel in the greenhouse, rolled it in newspaper, and set off for the lookout with a cardigan over my arm and the piping under it. I stopped a few moments at the lookout, but not for as long as I told the police. I didn't see anyone, there or in Beauregard Lane or Vauxlaurens. Charles couldn't have presented himself more helpfully. He was leaning on those railings with his back to me, looking at the water. I couldn't see anyone else, but that was the really dangerous moment. Until the actual blow, of course, I was safe – I was merely joining my husband on his walk in Candie Gardens.

188

'I was wearing rubber-soled shoes, and I was on grass until the last couple of steps. He didn't hear me. I'm strong, Janet, and it was easy. Just the one blow. When he'd fallen and I could see he was dead I threw the piping into the water. The splash was the loudest sound I've ever heard.

'I took the newspaper home and burnt it with the gloves. There was no blood. But I fell down on one important thing. I'd intended to rob Charles and bury what I'd taken somewhere in the Gardens, make it look like the mugger, or at least a copycat crime if the mugger turned out to have been busy elsewhere. When it came to it I couldn't touch him. Perhaps that makes you feel a bit better, Janet? No? Anyway, that was what made it go wrong. That, and the draft letter.'

'The letter? You didn't have to tell me you'd seen the letter.'

'Janet! I took it out of Charles's drawer. I handled it. With fingertips that must have been sweaty from shock. The first thing the police would do would be to test it for fingerprints.

'When I'd done the burning I went straight to the drawer again. The draft letter wasn't there. It wasn't anywhere in the house, I had all night to look. I was frightened then, Janet, because of the note Charles had scribbled on the draft, asking you to tell him what you thought of it.' Olivia looked at Janet's hands, rigid on the arms of her chair. 'And there was the danger, too, that he might have prepared the final version and had it ready to post. Perhaps have posted it already to await arrival. He was always ahead of events. I telephoned my club in London to see if it was there, and when it wasn't I asked them to let me know if any mail arrived. They didn't. So there was the potential double danger of the draft being with you, and the final version being – if it wasn't in London I knew it would have to be in Charles's office safe.'

'He wouldn't write the final version until he had my comments on the draft.'

'I'm sorry, Janet. I asked Jennifer Tomlinson to bring me the contents of the safe right away, when Charles was just the random victim of a mugger turned murderer and the police had no interest in them. After failing to rob Charles, I knew my biggest hazard was that the real mugger might have an immediately provable alibi, but I got the grace I needed. The letter was there, Janet, sealed, addressed and stamped ready for postage. Perhaps you didn't know Charles quite as well as you think you did. No doubt he would be pleased to have you approve his letter, but whatever your verdict he would write it as *he* wanted, so he wouldn't see any point in waiting for your comments.'

Tim thought the catch of breath was Janet's.

'I destroyed it, and then there was only the draft to worry me. I rejoiced, of course, at what I thought then was the fact that you and Douglas had been out to dinner that night – it meant you would have no reason to produce the draft in self-defence, as you're producing it now. As I knew, of course, that you would do when Tim had told us about Joly's alibi. You saved me the trouble of arranging this meeting, Janet.'

'Olivia –' Fear was back with Janet, the most terrible companion she had ever had. If they once stopped talking . . . 'You found some lead piping in your greenhouse?'

'Yes. When the mugger was first in the press there was a photograph of the weapon his victims had described. It rang a sort of bell with me, and then I remembered seeing a similar thing lying in a groove under the staging in the greenhouse. When I went to look it was still there. There was the danger that the gardener knew about it, and so I asked him what a piece of lead piping would look like. He told me, but he didn't use the piece in the greenhouse as illustration, so I knew he wasn't aware it was there. If Charles knew – it didn't matter.' Janet moaned. 'Are you sure you want me to go on, Janet?'

'Yes.' It was a whisper, hissing through the van. 'Tell me how you managed – afterwards.'

'I'll be glad to. I'm finding that I want to tell someone. It can't be Tim or Anna, and anyway you're my best friend.' Olivia smiled. 'The only way I could manage, Janet, from the moment I got up on Thursday morning, was to act as if I'd only been as far as the lookout. To myself as well as to other people. To play the role of the innocent inside as well as out. The feeling of numbness helped; it was like having a blank canvas on which I could paint any picture. Fortunately, of course, I wasn't expected to be my usual self. And although I was prepared to fake the odd loss of control, I found it came naturally. Although I couldn't cry.'

'You told Tim Charles had had an encounter with Joly.'

'He had – I told the truth. But pointing the police at poor innocent Joly was the worst thing I did. And when he died . . .' This time it was Olivia who moaned, a sound so tormented Tim brought his hands up to his ears. 'But it still gave me peace of mind for a few more hours. It let me stop worrying about the letter. About you, Janet. I started being glad to find myself secure in the island, in Saxon Lodge. Then Tim told us Joly was in the clear, and you arranged this meeting.'

Tim shifted uneasily in the silence, aware that there had never been more responsibility on his shoulders. When Ted Mahy made a thumbs-up sign round the door of the van he motioned him to get back in. 'Not yet,' he mouthed, hoping they were not two words he would regret for the rest of his life.

'Janet? I think I'll have some more lemonade.' The clink of glass. 'It's stifling. For you?'

'No.'

'Right.'

The straining ears made no sense of the vague sounds, until they heard a quavering cry. Tim raised his hand.

'Olivia!'

'The letter isn't in the bank, is it?' Olivia was whispering, now. How close was she to Janet Chapman? 'You couldn't bear to be separated from it, your reassurance that it wasn't all a dream. I've watched that hand of yours in the past few days, fluttering about. You played it so close to your chest, didn't you, Janet? Literally. But you were signalling what you were doing. The letter's taped to your body. Just – there.'

'You can see it, Olivia,' Janet offered eagerly. Olivia's hands were on the arms of her chair, Olivia's face so near to hers that it was blurred. 'You can handle it. I can tell the police I showed it to you and they'll expect to find your fingerprints.'

'That would be generous of you, Janet, if it wasn't so stupid. Do you really think I would give the letter back to you? Or that I need your permission to handle it a second time? But you're not thinking straight. Are you afraid I'm going to kill you, too?'

191

'I . . .'

'It wouldn't bother me now, but what would be the point?' Tim very slightly lowered his hand. 'Without the letter there's no way you can threaten me. If you tell the police about it and can't produce it they won't believe it exists. In fact they'll think it's a figment of your frustrated imagination, and be even more likely to believe that you killed the man who had had enough of you.'

'Olivia, please . . . No!'

'I'm strong, Janet, I wouldn't waste time struggling. And if you do, this knife might slip.'

Tim urged Ted Mahy out of the van.

'If you use it, Olivia' – Janet sounded as though she had been running – 'you'll be in trouble.'

'If I leave you holding it? Everyone knows about your affair with Charles, and how edgy it made you.' If the scene had been before Tim's eyes he could have closed them. But the nightmare scenario of his mind was inescapable. 'Better for us both, though, if I don't . . . That's wise of you, Janet, just stay still . . . Ah!'

Olivia had the blouse and bra strap down from Janet's left shoulder, revealing the neat plastic square. Janet gasped with pain as it was ripped from her skin. 'Sealed in plastic, so that you could even wear it in the pool. And no worries, obviously, about Douglas seeing it. Was it when you fell in love with my husband that you started shutting your bedroom door on yours?'

'He'd already stopped wanting to open it.'

Olivia was frowning. 'Janet! What does Douglas know about you and Charles? What does anyone know?' Her face cleared as she stared into Janet's. 'It's all right. I can see that you stuck to the bargain, too. Not that it matters, now I have the letter.'

'I told you, Olivia, you were to be the first to know the truth.'

'The truth!' Olivia gave a sudden harsh cry. 'And so I was. All right, Janet.' The men heard the shuffle of feet, and a quavering exhalation of breath. 'I'll leave you now. You may have some worrying moments with the police, but they can't convict either you or Douglas without evidence and eventually they'll have to let you both go. I should forget the letter

192

if I were you, or you could find yourself in the hands of the psychiatrists. They would be much more difficult to shake off. Goodbye, Janet.'

The Chapman pool was a long way down the Chapman garden, and Olivia met DS Mahy and the two uniformed men before she reached the gate.

She was swinging along at her usual slow rhythmic pace, the plastic square in her hand. When she saw Tim panting up behind the other policemen she stood still and smiled, not trying to conceal what she was holding.

'Tim! Janet's down by the pool. I thought you were going to see her in the morning. I still don't think she's well enough . . .' Her voice trailed away. The uniformed men were on either side of her, and Tim had never looked at her as he was looking now.

He put his hand out. 'I'll have that, Olivia.'

Belatedly she snatched, the only unconsidered gesture Tim had ever seen her make. He put the package into his pocket.

'*Et tu*, Tim,' Olivia said, swaying.

'It was for Janet,' he told her. 'We set it up for Janet.'

'Janet!' Her laughter was terrible.

'Take her to the car,' he told the uniforms. 'Search her. And wait for me, I shan't be long. Ask Inspector Robilliard or Sergeant Ozanne to follow me down in a few minutes and finish their job.'

A few spots of rain were beginning to fall as he sped across the lawn. Janet was lying very still in one of the chairs, one breast exposed under four red weals shaping a square on her skin. The rain was rapidly increasing, and as Tim came up behind her he was relieved to see her sit up and struggle her clothes back on to her shoulder. Then she put her head down on her knees.

'Janet . . .'

She moaned with shock, and he ran round to face her. 'It's all right. We have your conversation with Olivia on tape. It's all over.'

Slowly she raised her head and stared at him. 'All over? You had something set up?'

'Yes. We heard everything. We were ready to come –'

'And rescue Olivia? You thought it was me, didn't you? You were protecting her from me.'

'We were trying to get at the truth.' Tim shuddered, and she saw it.

'Oh, Tim, I'm sorry.'

'So am I. For all of us.'

'The letter . . .'

'I have it. It'll come back to you eventually.'

'Tim!'

'What is it?'

'No need to make it public. Things are bad enough for her. It doesn't matter now to me, except as my one and only love letter.'

'I'm afraid it's evidence, Janet. She'll come to trial.' If she had been able to go home before being taken to the station, she might not. But he was a policeman, and he couldn't permit her a way out of the hell to which he had consigned her. 'You said you were going back to England.'

'As soon as I can book a flight.'

'Good. You'll have to come back for the trial, I'm afraid, but by then you'll have established the break. Is there anything I can do for you now?'

'Could you ask Anna to come and see me? If she feels strong enough. I'd like to see her.'

'She'll feel strong enough.' Warmth flooded his anguish, easing it as he would try to ease Anna's. 'I'm sorry, Janet.'

She smiled at him. 'You loved Olivia. So did I. We still do.'

'Yes.' He touched her hand. 'Goodbye.'

He met the electronic wizards halfway up the garden, on their way to debug the lounging chairs. 'Thanks. I forgot to tell her you were coming, but she's in the picture.'

'We're sorry, Tim,' Inspector Robilliard said.

'Thanks.'

'Bit of a squeeze in the car. We'll take Ted Mahy back with us in the van.'

When Tim reached the car the uniformed sergeant gave up his place in the back.

'A kitchen knife,' he said as he got into the front passenger seat, indicating the plastic bag on the floor. Tim was close against Olivia, but felt no reaction to the sergeant's comment.

'We're going to St James,' he told her.

'Of course, Tim.'

Her relaxation seemed as total as ever, but when they were inside the station she turned and clutched him.

'Not me, Olivia.' He tried not to think of the imminent strip search, the hourly monitoring to ensure that she didn't find a way out. 'It can't be me. But I'll see you later, and so will Anna.' At least it was possible to evade her staring eyes. 'I'm so very sorry.'

'I'm – nothing. Goodbye, Tim.'

'Till later.'

He wanted to run out of the building, but he had to report as promised to his Chief, whose commendation might gratify him at some later date. Now he could hardly wait to get away. He rang Bradshaw, Jones and Coquelin before he left the station, asked for John Coquelin, and told him what had happened. Anna was out on a call, but John promised to send her to Tim's house as soon as she got back.

He drove home through a deluge. Between his kennel and the kitchen Duffy collected a coatful of water which he shook all over Tim. Tim fed him and the cat and prepared a tea tray, then spent the hour until Anna's arrival rearranging shelves of books and trying not to think of his last sight of Olivia. He kept going over to the window, and eventually Anna sped up his path to an open door.

'Oh, God, Tim.'

He kissed her wet face and hair. 'John told you. I asked him to. I'm so sorry, Anna.'

'I can't take it in. Why, Tim? She loved him.'

'He loved Janet. Olivia found a letter he was gong to send her in England, telling her their marriage was over. Suggesting she didn't come back.' Anna dropped into a chair. 'I'll make us tea and tell you everything I can remember. The cat's going to jump on your knee.'

When he came back with the tray the cat was still deliberating, but plumped for Tim so that he had to ask Anna to pour.

'How is she?' Anna asked.

'I don't know. Oh, I can tell you she was calm and quiet, as you'd expect, but I don't know. Why didn't I leave well alone?' The cat leaped the small space to Anna's lap, as if sensing Tim was about to fling himself out of his chair. For a moment Anna thought he was going to sweep the china figures off the old-fashioned mantel, but he dropped his hand and barged across the room to the streaming window. 'I've been a man for certainties,' he said without turning round, perhaps to himself. 'I thought justice was always the thing. But this piece of it does no good to anyone.'

'The Chapmans.'

'They would have been all right. As Olivia said, they couldn't have been convicted without physical evidence. And Olivia wouldn't have killed again.'

'Tim, the lead piping . . . She must have planned it. She was so calm that day we spent together. Knowing that the same night –'

'She did plan it. But she told Janet Charles had killed her first. I don't think you met the living woman. If Charles had been honest with her right away things could have been different. He should have been, but there was a callousness at the heart of him. It was in the letter, in that article he wrote that so upset Joly.'

'I remember what she said when I questioned her description of herself as lazy. "I move when I have to." I think it covers everything I've learned about her.'

'It covers her loyalty. She wouldn't change towards Charles any more than she would get unnecessarily out of her chair. That's why it was such an outrage, why she had to move against him. Oh, God.'

'Come here.' He swung back to her and she caught his hand and pulled him down beside her chair, provoking a rich purring from the cat. 'Has she been charged?'

'Yes. She made a statement right away pretty well repeating what we have on tape. The ghastly joke is that it's all down to me. I set the thing up to trap Janet . . . I'm forgetting – Janet told me she'd like to see you. I think it would be a kindness if you went as soon as possible, after I've told you all I know. Unless you're expected back at work?'

'Not today. When I've seen Janet I'd like to be expected back here.'

Douglas Chapman answered Anna's ring. He had a whisky glass in his hand.

196

'I'm sorry to disturb you, Douglas, but I think Janet wanted to see me.'

'She's upstairs,' he said. 'She's leaving me.' His pale blue eyes were puzzled, like a bewildered child's. Anna hadn't expected to feel sorry for him. 'Find your own way,' he suggested over his shoulder as he set off towards an open door the far side of the wide hall. 'Second on the left.'

Janet was in a chair by the window, her feet on a pouffe, her eyes staring beyond the rain-lashed garden. Although the rain had scarcely lowered the temperature, she had a rug across her knees.

'Janet.'

'Anna! Oh, I'm so glad you've come. Pull that chair over and forgive me for not getting up. The doctor's given me something and I'm floating.'

'Just as well after an ordeal like that.'

'Tim told you?'

'The truth about you and Charles as well.'

'I didn't want him to tell anyone, but he said the letter will have to be evidence. Anna, she loved him, she gave him superhuman rope, and it wasn't enough. It killed her, she told me. That's why she killed him. Perhaps if we hadn't tried to deceive her, hadn't underestimated her . . . She said that was the worst of all. We could have told the truth right away. We should have done. We were as much to blame –'

'No. But you should have given her her due. Your husband's just told me you're leaving him.'

'Yes.'

'Where will you go?'

'Back to England. I've never liked it here. I'm in a good job now, I'll get another.'

'Have you any family?'

'Not now. I'll stay in London. A hotel first, then a flat. I shan't have to ask Douglas for anything – when my father died last year he left me some money. Anna . . . You'll see her?'

'Later tonight.'

'Will you tell her from me that it's all right?'

'Yes.'

'Thank you. Anna . . . There's one other thing only Charles knew. I'd like to tell someone, and in a way you've

197

been there. Not as close as Olivia, but I couldn't . . . And I wouldn't want her ever to know. I was going to have a baby. I lost it on Saturday afternoon. On my own, here. It hadn't gone very far so I coped.'

'Oh, Janet. How terrible.'

'Douglas couldn't have children.' It was Janet's one small self-indulgence, to blame Douglas at last. 'You like Guernsey, don't you? Though perhaps now . . .'

'I still like it. You might have liked it too if you'd been running away from somewhere else. I suppose one person's prison is another's escape route. Are you well enough to travel?'

'I shall be by the morning. Anna . . . you really are sure that he didn't suffer?'

'I really am.'

When Anna went downstairs there was no sign of Douglas, and she let herself out of the house.

Dear Jane,

I'm looking out across a different green tonight, from the Bradshaws' big bright 1930s villa high on the other side of St Peter Port, with their lovely, silly old English sheepdog for company.

I'm glad I don't have to write it all down, although the reason I rang was that I didn't want you to find out from the media, as you did with the murder.

It's easier to write down the other thing I have to tell you than to say it over the telephone. It's about Tim Le Page and you'll already be smiling. It's hard to believe I've only known him a week, but we've shared some traumas and – well, there it was, suddenly on Monday night in his crowded little sitting-room. And yes, we went upstairs. It was never in my life more natural. How important? I can't say, except that I know it isn't on the rebound. And that I felt so at home pouring tea in his house this afternoon that I began to feel worried. That's a joke, I didn't, so perhaps . . . No, it's far too early to say. We don't even know if we've got anything in common apart from animals and the De Garde scandal.

I know I don't have to ask you not to tell Jimmy. If the time comes, I'll tell him myself.

Jane, I've just been to see her. She's in a cell at St James until tomorrow, when she'll be moved to the new prison at St Sampson. The irony's choking me: Charles was going to set her up in England, but she wanted to stay in Guernsey, and now she will.

It was a little spartan space, with a palliasse rather than a bed, and they'd taken her clothes. She was lying on the palliasse, staring at the ceiling. They go in every hour to monitor her breathing and see she hasn't managed to do away with herself, and they told me she hasn't spoken or eaten or looked at them. If she's still like that tomorrow they'll take her to the prison hospital.

She didn't speak to me, either, or look at me. While I spoke to her she went on looking at the ceiling. Janet had sent her a message – a sort of forgiveness, I think – but even when I gave her that she didn't have any reaction.

It was only when I got up to go . . . She turned her head very slowly and looked through me. Her eyes were as still as ever but her mouth was moving, so I waited. It took a few minutes but eventually, clearly, she said 'Jonathan'. That was to have been the name of her son.

How can I be so happy, and so sad?

Ring me or write to me soon.

Much love as always,

Anna.

You have been reading a novel published by Piatkus Books. We hope you have enjoyed it and that you would like to read more of our titles. Please ask for them in your local library or bookshop.

If you would like to be put on our mailing list to receive details of new publications, please send a large stamped addressed envelope (UK only) to:

Piatkus Books: 5 Windmill Street
London W1P 1HF

PIATKUS
The sign of a good book